Readers Love Eliana West

Be the Match

"*Be the Match* could have been a maudlin tale about childhood leukemia but it's not. It's a story filled with love, hope, resilience and overcoming more than one piece of bad news."

—Paranormal Romance Guild

A Homemade Hanukkah

"Grumpy/sunshine, forced proximity, two emotionally damaged characters, and a visit from a hundred-year-old cowboy ghost—this story packs some interesting and quirky twists."

—Rainbow Book Reviews

Dreidel Date

"This was just a really lovely story that shows how much we all have in common and was a holiday delight…there's also a bonus of a recipe!"

—Love Bytes Reviews

"[This] was such a wonderful, warm hug of a book to read.

—Nerdy Romantics Podcast

By Eliana West

Dreidel Date

EMERALD HEARTS
Be the Match
A Homemade Hanukkah
Once Upon a Hike

Published by Dreamspinner Press
www.dreamspinnerpress.com

ONCE UPON a Hike

ELIANA WEST

Published by
DREAMSPINNER PRESS

8219 Woodville Hwy #1245
Woodville, FL 32362 USA
www.dreamspinnerpress.com

This is a work of fiction. Names, characters, places, and incidents either are the product of author imagination or are used fictitiously, and any resemblance to actual persons, living or dead, business establishments, events, or locales is entirely coincidental.

Once Upon a Hike
© 2025 Eliana West

Cover Art
© 2025 L.C. Chase
http://www.lcchase.com
Cover content is for illustrative purposes only and any person depicted on the cover is a model.

Trade Paperback ISBN: 978-1-64108-841-1
Digital ISBN: 978-1-64108-840-4
Trade Paperback published July 2025
v. 1.0

To anyone who ever gazed at the stars and dared to dream—may you find your path, your adventure, and your own happily ever after.

Acknowledgments

Thank you to the Dreamspinner team. You are always such a joy to work with.

To Carmen Cook and Amber Lynne, thank you for always being there to listen, laugh, and offer words of wisdom.

To my readers, thank you for your kind words and for celebrating the beauty of diversity with me.

Chapter One

"Wow. I knew it was big, but seeing it up close—I don't think I've ever seen a boat that large in Lake Union before."

Benjamin Colton craned his neck, surveying the towering navy-blue-and-white hull. Bobbing alongside the massive structure, his kayak was like a tiny minnow next to an enormous whale.

"Technically, it's called a yacht, a megayacht," he said, taking in the gleaming teak-and-chrome details on the sleek modern vessel.

Benjamin read the gold lettering on the bow. *Faunus.* "God of the forest," he murmured.

"What?" His friend and neighbor Joy Anderson paddled over and angled her kayak next to his.

"*Faunus* is the god of the forest. Fitting name for the Huntington family yacht, I suppose," he replied with a resigned sigh.

Joy's eyes narrowed. "I'd heard it was big, but this is…."

"Totally obnoxious."

Joy raised an eyebrow. "Clearly you're not as impressed as everyone else."

Benjamin gave Joy a wry smile. They had met a couple of years ago when Joy and her husband, the famous musician Jason Anderson, moved into the house next door. At first they bonded over their mutual love of the outdoors, but as time passed, they discovered a deeper connection. Joy, a Black woman raised by two dads in an interracial marriage, and Benjamin, the child of an interracial heterosexual couple, shared a rare and profound understanding of what it meant to grow up with people questioning who you were.

"I don't disapprove of them. It's more that I don't approve of why they're here."

"Why are they here?"

"They want to buy my father's—" He grimaced. "—my stepmother's company."

"They want to buy DGD?" Hearing the shortened name his stepmother had adopted when she took over his father's company made him wince.

Benjamin nodded. "They want to buy it, and my stepmother is happy to get rid of it."

What started with a simple idea to make the outdoors more inclusive and accessible was now a lifestyle brand catering to a high-end clientele. The first small climbing gym his father opened almost twenty years ago grew into a chain of gyms and a line of outdoor gear designed with people's physical disabilities in mind. Drinking Gourd Designs grew into a successful business until…. Benjamin blinked back the tears that always threatened to fall with the memory of his father's death.

"Do they know what a shit show it is?"

"My stepmother is good at covering her tracks. She's betting they won't discover how badly the company's been hemorrhaging money until the deal is done."

A movement at the railing caught their attention, and Benjamin and Joy caught a glimpse of a man gazing at the Seattle skyline behind them.

"Wow, who's that?" Joy asked.

Benjamin studied the heir to the Huntington family empire. "That is Max Huntington, otherwise known as the Prince of the Wilderness."

On a clear, sunny Seattle day like that day, his hair glinted deep gold mixed in with lighter brown threaded throughout. Benjamin was too far away to see Max's eyes, but he knew from the pictures he'd seen they were a light greenish brown that reminded him of the moss that covered the trees in the rain forests he loved to hike.

The Huntingtons weren't royalty, even though the press treated them as if they were. They came from East Coast high society. They were already well-to-do before Max Huntington's parents took the family business to new heights.

"Benjamin," Joy whispered and tapped her paddle on his kayak. "He's watching you."

He'd been so caught up in his own appraisal, Benjamin hadn't noticed Max had turned his attention to him. The prince lifted his hand and waved. Even his wave set Benjamin's teeth on edge. Who did he think he was—the King standing on the balcony at Buckingham Palace?

Dipping his paddle in the water, Benjamin deftly turned his kayak away. "Let's go. I've got to get back. With the Huntingtons in town, my stepmother and the twins are going to be even more high-maintenance than usual."

"I suppose you'll get to meet him in person," Joy said, paddling to catch up.

"I doubt it," Benjamin snorted. "Remember, I'm just the help. I've been given strict instructions not to be noticed."

"I hate the way they treat you." Joy scowled. "I wish you'd leave. You know they'd be nothing without you."

Benjamin rested his paddle across his stomach and leaned back, tracking the seaplane circling overhead. "You know why I can't leave," he said, his voice heavy with resignation.

Joy gave him a sympathetic smile.

He picked up his paddle and dipped it in the water, and they continued their journey under the University Bridge and then its little sister the Montlake Bridge through the small canal that led to Lake Washington. As they rounded the bend, the beautiful home Joy shared with her husband came into view. A classic Pacific Northwest Craftsman style with modern touches, it was a newer build designed to fit into the surroundings as if it had always been there. The grounds were pristine, featuring rhododendrons, azaleas, dogwood, and Japanese maple trees.

When they reached the dock, Joy jumped out and tied up her kayak. "Do you want to come in for a cup of coffee?" she asked.

"I know you're trying to stall so I don't have to go home, and I appreciate it. But I've got to get back."

"Jason and I have been talking. We have plenty of room. Why don't you move in with us?"

His friend's offer brought tears to Benjamin's eyes. He swallowed past the lump in his throat. "I appreciate the offer. That's—it's generous and nice of you, but I can't leave. It's the only home I've ever known, and it's the only thing I have left from my parents. In eight weeks I'll be twenty-five, and Hyas House will be mine."

"What's left of it." Joy scowled. "It's outrageous the fees she's charging the estate as the executor."

"I don't care if she takes all the money. The only thing I care about is the house."

"I'm worried you won't have any funds left to pay the taxes and make the repairs."

"I'll figure it out."

"Jason and I could—"

"Joy, I'm not taking your money. But thank you, you're a good friend. Both you and Jason are."

Joy glanced toward Benjamin's house next door and sighed. "Okay, but promise you'll check in and let me know how things are going. I suppose with the Huntingtons in town you might not be able to come out for a paddle for a while."

He pushed away from her dock. "I'll try to make it out when I can."

With a few quick strokes, he arrived at his dock. Unlike the well-maintained one next door, this dock had seen better days. The wood was weathered and gray, and if you didn't know the right places to walk, you'd be in danger of falling through the rotted spots.

The dock reflected the condition of the rest of the property. Once upon a time, the house and grounds were as well-kept and beautiful as the house next door. Despite his best efforts, years of neglect had taken their toll.

Benjamin pulled his kayak up onto the lawn and made his way to the house, admiring the giant peach blooms of the rhododendron his mother had planted along the edge of the yard.

"The kitchen sink is clogged again," his stepmother called down from the upper deck. She leaned against the railing, her long straightened hair falling forward as she peered down at him. Even though she ran an activewear company, Benjamin never saw his stepmother wearing anything but suits that were so structured and tight it was amazing she could move or breathe. Today her suit matched the sky, a bright blue that coordinated with her eyeshadow, complementing her dark brown skin.

"I'll get my toolbox."

"Really, Benjamin." The disappointment was clear in her tone. "I'm surprised at you, wasting your time paddling around the lake when you have so much work to do." She sighed, twisting the large diamond ring his father had presented her with when he proposed. "I shouldn't be surprised. You've always been so selfish."

Benjamin bit down on the inside of his cheek. There was no point in arguing, and it would only result in his stepmother finding another excuse to create an expense that he'd be expected to pay. Her grand plans to tear down the house and build a McMansion were foiled when she learned she'd inherited everything but the house. It wouldn't have mattered if she had inherited it; Hyas House was designated a historical landmark and couldn't be altered.

She didn't have enough money to realize her grand dreams anyway. The lifestyle Rochelle Tremaine and her precious twins insisted on living wasn't cheap. Fancy cars, jewelry, clothes, and the pricy colleges the twins attended were a drain on the limited resources they had, along with the exorbitant salaries they drew. Their resources were limited because Rochelle ran the company on a shoestring budget, and the income the business generated couldn't keep up with their lavish lifestyle. She tapped her foot, waiting, hoping he'd talk back, but Benjamin knew how to play her game. He forced a smile. "You're right. I'll get right on it and take care of that for you."

They locked eyes, each waiting for the other to show a sign of weakness. After a few seconds, Rochelle turned on her heel. "Get it done, and don't be late getting to the office. It's important to make a good impression for the Huntingtons. Everything needs to be perfect when they arrive."

Benjamin waited until his stepmother was out of sight before he blew out a shaky breath.

"Eight weeks. You only have to get through eight weeks and then you'll be free."

Selling the company would provide a substantial payday, leaving Rochelle and her children free to live the Kardashianesque lifestyle they dreamed of, and Benjamin alone.

He took the narrow path toward the garage, heading straight for the room at the back he called home. A glass canning jar filled with wild sweet pea he'd found on his last hike sat on the windowsill of the only window in the room. It might have been small, but it offered a peekaboo view of the lake and cast a narrow beam of sunlight during the summer and a silvery cold shadow during the winter. Benjamin had brightened the rest of the room with alabaster-white paint, a thrifted bedside lamp, and a desk lamp.

He toed off his sneakers and set them at the foot of his bed next to a worn pair of hiking boots with bright emerald-green laces, a small tribute to his dad.

The more his stepmother stripped away his past, the harder Benjamin clung to any small connection to his parents. The shoelaces made it seem like his dad was with him whenever he went on a hike or camping trip. Spending time in nature and camping under the stars gave him hope and was Benjamin's way of keeping his dad's legacy alive.

Pushing away his sadness, Benjamin grabbed a bottle of water out of the refrigerator in the kitchen he'd built in one corner of his room. An old-fashioned ceramic water cooler provided water for cooking and doing dishes. It sat on the butcher-block countertop he'd thrifted, along with two narrow lower cabinets to support it. A hotplate, microwave, and dorm-size refrigerator made up the rest of the makeshift kitchen. It was bare bones, but along with what might be world's smallest bathroom—including a shower barely large enough to turn around in—it allowed him to dodge going into the main house unless it was absolutely necessary, thereby avoiding the pain of seeing how his stepmother had stripped away all traces of his mother and father's existence.

Benjamin settled at the small desk he'd found at a garage sale and put under the window. As he opened his laptop, he rubbed a spot behind his left ear, thinking about Max Huntington. What would happen when the Huntingtons arrived at the DGD offices? Would he be able to keep out of sight and avoid them? He took a few minutes to check his schedule and social media. One post in particular made him smile, bringing a moment of levity before he faced what he knew would be a stressful day ahead. With a heavy exhale Benjamin closed his laptop and went to the garage to get his toolbox. He didn't have time to daydream about billionaires or make-believe princes.

CHAPTER TWO

THE HULL of the *Faunus* towered over the other boats on Seattle's Lake Union. At its peak, the megayacht was six stories from upper deck to the waterline. The man and woman in the kayaks bobbing on the water three stories below caught Max Huntington's attention. The man with curly brown hair and dark brown eyes, who was watching him with curiosity, intrigued him. The late afternoon sun cast a golden glow on his pale, creamy brown skin. Max sensed the man knew who he was, but his expression made it clear that neither the megayacht nor Max's presence impressed him. Max wasn't impressed either. Narrowly squeezing through the Ballard Locks connecting Puget Sound to Lake Union, the *Faunus* was a spectacle that made the local news. The *Faunus*, the only megayacht currently moored in Lake Union, dominated every other boat on the lake. Even the seaplanes coming in for a landing seemed like nothing more than oversized seabirds when they flew past the 370-foot yacht. While there were plenty of elegant large yachts dotting the lake, it was rare for one of this size to moor there.

"It's beautiful here, isn't it?" Max's father said, joining him at the railing. "The trip through the sound was breathtaking."

"Was the expense to bring the *Faunus* here from the Caribbean necessary?"

"Your mother and I are planning on exploring more of the San Juan Islands and going to Vancouver Island when our business here is finished."

Max bit his tongue. His parents were constantly planning trips they never ended up going on. There was always another business deal to broker or social event that his mother insisted they needed to make an appearance at. The odds were when their trip to Seattle was finished, the *Faunus* would sail back to its home port with only its crew on board while his parents took the private jet to their next event. Max didn't intend on being there. He planned on heading back to Manhattan as soon as he could. The press may have dubbed him the Prince of the Wilderness, but his forest was made of glass and chrome. Not that he wouldn't mind spending more time outdoors, but lately trying to keep his parents from running Huntington Outfitters into the ground didn't allow much time for camping under the stars.

Max gave his father a knowing look. "We both know you weren't going to say no to Mother when she insisted it would be more convenient to conduct business and entertain on the *Faunus* than stay in a hotel."

What Max didn't say was that his mother never wanted to miss an opportunity to make a grand impression. The *Faunus* was proof of that. The same was true for their vacation home on Martha's Vineyard, the apartment in Paris, or the townhouse on the Upper West Side, the yacht—with accommodations for twelve guests and a crew of twenty-five—was carefully curated to impress.

Phillip Huntington eyed his son. "Is that a note of cynicism I hear in your voice?"

"You know I have concerns about this acquisition. I already have my hands full with overseeing opening the next round of stores in the UK. Why do we have to do this now?"

"We've been searching for an opportunity to get a foothold on the West Coast for quite a while," his father said with an exasperated sigh. "The Pacific Northwest is known for its outdoor lifestyle. Adding a homegrown company to our portfolio is a good move."

"Why this one? There are other companies based here that we should consider."

"Like that star one you mentioned?"

"Big Dipper Adventures," Max ground out. "I've mentioned it enough times you should remember the name by now."

The fact his father couldn't be bothered to remember the name set Max's teeth on edge. He wasn't listening, something that seemed to happen often these days. His parents served as co-CEOs of Huntington Outfitters, and Max had worked his way through every position in the company to earn his place as its president. It would be nice if his parents didn't micromanage him and allowed him to fulfill his role in a meaningful way instead of making him feel like nothing more than an empty figurehead.

"Have you made any progress getting information on the company?" his father asked.

Max shifted his gaze to the floating homes on the other side of the lake. He didn't want to see the patronizing expression in his father's eyes that would inevitably be there when he gave his answer.

"No."

Max could avoid seeing it in his eyes, but it was unmistakable in his father's tone. "I appreciate you're trying to help, but your mother and I feel this is a better option. Now, it's time to get ready to welcome Mrs. Tremaine and her children for dinner tonight."

With a dismissive pat on the back, his father left Max gripping the railing, trying to tamp down his frustration before it spilled over. His thoughts returned to the man in the kayak. He'd rather grab a kayak and paddle alongside his mystery man than entertain Mrs. Tremaine and her children. From what he'd seen of the Tremaine social media accounts, Max wasn't interested in getting to know them better. All of their posts featured the twenty-seven-year-old Tremaine twins, Monaco and Milan, playing at being socialites. They were doing their best to emulate another well-known family of social media influencers, whose only talent was being famous for being famous, and failing miserably.

"My mystery man," Max said under his breath with a laugh. What was it about the man in the kayak who'd captured his attention from a single glance?

Pushing away from the railing, he tried to stop thinking about his mystery man, but… he did it again. He took a deep breath and attempted to clear his head. A few weeks in Seattle wouldn't be so bad. He'd find someone to keep him entertained while he was here and then move on when the trip was over. That's the way Max preferred his love life. Nothing serious and nothing permanent. He was too focused on his career to be weighed down with the responsibility of taking care of someone else, and he was certainly not willing to settle down for no other reason than to make his mother happy. He scanned the lake, eyeing the houseboats on the other shoreline and wondering where his mystery man had paddled away to.

"Stop it," Max muttered to himself. The guy in the kayak wasn't *his* mystery man. So why was the idea of never seeing him again so disappointing?

"Bennett, will you arrange for a kayak to be delivered?" Max asked after returning to his suite.

His executive assistant paused from flipping through Max's closet and peered over his shoulder with a raised eyebrow.

"Feeling adventurous, are we?"

Bennett pulled another shirt out of the closet. With a frown he put it back and continued to go through the neatly hung shirts with a dismissive flick of his wrist. Bennett's accent became even more posh when he disapproved. The posh voice matched Max's best friend's regal bearing. He came by them naturally, being the second son of an earl.

"You know you're my executive assistant and not my butler, right?"

"I am fully aware of that. I also know I have better taste than you do."

Max couldn't argue. Bennett had impeccable taste. Max flopped onto his bed. Bennett had taken over management of Max's wardrobe when they first met at boarding school, insisting he was the only boy in their class who knew how to properly tie a Windsor knot.

"I don't care what I wear to this ridiculous dinner."

"Yes, but I do, and so does your mother. Life will be much easier for both of us if you show up for dinner with Mrs. Tremaine and the twins dressed like the gentleman you are."

"You know you could go home and take care of your own estate instead of harassing me?"

Bennett sighed as he continued to lay out outfit options on the bed. "You know very well it's not my estate. I am content in my role as the spare."

Max noted his friend's voice became even more proper and clipped, a clear indication of his growing annoyance. Max felt a pang of sympathy for Bennett, who had to deal with a family who was an even bigger source of irritation and disappointment than Max's own.

"Except for the fact that you love Goulding Hall and your brother, Mark, is a narcissist buffoon."

"Continuing to state facts isn't going to change anything." Bennett assessed the shirt, jacket, and tie combination he'd chosen. With a nod of approval, he held them out to Max.

"Come on, let's get this over with."

AN HOUR later Bennett kicked Max under the table again. He'd done it so many times since dinner Max's shin was starting to ache.

Bennett tipped his head to where Milan Tremaine and his twin, Monaco, were taking selfies. Again. During dinner.

"Rochelle, I must say how impressed Phillip and I are with what you've accomplished with DGD," Max's mother said.

Rochelle Tremaine pursed her overly filled lips and did her best to morph her expression into something that would have appeared like sadness if her dermatologist allowed any of her face muscles to work. "It wasn't easy with three children to raise."

Max frowned, glancing at the twins. "I thought you only had two children, Mrs. Tremaine."

"Benjamin doesn't like parties." Monaco flipped her long straight hair over her shoulder while she held her face up to her phone, stretching her neck at an unnatural angle a giraffe wouldn't attempt.

Her mother laughed, with a tremor of nervousness that Max picked up on. Bennett raised an eyebrow, indicating he'd caught it too.

"What Monaco means is that...." She dropped her voice to a conspiratorial tone, giving Max's mother an understanding glance. "Well, poor thing, I'm afraid he's a bit awkward. I've tried to guide him where I can, but I haven't been able to do much. He's... well, the poor boy doesn't have the manners or right appearance to represent DGD."

"I can't imagine." Max's mother gave her a sympathetic smile. "I hope he's grateful to have such a wonderful stepmother and stepsiblings."

Rochelle sighed dramatically. "You'd think so, but—"

"He's the worst," Milan interrupted with a scowl. "He's got no taste. He doesn't even have a TikTok account."

This time Max kicked Bennett, with a subtle motion for him to close his mouth while he watched Milan apply a heavy coat of lip gloss as he spoke.

"Why isn't he here tonight?" Max asked.

"Like I said, Benjamin is a bit awkward. He wouldn't be comfortable," Rochelle snapped.

There was a hardness in her voice that Max didn't like. So far he didn't like anything about Rochelle Tremaine and her children. Artificial was the word that came to mind. Nothing about their manners, voices, thoughts, or ideas seemed genuine. Something was off. This trip had his instincts on high alert. He'd been vocal in his opposition to the merger with DGD and overruled by his parents. They seemed determined to put aside any rational analysis of the business to make the merger happen. "They" mainly being his mother. He'd grown up admiring her drive and determination, but he'd come to realize there were times when those qualities were a detriment and not an asset.

"Well, I think our current company more than makes up for his absence. Don't you think so, Max?" his mother said with a nod and a scheming glint in her eye.

Oh no. His stomach sank. Max knew that look. He'd seen it frequently lately, mainly every time she was matchmaking.

He muttered something vaguely appropriate while taking a sip of his drink.

Business dinners weren't his favorite activity, and this one was a particular kind of torture. As soon as he could, he escaped to his suite, declining the twins' repeated offers to take him to their favorite club. He rolled up his sleeves, poured himself a glass of whiskey, and dropped onto the edge of his bed with a heavy sigh.

With barely one rap on the door, his mother walked in, wearing a disapproving frown. "Really, Max, I expected more from you tonight."

"More what, Mother?"

Kathrine plucked an invisible piece of lint from her impeccable dress. "You know what I mean. Mrs. Tremaine has two children, and we're going into business together—"

"Three."

"What?"

"Mrs. Tremaine has three children."

His mother waved a dismissive hand. "I'm only concerned with the two who can help us."

Max wrinkled his forehead in confusion.

"Max, darling, don't you see? A personal and business relationship with the Tremaine family is beneficial for everyone. We're trying to increase our diversity efforts, and you need a partner who can support you in social situations. Someone who understands our business and what's needed to be successful."

Max couldn't believe what he was hearing. He jumped up from his seat and slammed his glass down with enough force to make his mother jump.

"I am not interested in either of those two dithering idiots, and I've made my views on the merger with DGD clear. I'm bi, not desperate, Mother."

"Fine." His mother threw up her hands. "At this point I don't care. Pick someone. You need a partner in life who will—"

"Look good in pictures," Max repeated the line before she could. "Why isn't it enough for me to be good at my job? Although you wouldn't know I'm good at it since you won't let me do it."

Max voiced out loud the question he'd been considering for months. He'd earned his role as president of the outdoor clothing and equipment empire his parents had built from the modest-sized sweater company they'd inherited from Max's grandfather after he'd inherited it from his own father.

"Your father and I have made Huntington Outfitters into what it is today. You're young and still have a lot to learn."

"I'm almost thirty. I started in the warehouse and worked my way up the same as everyone else. I graduated from Yale, a school you didn't help me get into. And earned a master's in business and economics from the London School of Economics. With honors," he added for emphasis.

"You should have gone to Wharton instead of running off with Bennett. None of that matters anyway. You're still single, and I want to see you settled. You need a partner who can—"

"Mother, I swear, if you say one more word about marriage, I will go to the airport right now, take the jet, and leave."

The heavy silence that settled between them proved his point. His parents weren't going to carve out a space for him in their empire. It was okay for him to be the Prince of the Wilderness for the press, but he was trapped on a floating palace with nothing to do.

"It's late. We'll talk about this tomorrow," his mother said.

"Of course."

There was no good-night or quick motherly peck on the cheek when she left the room, and there would be no talk tomorrow. His mother would avoid the conversation like she always did. Max paced his quarters, eyeing the Seattle skyline outside the window. He wasn't opposed to marriage, to finding a partner, someone who he could share his success and failures with. A partner who challenged him. He *was* afraid of being saddled with his mother's choice, someone who had the right presence and nothing more. It didn't matter if they shared any chemistry or had anything in common.

CHAPTER THREE

"ON YOUR right."

Benjamin bit back a groan of annoyance, watching the man who'd invaded his peaceful morning run lap him… again.

And yes, he could be annoyed and still appreciate the view of his backside. But why was the Prince of the Wilderness running on an abandoned, overgrown track? Benjamin's track. A quiet place where he could have a little solitude and peace away from his stepfamily. Wasn't there a gym Max Huntington could work out in on that ridiculous yacht? But if he'd done that instead of showing up at Benjamin's track, Benjamin wouldn't have gotten the chance to see the Prince in person and find out for himself that pictures didn't do him justice. The steady thump of steps came toward him once more, and he could have sworn he felt the Prince's breath tickle the back of his neck as he started to pass.

"On—"

"I know!" Benjamin shouted.

He immediately regretted his exasperated outburst when the Prince's footsteps faltered and he stopped, looking over his shoulder at Benjamin. Max Huntington rested his hands on his hips, breathing heavily, his gaze traveling from Benjamin's feet until he met his eyes. Benjamin silently cursed his outburst and stopped his slow, measured progress around the track. When Max tilted his head, recognition flashed in his eyes.

"We've met, haven't we?" he asked, walking toward Benjamin with a friendly smile.

It wasn't fair for such a hot guy to also have a deep, sexy voice with a posh East Coast accent.

Benjamin took a step back as Max approached. "No, we've never met."

But Max continued to study him, his eyes roving over Benjamin's face and traveling down his body before returning, his smile becoming something more than friendly. His eyes lit up, and he snapped his fingers. "Kayak."

Shit. How in the world could Max have recognized him from that one brief moment?

"You and a woman were kayaking by the *Faunus*," he continued. He came forward with his hand outstretched. "I'm Max."

Their warm hands met, both still damp from sweat, and a frisson of awareness jolted Benjamin, making him quickly pull out of Max's grasp.

"Was that your girlfriend?" Max asked with a hopeful glint that caught Benjamin off guard. Max couldn't possibly be interested in him. He was too ordinary for the Prince of the Wilderness.

"Joy and her husband, Jason, are my neighbors. She's a friend," he said, watching Max's eyes light up and his smile grow.

"I suppose you have a name as well?" Max asked, his accent and tone combining to make it a demand as much as a question.

Benjamin stiffened. "I do, but you don't need to know it."

He blew out a shaky breath, keeping an eye on Max, who was still watching him with his arms folded in front of his chest. A well-toned chest Benjamin wanted to press his hand against, wanting to make sure it felt as firm as it seemed.

"I suppose that makes sense." Max nodded and continued with a hint of mockery in his voice. "Wise, actually. Young men shouldn't give their names to strangers."

Benjamin lifted his chin. "Exactly."

The corner of Max's lips tipped up into a confident smile. "I suppose the best way to remedy the situation would be for you to join me for coffee, where we get to know each other, and then we won't be strangers anymore and you can tell me your name."

"Oh no," Benjamin backed away, tugging on the edge of his worn T-shirt, comparing his thrift-shop clothes to Max's shoes, which cost more than his entire outfit. "That wouldn't be a good idea."

What was happening? Was Max flirting with him? His heart began to pound faster than from his run, and his lips tingled with anticipation as he imagined Max kissing him. Bad idea. He shouldn't be flirting with Max Huntington, if that's what was going on and it wasn't wishful thinking.

"I promise I'm a decent guy with honest intentions."

"Still no," Benjamin said, continuing to inch closer to where his Jeep was parked. "It was, uh, nice to meet you, Max. I've got to go. Bye."

He turned on his heel and sprinted to his Jeep. He tipped the visor down, and his keys dropped into his hand. In less than a minute, Benjamin was pulling away, sneaking a glance in the rearview mirror at Max, who was watching him with a frown as he drove away.

With a shaking finger, he pushed buttons on his phone, and his best friend's voice rang out on speaker.

"Hey, doll, what's up?"

"I met the Prince of the Wilderness."

A pause and then, "Bubbie's making pancakes. Come for breakfast. We want to hear everything."

FIFTEEN MINUTES later Benjamin pulled up to the little postwar bungalow his best friend, Aspen, shared with their grandma in Maple Leaf. A short walkway lined with small rosebushes led to a front door painted lavender. The color complemented the rest of the house—deep gray accented with white trim. Blue hydrangeas planted under the front window completed the cottage effect. When Aspen first moved in, the house wasn't as cheery as it was now. Their Bubbie, Gwen, barely had enough for herself with the small pension she lived off of. She couldn't afford to take in her sixteen-year-old grandchild, but she did it anyway, without blinking an eye. Over time their roles reversed. Aspen's success as a freelance coder gave them the means to restore their grandma's house and take care of her.

Benjamin had made it halfway up the walk when the door opened and Aspen poked their head out and waved him inside. "I've been dying. What took you so long?"

"I came as fast as I could without getting a speeding ticket."

Aspen ushered him into the bright cheery kitchen. They'd remodeled last year, and Benjamin loved the traditional cherry cabinets with classic marble countertops.

Aspen's grandma, Gwen, stood at the bright green commercial-style stove that matched the green tile backsplash. Her sparkling pale blue eyes were a slightly faded version of her grandchild's darker blue ones. She wore her silver-gray hair in a short pixie cut that framed her face and emphasized her large eyes. Despite being almost seventy, she had hardly a trace of a wrinkle on her face.

"Perfect timing," she said, flipping a pancake onto a plate and pouring another perfect circle of batter onto the griddle.

Gwen Brown reminded Benjamin of a little bird, always flitting around. The woman was in constant motion. People often underestimated her. They soon learned that, despite her appearance, Gwen Brown wasn't a frail little old lady. Aspen's Bubbie had a quick wit and a sharp tongue. If she loved you, you were loved fiercely, but if you were on her bad side, that fierceness could take you to your knees in a heartbeat. Something Benjamin witnessed firsthand when he and Aspen showed up on her doorstep after Aspen's parents kicked them out. Benjamin sat on the sofa with his arm around his best friend's shoulder while Gwen called her son and daughter-in-law and proceeded to read them the riot act, calling them out for refusing to accept Aspen and their nonbinary identity. Benjamin had watched with a pang of envy, wishing he had someone who would stand up to his stepmother the way Gwen defended her grandchild. Gwen would do it for him in a heartbeat. She'd offered more than once, but she also respected Benjamin's fear of doing anything that might jeopardize his inheritance.

"Here, honey, I made a fresh pot." Aspen's grandma slipped a cup of coffee in front of Benjamin as soon as he slid into the built-in banquette in one corner of the kitchen. "I'll have more pancakes ready in a minute."

"Thanks, Gwen." Benjamin took a sip and gasped, struggling to get air into his lungs. "Good Lord, Gwen, how much whiskey did you put in this?"

Gwen continued flipping golden circles. "Aspen said you'd had a traumatic experience. I figured you could use it."

Aspen rolled their eyes and replaced Benjamin's mug with theirs, whispering, "This one isn't ninety proof."

Benjamin snorted a laugh and took a sip of the milder brew.

Gwen returned to the table with a plate piled high with pancakes. "Eat up."

Benjamin managed to wolf down a few bites before Aspen squirmed in their seat. "I can't stand it anymore. I need to know everything that happened with Max Huntington."

Gwen fanned herself. "Is the Prince of the Wilderness as hot as he looks on the latest cover of the Huntington Outfitters catalog?"

"That rugged windswept vibe is so hot." Aspen said.

Benjamin stuffed another bite of pancake into his mouth and nodded.

"And…?" Aspen waved their hand, encouraging him to elaborate.

"I—" Benjamin avoided their curious gaze. "I ran away."

Aspen almost spat out their coffee.

"I got flustered, okay. He was being charming and wanted to know my name."

Gwen patted his hand. "Why don't you start at the beginning and tell us everything."

When he finished sharing the details of his encounter with Max, Aspen let out a low whistle. "He's going to find out who you are when the Huntingtons show up at the DGD offices this afternoon."

"I know." Benjamin pushed the remains of his pancakes around his plate with a sigh.

"I'm sorry, sweetheart, but I don't think there's anything you can do to avoid him," Gwen said.

Benjamin rubbed his stomach, trying to ease away the nervous knots.

"What are you going to say when he comes in?" Aspen asked.

"Nothing." He shrugged. "Rochelle made it clear that I'm supposed to stay in the background and not get noticed, and that's what I'm going to do."

Aspen and Gwen exchanged an angry glance.

"It's not fair." Aspen clenched their fist. "It's your father's company. His legacy."

Benjamin smiled at Aspen's passionate statement. Aspen was loyal to a fault, and they were right. Drinking Gourd Designs was his father's baby. It wasn't fair that it was being sold. But his father's company hadn't existed in a long time.

"It may have been my father's legacy, but he wouldn't recognize his company now. DGD doesn't have anything to do with his original idea to make adaptive outdoor equipment. Now it's…." Benjamin pushed his plate away with a heavy sigh.

"A bunch of overpriced crap designed for people who never actually go outside," Gwen said.

"DGD is a high-end outdoor lifestyle brand that caters to an exclusive clientele," Aspen parroted the company line in a mocking tone.

Benjamin drew in a shaky breath. "If the Huntingtons want to waste their money on DGD, that's their business and nothing I'm going to need to worry about. The Prince of the Wilderness isn't here for me."

Aspen raised an eyebrow. "From the way you described your encounter, it sounds like he'd like to be."

"First, *encounter* makes it sound as if we were in a Lifetime movie. Second, even if Max was interested in me, we both know all the reasons why that's not a good idea. I can't afford to do anything that will upset Rochelle."

"My sweet boy, you may think you're hiding in the shadows, but you shine like the star you are. Someday everyone will know you're the brilliant young man who carried on his father's vision in a wonderful and unique way," Gwen said.

Benjamin leaned over and gave Gwen a kiss on the cheek.

"You're in the home stretch," Aspen said. "And then you can kick your ugly stepmother and those two ugly twatwaffles to the curb."

"Exactly. Which is why I can't do anything to ruffle my stepmother's feathers. If I'm lucky, I'll have enough money to pay taxes on Hyas House and be able to take care of the most important repairs—the roof, the plumbing, and the electrical."

Aspen frowned. "I'm worried. Rochelle is doing everything she can to drain your trust fund with her—" They curled their fingers in the air. "—executor fees."

Gwen uttered a string of curses under her breath before she said, "I still don't understand how she's getting away with that crap."

"You can get away with a lot when you're fucking the head of the bank's trust department," Benjamin replied flatly.

Aspen and Gwen didn't respond. What could they say? They knew he was right. Benjamin had learned quickly not to underestimate his stepmother's greed. When Rochelle and the twins ran through the money she'd inherited when Benjamin's dad died, she turned to Benjamin's trust fund as a source of income, since she couldn't sell the house. It was the one thing Rochelle couldn't take away from him. The trust specified that the house belonged to Benjamin and could not be sold. His stepfamily could live in the house until he received his trust. All he had to do was hold on until his birthday and he'd be able to reclaim his home.

Even as understanding as Aspen and Gwen were, Benjamin knew they didn't understand his connection to the house. Hyas House was important. It was the last house designed, at least in part, by Seattle's first Black architect, Benjamin McAdoo. It was considered an architectural landmark, a masterpiece of mid-century modern design. It was also the house Benjamin's mother designed for her senior project. Benjamin McAdoo was her professor at UW and worked with her on the project. It was the last thing he designed before he passed away. Their bond was special. His mother honored her beloved mentor by naming Benjamin after him. Benjamin's memories of his mother, the few memories he had, were tied to the house. Hyas House was home.

But first Benjamin had to figure out how to get through the Huntingtons' visit to the DGD offices today. What would happen when Max discovered who he was?

He held his coffee cup toward Aspen. "I think I'll trade you back for that ninety proof now."

CHAPTER FOUR

ROCHELLE TREMAINE'S assistant had a tell. Max hoped he didn't play poker, because he would lose every cent.

The meeting he'd been dreading suddenly became a lot more interesting when Max arrived at the DGD offices. The cute guy at the track worked for DGD. Max didn't know his name yet, but that wouldn't be for long.

He'd held out his hand to greet his mystery track man when Milan, Rochelle Tremaine's son, hooked his arm through his.

"He's not important," he said, guiding Max away with a dismissive wave.

Max glanced one more time at the assistant, who busied himself organizing folders, doing everything in his power to avoid Max's gaze.

"Welcome to DGD," Milan said, pushing Max toward the conference room. "As you know, DGD is a high-end outdoor lifestyle brand that caters to an exclusive clientele."

Milan rambled off the company tagline while Max's parents walked ahead of them, busy chatting with Rochelle.

Bennett came up behind him and murmured, "For a successful company, these posh offices are oddly quiet."

"Where is everyone?" Max asked.

"Oh, I'm sure they're at another meeting or at the warehouse," Milan said.

That was the beginning of a litany of excuses and evasive answers to the questions Max asked for the next hour. He sat at the table with his parents and Bennett on one side and Rochelle, Monaco, and Milan on the other. But it was the assistant, who'd slipped in after they were all seated and sat quietly in the corner with a laptop balanced on his knees, who kept Max's attention. Monaco had jumped up and snatched the files from his hand when he came in and then shoved him toward the chair he now occupied.

Max nodded along to the conversation, only half paying attention while he kept an eye on the assistant. Watching him was much more interesting and safer than engaging with the twins. He was doing everything he could to avoid making eye contact with either of them. The last time he did, Milan kept using his pen to show off his oral skills while the other one…. Bennett choked on his tea when Monaco batted her eyes so hard one of her false eyelashes came halfway unattached. She didn't notice until her brother elbowed her and whispered in her ear. In unison they rushed out of the room. A few minutes later they returned, and Monaco's eyelashes were reattached, with even more mascara piled on.

Unlike the twins, who were squeezed into skintight activewear, the assistant wore a pair of jeans with a Smokey the Bear T-shirt under a black blazer.

"Our unique and original designs are the reason DGD is a leader in the Pacific Northwest activewear scene." Rochelle said.

Max glanced at her assistant again. Sure enough, his fingers hovered over the keyboard for a heartbeat before he typed. It didn't take long for Max to figure out each hesitation coincided with an exaggeration or possible lie that Rochelle told. Even though he couldn't see the assistant's lips, Max was confident they were pursed behind his screen. Soft full lips that Max was starting to have dirty thoughts about. He had to concentrate, making sure he kept track in his own notes of each statement that coincided with one of the pauses. These he would review with Bennett later.

As soon as the meeting ended, the assistant retreated. He was at his desk at the entrance when the rest of them left the conference room. Receptionist and assistant—how many other roles did this man play, Max wondered, observing the still-empty cubicles on his way out.

With the rest of his party busy paying each other compliments, Max edged closer to the reception desk. The assistant stared intently at his computer, refusing to acknowledge him. He didn't take his attention from his computer, but his eyes flicked to where the Tremaines and Max's parents were saying their goodbyes.

"Stop it," he said in a panicked whisper.

"Stop what?"

"You're hovering."

"I simply wanted to make an appointment with you to review the accounts. I have some questions about the last quarter's earnings."

"I'm sure Ms. Tremaine will be happy to help you with whatever you need."

"I'd rather talk to you. You're the one who's done all the work, aren't you?"

He pressed his mouth into a thin line.

"Is there a problem, Mr. Huntington?"

Rochelle Tremaine appeared at his side. She glared at her assistant for a second before turning to Max with a smile as frozen as her Botoxed forehead.

"Not at all. I was simply asking if I could make an appointment with your assistant to go over your last quarterly statement. I have a few more questions."

Rochelle didn't even need to have a tell; her discomfort was obvious.

"Well, I-I'm sure Benjamin can send you anything you need. There's no reason for you to meet with him."

Benjamin. Max schooled his expression. His mystery man was a mystery no more. So this was the awkward stepson who was too shy to socialize.

Max wanted to press the point, but then he caught the hint of fear in Benjamin's eyes. He gave the slightest shake of his head, continuing to type away as if he wasn't a part of the conversation.

Max hesitated before he backed down. "I'll have my executive assistant, Bennett, follow up."

Rochelle's smile became a bit less brittle. "Excellent. Ah, here's Monaco. I'll let her escort you out."

Ugh, the eyelashes again. They were so long and thick with mascara, Max wondered how she could see to find the way out. But he had played his fair share of poker in boarding school and had a very good poker face. He smiled and offered his arm to Benjamin's stepsister without showing his annoyance. He snuck a peek over his shoulder as he was led away, noting the way Rochelle was leaning over the desk pointing a finger in Benjamin's face. He'd gotten Benjamin into trouble, and now he felt like an ass.

Monaco pressed herself to his side. "Seattle is known for its seafood. I'd be happy to be a sushi platter for you anytime."

Even a professional poker player would have had a hard time keeping a straight face with that line. Of course she said it right as they reached Bennett, who was waiting for him by an SUV with blacked-out windows. His friend did a terrible job trying to cover his laugh with a cough. Not that it mattered. Monaco was too busy trying to wrap her leg around Max's and climb him like a tree.

Instead of helping, Bennett said, "I've made a comprehensive list of the top sushi restaurants in the city, sir."

Max shot him a glare that only made Bennett's eyes twinkle even more with amusement.

He managed to untangle himself from Monaco's tentacles with only a slight stumble. Max straightened his tie as he maneuvered himself closer to the car and put his hand on the door handle, prepared to make a quick escape.

"Thank you, Monaco. I'm sure our paths will cross again as we begin our negotiations."

He jumped into the car, and Bennett immediately slammed the door on whatever reply Monaco tried to get past her overly inflated lips.

"Well, I think that went extremely well," Max's mother announced with a smug smile from the back seat.

His father peered over his reading glasses at her for a moment before going back to the sheaf of papers in his hand.

"Before you get too excited, I have a few concerns. Bennett and I have been reviewing DGD financials, and we would like to dig a little deeper."

"Darling, we have a whole team of accountants who've been over everything, and there haven't been any red flags."

"I'm aware of that, Mother. I would appreciate it if you would take my concerns more seriously. I think I've proven that my instincts and my business experience are a valuable asset."

His mother pursed her lips and turned to stare at the Seattle skyline outside the tinted windows.

"I don't appreciate you holding one mistake against me," she said in a steely voice.

Only it wasn't one mistake. Lately the drive and determination that had been his mother's greatest asset had become a liability. Six months ago, his mother wanted to acquire a small supplier of outerwear. She was so excited about the potential for increased profits she hadn't done her due diligence or allowed their accountants and legal team to do theirs.

Max had tried to voice his concerns, but his mother shut him down, and his father, as always, sided with his wife. She'd done something similar the year before, signing a contract with a supplier that claimed their products were certified organic when they were anything but. She'd become reckless in her pursuit of growing the company and making even more money. Growing their family assets into the billions wasn't enough for Kathrine Huntington. She wanted more. Max kept waiting for his father to step in and be the voice of reason, but Phillip hadn't intervened. They'd always had a strong partnership and loved each other. Max admired their devotion but not how their devotion made them blind to each other's faults.

"Why is acquiring DGD so important to you anyway?" Max asked.

His father put down the stack of reports that he'd been reading. "They have a strong foothold in the Pacific Northwest and a long track record."

"We don't need a high-end outdoor brand. It's more fashion than function, and that's not who we are at Huntington Outfitters."

His mother swatted away his objection with a wave of her hand. "Mrs. Tremaine and her twins have tapped into the high-end outdoor apparel market with innovative and imaginative designs. That's what I'm interested in."

His father added, "In the right hands, the original designs for adaptive equipment Mr. Colton developed before his passing could be a valuable asset."

Max dipped his head in acknowledgment. The equipment designs were the only element of this deal he and his parents were in agreement about.

As soon as Max returned to his suite on the *Faunus*, he threw himself into a chair and loosened his tie.

Bennett followed him in. "I don't know about you, but I could use a shower and a drink. I can't think of anything else that will get the stench of whatever perfume the Tremaine twins bathed in." He eyed the large amount Max had gotten up to pour himself. "Drowning our sorrows, are we?"

"Are you telling me that's not a good idea?" Max asked as he returned to his chair.

Bennett accepted the glass Max offered and took a seat across from him.

"I couldn't help notice you watching their assistant."

"He's more than an assistant. He's the awkward stepson, Benjamin, and my mystery man from the track."

Bennett's eyebrows shot up. "Interesting."

"Did you notice his tell?"

"His tell?

"Every time his stepmother or stepsiblings said something he disagreed with, he'd pause and take notes. I marked every pause on the presentation, and I want to go back and take a closer look at those points."

"Clever." Bennett nodded in approval.

Max sat down with his laptop and started typing, talking to himself as much as Bennett. "Why does Mrs. Tremaine want to cut her stepson out?"

"What makes you say that?"

"The way she talked about him at dinner, and the way she treated him at the meeting today."

Bennett tapped his finger against his glass. "Interesting."

"I need to talk to Benjamin without his stepmother hovering. Meanwhile let's go over the numbers again. We're missing something, I can feel it. I want to check on their claim that all of their clothing is sustainably resourced. We've been down that road once, and I don't want to make that mistake again."

Bennett winced. "Your mother's impulsive decision cost the company a pretty penny."

"Which is why we're going to do everything we can not to let it happen again." Max thought about his backup plan that he hoped would guide his parents to a better option. "Anything on Big Dipper Adventures yet?"

Scrolling through Instagram one night, he'd stumbled on an account for an outdoor adventure group. Their slogan, Outdoor for Everyone, caught his eye. Big Dipper Adventures sponsored hiking and camping trips for different minority groups. This was the kind of business model Max wanted Huntington Outfitters to be associated with. For the last year he'd been trying to find the owner. He'd learned from the locations pictured on the group's Instagram account that they operated somewhere around the Seattle area. It was his curiosity about the group, more than acquiring DGD, that motivated him to come on this trip.

Bennett sighed. "Nothing."

"There must be something."

"Whoever it is, I have to say they're doing a masterful job of staying hidden."

There was a note of appreciation in Bennett's voice. He was just as intrigued as Max was, and between the two of them, he was confident they'd figure out the mystery of Big Dipper Adventures. Now he had another mystery to solve: What was Benjamin's story?

Chapter Five

"What?" Max snapped at Bennett.

Bennett gave him one of what Max called his British smiles, mildly amused and calculating at the same time. "We've been skulking in this parking lot for—" Bennett checked his watch. "—almost thirty minutes."

"We aren't skulking, we're waiting. And stop looking at me like that."

"So the young Mr. Colton has piqued your interest."

"Good Lord, stop making it sound like we're in a Mills and Boon novel from the sixties."

"Well, whatever he's done, there's Benjamin coming out of the office now."

Max jumped out of the back of the SUV and called out to him.

Benjamin stopped. He glanced over his shoulder nervously before heading toward them with a frown.

"You can't do this," he said with a thread of anger in his voice.

"I won't keep you. I want to talk to you."

"I can't be seen talking to you," he said, glancing toward the office again.

Max nodded. "Okay, I understand."

He nodded to Bennett and closed the door to the SUV, motioning to the driver to leave.

"What are you doing?" Benjamin said with a note of panic in his voice when Max fell in step with him as he walked toward his Jeep.

"Well, obviously I'm going to need a ride, and I'm hoping you can help me out."

He'd barely gotten into his seat before Benjamin was peeling out of the parking lot. Max grabbed the roll bar, suppressing a yelp of alarm.

As soon as they were a few blocks away from the DGD offices, Benjamin turned onto a quiet side street and pulled over, coming to a stop with a jerk that would have launched him out of his seat if it weren't for his seatbelt. Benjamin turned to him, leaning his elbow on the steering wheel. "What. Do. You. Want?"

"I-I only wanted to talk," Max stuttered, taken by surprise at the anger and frustration in Benjamin's voice. His charming smile usually worked better than this.

Benjamin bowed his head and sighed. "You're making my life difficult."

"I'm not doing it on purpose, I promise. I'm… curious about you, and I want to get to know you better, that's all."

"There's nothing to know about me. I'm nobody."

Max reached out and lifted Benjamin's chin with his forefinger. "That's not true," he said, gazing into Benjamin's warm brown eyes. "I think you're someone."

Benjamin swallowed. "I… now's not a good time."

Max reluctantly let his hand drop "Why? I need to understand why."

"You're not going to let this go, are you?"

Max slowly shook his head. Now that he'd touched Benjamin, he definitely wasn't going to let this go. Not when he wanted more.

After a few moments, Benjamin exhaled with a resigned sigh. "Three questions. I'll answer three questions."

Max gestured toward the traffic on the street. "Do we have to do this here?"

"I have to get home. I can drop you off at your yacht."

The abrupt dismissal caught him off guard. "Sure."

They didn't talk on the drive back to the *Faunus*. Max studied Benjamin's profile as he maneuvered the ancient forest-green Jeep through the city streets toward the dock on Lake Union. The strong set of Benjamin's jaw told Max it wasn't going to be easy to get the information he wanted out of him. Benjamin pulled up to the boat but didn't park. He put the Jeep in neutral and pressed his palms against the steering wheel, clearly trying to make up his mind.

"I'll meet you at the track tomorrow morning. Three questions, that's it."

"I'll be there."

The minute Max was out of the Jeep and had shut the door, Benjamin took off without looking back, leaving Max standing on the dock trying to figure out where he went wrong.

"Thinking deep thoughts, are we?" Bennett ambled toward him a little while later. Even in a pair of navy board shorts and fitted T-shirt in the same shade of blue, Bennett appeared aristocratic. Leaning against the railing at the bow next to Max, he studied him with a scrutinizing gaze. "I take it things didn't go well with our intriguing Benjamin."

"I touched him."

Bennetts eyebrows arched almost to his hairline. "Do we need to make a report to HR?"

Max gripped the railing. "He's intriguing, and… I want to learn what his story is."

"Need or want?"

"Both." Max groaned. "I don't know."

"Well, this is new."

"Don't be rude," Max grumbled.

Bennett turned and propped his elbow on the railing. "You know you can't shag Benjamin for a few weeks and then up and leave. This one is different, and mixing business and pleasure is never a good idea."

"I've never done it before."

"You're tempted to do it this time, aren't you?"

Max remained silent.

Bennett smirked. "This is going to be interesting. For the first time in your life, you're going to have to work hard."

"I work my ass off," Max bristled.

"At Huntington Outfitters, absolutely. In relationships, not so much. You're the Prince of the Wilderness. There's always a potential partner waiting in the wings. The most effort I've ever seen you put into getting a date was the time you showed up on that model's doorstep with a Prada handbag." Bennett leaned forward conspiratorially. "I hate to break it to you, but she was only playing hard to get. She'd already been texting her friends about how she was going to snag a prince, but she was going to make him pay for it first."

"I was twenty-four. It was a moment of… of insanity," he sputtered. "And you're never going to let me forget it, are you?"

"Benjamin doesn't strike me as someone you can dazzle with your money. And from what I've seen, your usual charm isn't going to work either. Is there any point in putting all this effort into a relationship with someone when the *Faunus* is going to sail away in a few weeks?"

"Who says there'll be anything between us? I'm curious, that's all."

"If that's what you want to call it."

"You're dismissed." Max said waving Bennett away.

"Yes, your majesty," Bennett answered with a bow.

"Smartass."

"Every ruler needs a court jester."

Max watched Bennett walk away. His best friend was the furthest thing from a court jester. He was pragmatic, wise, and had a razor-sharp tongue, and Max valued his opinion. That didn't mean he always appreciated it.

THE NEXT morning Max waited in his car at the track for Benjamin to arrive. He took a sip from his second cup of coffee, trying to clear the cobwebs from a sleepless night.

Three questions. Max lay awake most of the night strategizing what his three questions would be. That wasn't the only thing keeping him awake. How could one brief touch have had such an effect on him? He'd tossed and turned, imagining running his fingers through Benjamin's soft curls, then letting them trail down his neck, over his collarbone. He groaned, shifting in his seat. Last night his fantasies ran away from him, and he ended up jerking off under the covers like a schoolboy.

Max paused mid-sip as he caught sight of Benjamin's Jeep pulling into the parking lot. Instead of parking next to him, Benjamin parked a few spots away. Benjamin wasn't going to make this easy. He thought about what Bennett had said. Determined, he got out of the car and met Benjamin at the entrance to the track.

"Morning," he said with a smile.

"Morning," Benjamin replied, sounding more resigned than happy to be there.

"Do you want to get a run in first?"

Benjamin eyed the track for a moment. "I'd rather not get lapped by you like the last time, so I guess not."

"I can make an adjustment."

"Fine," Benjamin said and headed for the track.

"Do you come here to run often?" Max asked as they stretched.

Benjamin stopped stretching his calves. "Maybe two or three times a week, whenever I can and when it's not too rainy or snowing." He set off at a slow jog. "By the way, that's one," he called out over his shoulder.

Dammit. Max took off after Benjamin and fell into step with him. He spent the first three laps trying to think of something to say that wasn't a question. Their paces matched well. The first time Max saw him at the track, he ran circles around him out of frustration. Taking out his annoyance on being cajoled into coming on this trip by his parents and their refusal to include him in the decision to acquire DGD. This time it didn't take much effort to make a slight adjustment for the two- or three-inch difference in their height. It also afforded Max a perfect view of Benjamin's toned shoulders.

Max let the laps pass in companionable silence, the only sounds their rhythmic breathing, birds stirring awake, and the occasional hum of seaplanes overhead. By the sixth lap, Benjamin slowed to a walk, resting his hands on his hips as he caught his breath.

He tugged up his tank top to wipe the sweat from his face, revealing a glimpse of his flat stomach and the trail of hair leading from his navel and disappearing beneath the waistband of his shorts. Max's gaze lingered for a moment before he turned away, his thoughts spinning. The more Benjamin revealed—both physically and personally—the deeper Max's curiosity grew, leaving him wanting to uncover every layer of the man in front of him.

Max inhaled as his heartbeat slowed. "Your mother has a different last name." It wasn't a question but a statement, Max thought, proud of his cleverness. "Why—" He paused, wanting to structure the question to get as many answers as possible. "—has your stepmother always hated you, and is that why she treats does you like an employee instead of family?"

The corner of Benjamin's lip curled up. "A better question."

"And?"

Benjamin gestured toward a small set of bleachers dotted with rust. They walked over, and Max straddled the bench, mirroring Benjamin's pose when he sat down.

"I don't know why my stepmother didn't take our last name. And I don't know why she hates me." Benjamin huffed a laugh. "I've been wondering what I did wrong since the day my father married her. Over the years I've come up with a few theories. Jealousy, greed, and race." He ticked the reasons off on his fingers.

"I get jealousy and greed, but I don't understand what race has to do with it. You're both Black."

"Not all Black folks are down with the swirl."

"Down with the swirl?"

"My mother was white. I'm mixed." He lifted his hand in a spiral. "Like the soft-serve cones of chocolate and vanilla swirled together. It's funny, she could accept having a gay stepson. But not a mixed one. Add to that, I'm Jewish, and that she absolutely couldn't accept."

"Jewish." Max's eyebrows went up in surprise.

"Yup, I'm all the things. Too many for my stepmother." Benjamin cleared his throat. "Even though you technically asked two questions as one, I'll let you ask another one."

Max locked eyes with Benjamin, seeing a combination of hurt, uncertainty, and secrets hiding in their brown depths.

"What secrets are you hiding?" He was asking the question to himself, but the words slipped out of his mouth.

Benjamin dropped his gaze, his mouth pressed into a thin line.

Max retreated so safer ground. "What was it like? The business, before your stepmother took over?"

Benjamin's face lit up. "Dad started Drinking Gourd Designs because a friend of his lost a leg in a car accident. Dad wanted Charlie to be able to go climbing with him. He designed special clamps that would work with Charlie's prosthetic. When another disabled climber saw what my dad did, she asked him to make some equipment for her. My dad took his engineering degree and combined it with his love of nature, and the rest took off from there."

"Your dad was a genius."

Benjamin smiled. "He was."

"You must miss him."

"Every day," Benjamin said with a slight quaver in his voice.

Max reached out and covered Benjamin's hand with his. "And you've been on your own ever since."

Benjamin nodded and leaned back, breaking contact. His watch pinged with a message, and he grimaced when he read it.

"That's all the questions you get," he said, rising.

"Can we do this again? Talk some more? Maybe over dinner?"

Benjamin shook his head, backing away. "I already told you—if my stepmother found out I'd been seen with you outside of the DGD offices, there'd be hell to pay. Good luck with your deal, Max. I hope you get what you want."

With that, Benjamin turned on his heel and jogged back to his Jeep. He pulled out of the parking lot so fast the Jeep wobbled, flirting with going up on two wheels.

"I plan on it," Max murmured, watching Benjamin drive away.

Chapter Six

Aspen checked on the group before they bumped Benjamin's shoulder. "So… how's it going?"

"I don't know." Benjamin stretched his neck, looking up at the sky framed by evergreens. "I'm trying to stay out of the way, but Max keeps trying to talk to me. I knew I was going to be in trouble when he figured out who I was. Rochelle rips me a new one anytime she catches me talking to Max. I'm not instigating it, but she doesn't care."

"What does he want?"

"I wish I knew. He asks me for reports he doesn't need. I think he does it as an excuse to talk to me. I'm counting down the days, Aspen. I'm so close to getting Rochelle and the twins out of my life once and for all. She's held the house over my head since my dad died, and in a few more weeks she'll never be able to do it again."

Aspen reached for Benjamin's hand and gave it a reassuring squeeze. "Sorry, I guess I got caught up in my own fantasy of being swept off my feet by a handsome prince."

"Someday your prince will come."

Aspen laughed, giving Benjamin a playful shove.

"Come on, we've still got a mile to go and then the return hike. Bubbie's got roast chicken and chocolate babka waiting for us when we get back."

"Come on everyone. Summit's near!" Benjamin announced to his hiking companions.

A few hours later, Aspen raised their hands over their head as the wind whipped through their hair. "Great hike," they shouted over the road noise.

Benjamin grinned at his friend, breathing in the late spring air. No more June gloom. Summer had arrived with bright blue skies and warmer days. On a day like today, when Benjamin got away from his stepfamily to spend time in nature, all of his worries disappeared.

"Bubbie, we're starving," Aspen announced when they walked in the door of their house.

"Come sit down and I'll get you fed," Gwen called out.

Benjamin's stomach growled when they went into the kitchen. The aroma of roast chicken filled the room as soon as Gwen opened the oven.

The smell brought a wave of childhood memories Benjamin tried to keep buried. Warm kitchens, hands plunged into sticky dough, the soft glow of Shabbat candles.

"Ben? Sweetheart, what's wrong?" Gwen grasped his arms, looking up at him with worry etched on her face.

He blinked, returning from his memories. "Sorry." He cleared his throat. "I was… remembering."

Gwen nodded with an understanding look in her eyes. She pulled him in for a tight hug and then gestured for him to sit down. Within minutes, Gwen had filled the table with chicken, roast potatoes, and salad.

"Good hike?" Gwen asked, taking her seat.

"Wait until you hear what happened," Aspen started and spent the next half hour regaling their grandma with stories from their afternoon.

Gwen gave Benjamin an extralong embrace when he left that night. "I wish you'd come and stay with us. It hurts my heart every time you leave to go back to that room in the garage."

"A few more weeks, Gwen. Do you know what I want to do on my first night in the house? Have a Shabbat dinner. I don't care if it's Friday night or any other day of the week. I want you and Aspen to come for dinner, and we'll light candles."

"We'll be there. Always. And—" She waggled her finger at him. "—you can call me Bubbie. You are as much my grandson as Aspen is my grandchild. I hope you know that."

Benjamin blinked back tears. "Thank you, Bubbie."

As night fell, Benjamin returned to Hyas House. He parked his Jeep next to the garage. His stepmother didn't like seeing it parked in front of the garage. She deemed the vehicle too dilapidated; it reflected poorly on their image. Sometimes Benjamin wondered if Rochelle didn't like seeing it because it reminded her of Benjamin's father. But that would have to mean she loved him and he was something more than a means to an end.

After going into his room, Benjamin closed the door and leaned against it with a resigned sigh. He pulled out his phone, dread pressing on his chest. It was a small indulgence he allowed himself when he went hiking. Now he'd pay the price.

Benjamin swore under his breath when he saw his screen. Twenty-seven missed messages.

Monaco: *What's my password?*

Milan: *I downloaded another virus on my laptop. Oopsie!*

Rochelle: *I need an updated employee salary report on my desk first thing in the morning.*

The bathroom shower was clogged again, dry cleaning needed to be picked up, the list went on and on.

"You can do this," he whispered.

TWO DAYS later he pulled up to the track and dropped his head to the steering wheel with a groan.

"Good morning." Max, leaning against the driver's door of a sleek black Mercedes coupe, grinned at him.

Benjamin got out of his Jeep, watching Max warily. "Can't you run on the treadmill at the gym like everyone else?"

Max took in his surroundings. "I like this place. It's quiet here. If I go to one of your gyms, I'll feel like I'm on display."

"Not my gym."

"I've been wanting to ask you about that," Max said, following him to the track.

"Do we have to do this?" Benjamin asked.

Max stopped, eyeing him with a frown. "You have dark circles under your eyes."

"So what?" he snapped back.

Max moved closer. "That was rude of me. I apologize."

"Fine." Benjamin started walking around the track. He was tired, too tired to run, but he needed a break. His stepmother's and stepsiblings' demands were never-ending since his last hiking trip. If they wanted to run him ragged before his birthday, they were succeeding. Max was ruining all his plans to have time alone, throw himself a pity party while he ran, and possibly allow himself a good cry.

"Benjamin, wait." Max grabbed his arm. "I wanted to talk to the one Tremaine who has the most common sense."

"I'm not a Tremaine, so you're out of luck." He sighed when Max wrinkled his forehead. "My stepmother never took my father's name," he explained.

"What's your name?" Max asked softly.

Benjamin looked down at Max's hand, still wrapped around his forearm, and then into Max's gray-green eyes. Who knew a pair of eyes could be such a potent truth serum? "Benjamin Colton. My dad—" His voice broke. "My dad was Joe Colton. DGD started out as Drinking Gourd Designs. Now there's nothing left. Everything he built… there's nothing left." He turned away, pressing the heels of his hands against his eyes. "I'm too tired for this."

Max's palm pressed between his shoulder blades. "I didn't mean to upset you, Benjamin."

He stiffened at the contact. An image of standing in the circle of Max's arms flashed in his mind. His heart whispered he'd find warmth and comfort in Max's embrace. When was the last time he'd hugged someone other than Aspen or Gwen? Dating? Forget it. He was too busy surviving and trying to hold on to what little he had left from his parents. Besides, what was he going to do? He didn't have a home to bring some guy back to, only a dingy room in the back of a garage. Benjamin didn't have anything to offer anyone and wasn't someone anyone would want.

"Can we sit over there and talk?" Max asked, pointing toward the bleachers by the track where they'd sat before. "We don't have to talk about DGD or your stepmother. No ulterior motive, I promise. I only want to learn more about you."

Benjamin turned to face him. "Why?"

"Well…." Max smiled. "For one thing, I think you're cute."

Ben dropped his chin, feeling the heat in his cheeks.

"I'm also convinced that you're the smartest person in your family."

"This is a bad idea." Benjamin shook his head. "I can't—I have to avoid getting on my stepmother's bad side."

While he was talking, Max somehow maneuvered him over to the bleachers, and now they sat side by side on the bottom bench.

"Why do you stick around? Once the DGD sale is completed, you'll have money to do whatever you want."

Benjamin snorted, rolling his eyes. "I won't see any of that money."

Max frowned. "Of course you will. It was your father's company."

"Spoken like someone who's never been denied anything. I was twelve when my dad died and my stepmother took over the company. Drinking Gourd Designs was part of my trust. When she reincorporated as DGD, I was cut out."

"That's… that's… how?" Max sputtered. "Wasn't there a trustee for you?"

"Yes. But if he's sleeping with my stepmother, then my best interests aren't his top priority."

"Back to my first question. Why do you stay?"

"Hyas House."

"What's Hyas House?"

"It's my home. My mother studied architecture at the University of Washington and designed Hyas House as her senior thesis, working with her professor and mentor Benjamin McAdoo. He's my namesake, the first Black architect in Seattle. Hyas is a word for 'big' in Chinook Jargon. My mom was inspired by Native American Cedar Plank house design and built Hyas House to resemble a traditional longhouse with modern elements. The house is designated a historical landmark, and it's the only thing I have left from my mother. It's the one part of my trust my stepmother can't touch. In four weeks, I'll be twenty-five. Rochelle and the twins will have to leave, and I can live there again."

Max grimaced. "Wait, you don't live in your own house?"

"Kind of."

"What does that mean?" Max asked with growing anger in his voice.

"I live in the garage."

Max jumped up, threading his fingers through his hair. "This is outrageous. You need to—"

"Nope." Benjamin stood and held his palms up. "You don't get to walk into a situation you don't have a clue about and think you can fix it. I've been dealing with Rochelle and the twins since I was twelve. You met them a week ago. You don't know anything about me or my mom and dad. I bet you didn't even do any research about my dad before you made the offer for DGD. You don't care about me. You'll sail away on your floating palace in a few weeks, and you'll never see me again. You don't get to play Prince Charming coming to the rescue." He poked Max in the chest. "Do. Not. Interfere."

Max caught Benjamin's hand, lacing their fingers together as he pulled him closer until their chests brushed. Now standing at the same height, their eyes locked. Max's hazel gaze, flecked with streaks of gold and gray, held Benjamin captive. For the first time, Benjamin caught sight of the faint constellation of freckles dusted across Max's nose.

"I won't, Benjamin." Max said in a gentle, reassuring voice. "One more question. Is hugging not your thing?" Max asked, tilting his head with a curious smile.

"Why?" Benjamin frowned.

"You kind of froze when I hugged you," Max said softly, his tone gentle but probing.

"I don't do it often."

"Hug people?" Max asked, his brow furrowing.

"No, have people hug me." Benjamin swallowed hard. He stepped back, creating space between himself and Max's tempting closeness.

"Can I see you again?" Max asked.

"That's two questions."

"I lied." Max winked.

Benjamin licked his lips. "I can't. Not outside the DGD offices. If Rochelle thought I was trying to interfere with the sale or anything—listen, she uses any excuse she can find to impose executor fees." He made air quotes. "I'll need every penny I've got when I get the house to pay taxes and for repairs."

"I understand."

"I'm sorry."

Max shook his head. "You don't have anything to be sorry for. You're right, I shouldn't make assumptions about a situation I'm not familiar with. But you're wrong too. I do care, and I won't sail away and forget about you, Benjamin."

"That was harsh. I shouldn't have said that. Ignore that stuff I said, I'm tired, it's been a long week. I should go." He started backing away. "Will you be at the DGD offices today?"

"Do you want me to be there?" Max asked, with a glint of hope in his eyes.

Tempting. So damn tempting. Benjamin snuck a glance at Max as they walked toward their cars. He'd been so focused on staying afloat, the attraction he was feeling was like being in his kayak on a stormy day, being tossed by the waves.

"I wouldn't be disappointed if you were there," he admitted.

Max flashed him a smile that made Benjamin's heart beat faster and held his hand out. "Phone, please."

Benjamin handed over his phone and watched while Max put his number into Benjamin's contacts. As Max's thumbs flew over the keyboard, Max's phone buzzed from his pocket.

"Now I have your number." He handed Benjamin's phone back to him with a satisfied smile. He held his hand out. "I'm glad we're friends, Benjamin."

Benjamin put his hand in Max's. "I… thank you."

Being friends with Max was a nice idea, but Benjamin couldn't risk being anything more.

CHAPTER SEVEN

MAX'S MOTHER greeted him when he walked in for breakfast. "I've hardly seen you since our visit to the DGD offices. What have you been doing?"

"Bennett and I wanted to take some time to explore the city." It wasn't a blatant lie. He'd spent the last week stalking the track where he'd first met Benjamin and visiting every outdoor clothing store in the city. Big chain or small mom-and-pop, he asked about Big Dipper Adventures and checked for flyers on their bulletin boards. Anything that might give him a clue to track down the elusive owner. He didn't have any success learning more about Big Dipper Adventures, but he did find out a lot about DGD.

"What did you think about our meeting with Rochelle and her twins?"

He hovered by the buffet, taking his time to doctor his coffee to his satisfaction. "It was… interesting."

His mother's gaze swept over him, and her nose wrinkled. "Really, Max, you could have at least showered before you came to breakfast."

It may have been early, but his mother was flawlessly styled and dressed as usual, her hair in a sleek blond bob that framed her face. In her late fifties, Kathrine Huntington's appearance was still smooth and unlined. Her eyes were a lighter shade of hazel than his and harmonized with the pale green-gray silk blouse she'd paired with trim pants in the same color. Coiffed, coordinated, and determined, he'd never known his mother to be anything else. She'd used all three elements to become successful in business and at his father's side, the other half of a powerful society couple.

He walked around the sleek rosewood dining table and gave his mother a kiss on the cheek as she tried to wave him away. "I went for a run."

His father stopped reading the sheaf of papers in his hand. "You should have worked out at one of the DGD Gyms."

Max sank down into one of the plush upholstered dining chairs with a sigh. "I prefer not to be on display when I work out."

Plus he'd rather hang out with Benjamin and talk more. But once again, this morning he'd had the track to himself.

"Where did you go?" his mother asked.

"I did a run around the lake."

His mother frowned. "Hardly safe, dear."

Max poured himself a cup of coffee. "What wouldn't be safe about it?" He took a sip and nodded appreciatively. Their chef was clearly taking advantage of Seattle's coffee culture. "Seattle is as safe as any other city."

His mother made a disapproving noise but didn't argue.

Max took a seat at the table and continued to stir his coffee, calculating how he wanted to approach the next subject.

He took a sip of coffee and asked. "Did you know the man who was introduced as Mrs. Tremaine's assistant was her stepson?"

Phillip Huntington narrowed his eyes. "Who?"

"That drab boy at the reception desk," Kathrine said.

Max frowned at his mother. "That's not very nice."

"All I'm saying is compared to his stepbrother and sister he's—" She shrugged. "—nothing."

Max took deep breaths, trying to calm the frustration rapidly building.

His mother's statement finally registered with his father. "Wait, that's the stepbrother?"

"You weren't paying attention, dear," Max's mother said. She got up from her seat and removed his cup, then went over to the sideboard and poured him a fresh cup of coffee. "The boy who took notes in the meeting is Rochelle Tremaine's stepson. The poor thing is lucky to have such a wonderful woman to take care of him after his father died."

Max thought about how Monaco and Milan had their social media celebrity pout perfected. Benjamin wasn't awkward; he didn't put on airs and didn't seem to care what anyone thought of him. Not once did Rochelle Tremaine refer to Benjamin as her stepson or acknowledge any family connection at all.

They'd all been sitting around discussing the sale of his father's company without acknowledging the son of its founder.

"You don't believe all the flattering crap you're saying about Rochelle and her kids, do you?"

His mother winced. "They can be a bit over the top. But she's a single woman running a successful business, and I respect that."

"About that. I've been doing some research on DGD. The company has transformed quite a bit since it was founded."

His father set his paperwork aside. "My focus is on the future and expanding into a new market with this acquisition. There's no reason to revisit the past."

Max frowned. "I still have misgivings. Have you looked at their social media platform? They don't present the inclusive image we've pivoted toward."

"You wanted to steer us in that direction. I'm still not convinced it's the right move," his mother said.

"Promoting inclusivity? What's wrong with that?"

Kathrine clasped her hands in front of her. "Will customers be able to relate to models who aren't… fit? That doesn't match the impression we want to give as an outdoor company. And we know most minorities aren't… the outdoor type."

Max groaned. "You're joking, right? Please tell me you don't believe what you're saying."

HIs mother responded with a scowl.

"There are other interesting minority-owned businesses that I'd like us to consider."

Max's father scoffed. "This is about that Big Dipper Adventures thing you're obsessed with, isn't it?"

"I'm not obsessed. I admire the untapped market they've found. Focusing on outdoor adventures for diverse communities is a brilliant move. Spaces for their LGBTQ inclusive hikes fill up months in advance, and they provide rentals of specialized hiking equipment for disabled hikers."

"Set up a meeting," his father said with a dismissive wave of his hand.

Max shifted in his seat. For months he'd been trying to find out who owned the company and set up a meeting, but the identity of the person behind Big Dipper Adventures was one of the best kept secrets in the outdoor industry.

It was a post from a month ago, with a picture on a trail by Lake Union with the caption "Even if there's only time for an urban hike in your hometown, it still counts," that gave Max the breadcrumb he needed. It was the reason he'd run around the lake that morning.

"In the meantime, we still have our deal with DGD to complete. I'd like you to consider another deal, Max. With the right coaching, Monaco or Milan would make a good companion who would—"

Max got up from his seat and threw his napkin on the table. "How many times do I have to tell you I'm not going to let you pick a partner for me. Not interested."

"Fine, then what about that lovely man we met at—"

"You mean the investment banker thirty years older than me who liked to brag about his—" Max made air quotes. "—assets?"

His mother pursed her lips. "Darling, you need a partner. Someone who will represent you and the company with elegance and grace. We have an image to uphold."

Max snorted and shook his head. He was thankful his parents accepted his bisexuality, but that acceptance came at a price. His mother threw any eligible man or woman in his path as a potential husband or wife.

"What about having a partner who I love?"

"Well, of course. But it's important that you have someone who shares your vision for the future," his father added.

Max knew his parents loved each other, and they were also a powerhouse couple. They may not have inherited his grandfather's love of the outdoors, but together they took their business savvy and the growing popularity of hiking and the outdoors to build the modest company they'd inherited into a billion-dollar lifestyle brand. His parents were a team, supporting each other through good times and bad. Yes, there was love, but over the years their love had become tempered with ambition. Finding the right partner wasn't what troubled Max. It was the shared vision for the future comment that struck a nerve with him. Right now he wasn't sure what the vision was.

"Don't be too quick to dismiss Monaco or Milan as a potential partner, dear. Take some time to get to know them while we're here," Kathrine said.

Max headed for the door. "I'm done with this conversation."

"What in the world has gotten into him?" His mother's voice followed Max down the passageway.

Retreating to his suite, he stripped off his sweats and stepped into the shower, letting the hot water wash away the tension from his conversation with his mother. When he emerged, Bennett was organizing a stack of papers on his desk. He threw on a pair of khakis and a blue Oxford shirt, eyeing his friend and muttering under his breath as he worked.

Bennett rolled up the sleeves on his shirt and raised an eyebrow at Max. "I could hear you cursing in the shower."

"It probably won't be the last time."

"That bad?"

"I didn't even get to talk to them about what we've heard about the Tremaines." Max ran his hands through his wet hair with a frustrated grunt.

"Do you want to talk about it?

"No, there's no point."

Bennett gave an understanding nod. They'd spent more time than either of them wanted trying to figure out their family dynamics.

"You're not going to get any work done on this barge. Let's get out of here."

"Barge?" Max snorted a laugh.

Bennett began shoving papers into his bag. "The point is we need a change of scenery. Let's find a pub we can work at."

Max pulled himself up and followed his friend's lead, pausing to grab his messenger bag. "A sound plan."

As soon as they stepped off the boat, Max took a deep breath, squinting at the clear blue sky. The mix of green forests, mountains, water, and sky made an intoxicating elixir.

"Let's find a place close to the DGD offices."

Bennett raised an eyebrow at his suggestion. "I'm sure we could set up shop there if we wanted."

Max weighed the option. He'd suggested a place close by, hoping to catch a glimpse of Benjamin. He'd be guaranteed a chance to interact if they worked in the offices, but how much work would they get done with Mrs. Tremaine and the twins underfoot? Then again, an unannounced visit to the offices might prove interesting.

"Good idea."

Bennett paused. "What are you scheming?"

"Don't you think an impromptu visit might prove interesting? So far we've only seen what Mrs. Tremaine wanted to present to us. Maybe if we drop by unannounced, we'll get a better idea of what's truly happening at DGD."

"Brilliant."

Benjamin jumped up from his desk, a hint of a smile on his lips when they walked in. He walked toward them, twisting his hands in front of him.

"Mr. Huntington, Mr. Goulding, what can I do for you?"

"We were feeling a bit claustrophobic on the *Faunus* and wondered if we might make use of your conference room," Bennett said.

"Oh, um, well, my stepmother and the twins aren't here right now. But I…. Sure, of course. If you'll follow me, I'll get you set up."

Benjamin led them through the office toward the conference room. This time the desks and cubicles were occupied, but there was a general air of gloom in the offices.

Then Benjamin offered them coffee or tea and to run out for pastries if they wanted. Max reassured him they were fine. As soon as he shut the door of the conference room, Bennett muttered, "Bloody hell," under his breath.

"It is a bit strange, isn't it?"

"The staff is walking around like they're at a funeral."

"Let's take a closer look at their payroll," Bennett said, pulling out his laptop.

They worked for about an hour, with Benjamin checking in on them, bringing requested files, and answering their questions. Max noted with satisfaction that Benjamin seemed more relaxed around him.

Abruptly Mrs. Tremaine burst into the room. A smile quickly replaced her slightly panicked expression.

"What a pleasant surprise. I wish I'd known you were coming. I would have rearranged my schedule so I could be here to welcome you."

"I hope we haven't inconvenienced you. We felt like a change of view."

"No, not at all," she said with a gleam in her eyes that said it was a big annoyance.

She smoothed her hands down her skintight dress and perched on the edge of the table. "Do you have any questions, or is there anything I can help you with?"

"No, not at all. Your stepson has been a perfect host." Max didn't miss the slight flinch when he referred to Benjamin as her stepson, not her assistant.

Mrs. Tremaine's eyes narrowed. "I would prefer if you worked with me. Benjamin doesn't understand the business the way I do."

Max bit down on the inside of his cheek, resisting the urge to correct her. Instead he steeled his expression and said, "Thank you for letting us know. I'll be sure to remember that going forward."

Bennett shot him a knowing look. Now that Max had learned more of Benjamin's story, the way Rochelle dismissed her stepson set his teeth on edge. Benjamin had asked him to mind his business, but how could he stand by and let Rochelle treat him so heartlessly? He wasn't going to let it go.

CHAPTER EIGHT

THE SUNLIGHT on Lake Washington made the water glitter like diamonds, and the sound of a child laughing filled the air.

"This is nice." Max admired the view.

"This is paradise." Ryan Blackstone watched over his shoulder, where his son was playing on the lawn with Ryan's husband, Dylan, and their six-month-old baby girl.

"Your life has changed since I saw you at the executive round table… when was that?"

"Three years ago." Ryan shook his head. "I think back, and I feel so disconnected, like I'm seeing a stranger's life."

"I'm so sorry to hear how badly your parents reacted to your coming out."

"I appreciate that. My story is one of many. Dylan can say the same thing."

"Yeah, but yours made the national news. I should have reached out when I read about the hostile takeover your parents and sister attempted. My only excuse is I was dealing with the mess my parents made with a botched acquisition." He grimaced. "It's been a tug of war with my parents—trying to get them to give me more control of the company. They made me president but refuse to let go of the reins."

"I'm glad you reached out while you're here."

Max took a sip of his beer and watched the boaters on the water, wondering if Benjamin was out there with the other kayakers gliding across the lake. He felt a small kernel of guilt in his gut. He'd reached out to Ryan because he genuinely liked him. Ryan had proved to be a smart, no-nonsense financial wizard. Max respected his business savvy and his ethics. When Ryan came out of the closet and his uptight conservative family attempted to take over his company and take custody of his son, every boardroom in the country was buzzing with the scandal. Max read the interview Ryan gave in the aftermath, telling the story of falling in love with his son's bone marrow donor and how both of their families rejected them. The respect Max already had for Ryan grew tenfold watching how he stood up to his family's hateful prejudice.

As happy as Max was to visit and see Ryan so content and settled, there was another reason for his visit. After Benjamin shared more of his story, Max became an amateur sleuth, researching everything he could find about Benjamin and his family. It was a fluke that he found an article about the musician Jason Anderson purchasing a home in Seattle that mentioned his new home was next door to Hyas House. Max remembered Ryan mentioning Jason was a friend. When he reached out to Ryan and learned Jason was his neighbor now, he finagled an invitation.

Now he sat two houses down from Benjamin's home.

"I like this neighborhood. You've found a great place."

"We love it here." Ryan said.

"And you get to live next door to Jason Anderson. That's pretty cool."

"Jason and his wife, Joy, are good friends."

"How about your other neighbors, the ones who live in that cool house down the street?" Max groaned inwardly, hoping he didn't sound too obvious.

Ryan's mouth twisted as if he'd eaten a lemon. His husband, Dylan, came down to the dock and perched on the arm of Ryan's chair, slinging his arm around his husband's shoulder.

"Mrs. Lieu is taking the kids for dinner." Dylan paused when he saw Ryan's expression. "Why are you making a face?"

"Max asked about Hyas House."

Dylan made the same face as his husband.

"Sorry, I didn't realize it was a touchy subject," Max said.

"Not so much touchy as infuriating," Dylan said.

Ryan rubbed his husband's back. "This is a little awkward. The woman you're here to do business with, Rochelle Tremaine, lives in that house."

"With her evil twin spawn," Dylan spat out.

"Easy, babe," Ryan said. "I know you and Benjamin are good friends, but Max is doing business with these people." Ryan leaned forward. "I've got to ask—why are you doing business with the Tremaines?"

"It's not what I wanted at all. My mother's determined to push the deal through and foist either one of the Tremaine twins off on me. She's convinced I need to get married, and I should have a partner who will make the right impression standing by my side in the press. It doesn't matter if I love them or not. Only that they keep up family appearances."

"Are you kidding me? Those two?" Dylan exclaimed. "They've got a reputation for making a spectacle of themselves."

Max sighed. "My mother has gotten it into her head that she can… I don't know, retrain them or something."

"Monaco or Milan?" Dylan asked.

"Either. She's accepted I'm bi. She's…." He took another swig from his bottle and shook his head. "I don't get it. My dad is indifferent and defends whatever my mom does no matter how much it costs the company. Lately I find myself thinking about walking away from the whole thing."

"That's pretty heavy," Ryan said with a sympathetic smile. "I've been there." He gazed at Dylan and reached up to gently caress his face. "I would have walked away from all of it. Instead I decided to fight for what I wanted." Dylan pressed his forehead against Ryan's for a second.

Max felt like an intruder, witnessing the love and trust between the two men. A heaviness settled in his chest, an unfamiliar feeling that caught him off guard. He didn't recognize it at first, and then he realized what it was. Jealousy. Max wanted what Ryan and Dylan had found. Love wasn't supposed to be a strategic partnership. Max resolved that no matter what his mother wanted, he would hold out for a meaningful relationship.

"I'm getting the sense you don't support Huntington Outfitters purchasing DGD," Ryan said.

"I don't like it. Something's off. On paper everything appears straightforward, but it doesn't pass the sniff test. Do you know anything I should know?"

Ryan shook his head. "I haven't dealt with Rochelle Tremaine in any business capacity. Dylan, has Benjamin said anything to you?"

"Benjamin's a quiet guy. He's had a pretty shitty time since his dad died. Rochelle is doing her best to reinforce the evil stepmother stereotype. He turns twenty-five in four weeks and gets Hyas House and whatever's left of his trust fund. I don't think there's going to be anything left. Rochelle's been making Benjamin pay for every lightbulb and repair on the house out of his trust and charging him crazy trustee fees. I didn't realize until recently that he doesn't even get paid to work at DGD. His salary goes toward paying Rochelle's fees."

Dylan's revelation made Max's blood run cold.

"I wanted to report her for fraud, but Benjamin begged me not to. He's terrified of losing Hyas House. It's more than a house to him. It's a connection to his parents, to what it meant to have a family." Ryan said.

"WHERE HAVE you been, Max? Monaco and Milan came by to take you to dinner. It's rude of you to ignore our hosts."

"They may be your hosts, but they're not mine. I have no intention of going to dinner or anywhere with the Tremaine twins."

"Honestly, Max, what's gotten into you? You've become so stubborn and difficult."

"Refusing to marry whoever you throw at me isn't being difficult. Don't you think I'm worth more than a marriage that's nothing better than a contract? I'm your son, not an investment."

"You need to settle down. I want to be sure you have the right partner before I hand over the reins of Huntington Outfitters," she said with steely determination.

"What about being confident in my abilities to run the company? Shouldn't that matter more?"

"Yes, of course," she said with a dismissive wave of her hand. "All of that matters, but you need the right person by your side. Someone who understands the pressure and who will present the right image. I've spent most of my life building up the Huntington brand. I won't allow some common nobody to represent my company or my family."

Max knew she didn't even hear herself. The words "my company and my family" stung like a slap in the face. He believed that it was *their* company, all of theirs as a family.

"It's late, and I have a headache," he muttered and walked away. Max returned to his cabin and took his suitcase out of the closet. He yanked open a drawer and grabbed a handful of T-shirts blindly. Frustration and anger fueled his need to escape his mother's suffocating grip on his life and career. He was exhausted by the relentless battle of wills their relationship had become. An image of Benjamin flashed in his mind, and he dropped the bundle of clothing. Resting his hands on the dresser, he drew in a few calming breaths. Something new took up space where his anger had churned in his gut before. Shame. He closed the drawer and put his suitcase back in the closet. He couldn't run away because he was unhappy. Benjamin didn't have that luxury. Every day he had to face his struggles and worries head-on. Benjamin couldn't go to the airport, jump on a private jet, and fly away. "There's too much at stake," he said to himself. This wasn't about his relationship with his mother or Huntington Outfitters; Max wanted to stay for Benjamin… and for himself.

"HOW WAS your evening?" Bennett asked when Max found him lounging on the upper bow deck, ensconced in one of the teak deck chairs with his laptop balanced on his lap. He snapped it closed when Max approached, but not before Max saw the email from Bennett's father.

Max dropped into the deck chair next to him. "Insightful."

"Interesting word choice. Do you care to share what you've learned?" Bennett's English accent was even more clipped and pronounced than usual. Not a good sign. Whatever was in the message from his father, it wasn't good.

"It's not so much what I've learned as what I've confirmed. We shouldn't be doing this deal with DGD."

Bennett put his laptop aside and leaned forward. "I agree. The research I've been doing the past week doesn't paint an attractive picture. There's been an increase in employee turnover. That's normal. There's always turnover that happens with a sale. But this is a long-term problem. Employees resign as fast as they come in. It doesn't help that DGD pays well under the industry standard. They've been filling the gap using interns. And as for our young Benjamin…." Bennett made a noise of disgust. "He's being paid minimum wage while his stepsiblings are drawing huge salaries."

Max remembered Dylan's comment about Benjamin's salary going toward his stepmother's executor fees. How did he have enough money to live on? And where else was Rochelle cutting corners?

"I'm doing more investigation into the day-to-day administration of the company. I've tracked down a few former employees, but no one is willing to talk. Rochelle has done a thorough job of intimidating her employees, making them sign noncompetes and NDA's. I've also found this." Bennett reached for his laptop, reopened it, and handed it to Max.

Max frowned at the social media profile. "Who in the hell is BirchBitch206?"

"That's a mystery, but whoever they are, they have a wicked sense of humor. Their reviews of the DGD gyms and apparel are biting. As if that weren't bad enough, the comments are as scathing. If the sale goes through, we're going to have a lot of work ahead of us to repair DGD's reputation."

"And we have no idea who's behind this?"

"Whoever created the account is incredibly tech savvy. The information is behind a firewall and layers of security none of our tech guys have been able to get through."

Max pinched the bridge of his nose. "Great," he muttered. "I have no idea what my mother's definition of due diligence is."

He read the review again and snorted a laugh.

I thought the newest DGD Gym would be a haven for sculpting glutes that could crack walnuts and achieving a level of core strength that rivals a circus acrobat. But oh, how the mighty (and mildly sore) have been deceived. Allow me to elaborate.

Is this a gym or are we going to da club? There are more mirrors than gym equipment. Vanity thy name is DGD....

The review went on with biting critiques of everything from the music to the heavily scented soaps in the changing rooms that smelled like—Max reread the comment—*Gucci in a freshly manured rose garden.*

His eyes flew to Bennett, whose face was lit up with amusement.

"I think they have a real shot at becoming a presidential speech writer."

"First Big Dipper Adventures and now this. Dammit, why can't we find any of these people?"

Bennett leaned back and steepled his fingers. "Ah, now there is where I have some good news. A last-minute spot opened up this weekend." Bennett's lips curled into a mischievous grin. "You're going on a hike."

Chapter Nine

THERE WAS something about heading east on I-90, where the urban sprawl gave way to mountains and forests, that always felt like home. Benjamin and his dad had spent all their free time camping and hiking, exploring every trail across the Pacific Northwest. He loved it all, but seeing the sign for the Snoqualmie Forest always brought a special smile to his face. His dad's presence lingered here in the trees and on the trails.

This was where Benjamin and his dad would lay in their sleeping bags under a canopy of stars, his dad weaving stories about each constellation. During their last summer together, they'd turned it into a game. For every constellation Benjamin could name, along with its stars, he'd earn a dollar; if he missed one, he'd owe a dollar back. He only missed one. His dad had made a big deal of it, even drafting an official contract for them to sign, complete with exaggerated ceremony. The memory was etched into Benjamin's heart, and he cherished it.

"We have a fun group today." Aspen said when they parked by the trailhead.

"Has everyone participated in the group calls?"

For this particular hike, they offered weekly group calls a month ahead to give participants extra time to ask questions.

"Most of them have dialed in at least once, except our last-minute substitution."

The sun added an extra sparkle to Aspen's cobalt-blue glitter spandex shorts. Today they'd paired them with a Big Dipper Adventures T-shirt bedazzled with gold crystals that formed the constellation on the front of the shirt. Aspen completed their ensemble by wearing gold glitter eyeshadow that brought out the flecks of gold in their hazel eyes, and more gold glitter in their dark brown hair.

"Good. Thanks for taking care of the advance work." Benjamin jumped out of the driver's side, and they started their routine double-checking of the supplies in their packs.

Benjamin was as eager as his clients to get going. He needed this hike as much as the participants. It had been a stressful and unsettling week since the Huntingtons arrived, and he'd been looking forward to some time in the mountains. Today's hike was an easy one, but Benjamin always made sure he was prepared for any emergency. For the Overcoming Your Fears hike, that meant having brown paper bags on hand in case someone started to hyperventilate.

When Benjamin paused to scan the horizon, the sky stretched out in a brilliant blue without even a whisper of clouds. The sunlight cast long shadows from the evergreens that framed the view. The temperature had already climbed into the upper 60s, with a light breeze carrying the earthy scent of pine. By afternoon it was expected to reach the low 80s, promising the kind of day that locals cherished. A Pacific Northwest summer day, perfect for outdoor adventures or simply soaking up the sun. Once he had his pack organized, Benjamin set it down with Aspen's. He took a deep breath, filling his lungs with the evergreen-scented air. Days like today made the bad days bearable.

"Here they come," Aspen announced as the first of their hikers began to arrive at their meeting point.

"You ready?" he asked Aspen.

They nodded with a grin. "I've been looking forward to this hike all week. One of the participants is a total cutie. He listed his pronouns as he/him and identified as LGBTQ. Maybe if I help him overcome his fear of spiders, he'll reward me later." Aspen waggled their eyebrows.

"Sometimes I wonder if the only reason you do this with me is to get dates," Benjamin said with a teasing laugh.

"That and get inspiration for my act. I've been thinking I could start having Theresa use a backpack on stage," Aspen tapped their chin with a thoughtful gaze. "Maybe something with a roasted marshmallow on a stick."

Aspen was one of the most creative people Benjamin knew, and he had no doubt they'd pull it off. He could easily picture his best friend on stage in their drag persona, Theresa Hugger, doing naughty things with a roasted marshmallow. The idea had him chuckling with anticipation.

Aspen's parents had been appalled when they discovered their son's costumes and makeup. Gwen was the complete opposite, encouraging their creative side. In their Bubbie's house, Aspen was allowed to flourish, and their creativity was seen as an asset, not a drawback. Aspen's parents weren't the only ones who didn't appreciate Aspen's talents. A lot of people underestimated them, assuming they were nothing more than an airheaded twink, based on their looks, but Aspen was so much more. They were offered full scholarships to Stanford and Harvard but chose the University of Washington and stayed in Seattle to be close to Gwen and help Benjamin with Big Dipper Adventures. Benjamin almost felt sorry for anyone who underestimated his friend. Almost. Anyone who didn't appreciate the bright, loyal, and loving person Aspen was didn't deserve to be in their orbit.

"Everyone's here except our last-minute sign up," Aspen said as they ticked another name on their tablet a few minutes later.

"Maybe they had a last-minute case of nerves. Let's go ahead and get started."

Aspen turned to the group with one of his dazzling smiles. "Welcome, everyone, I'm so happy to see you all in person. A few of you I've met online." He gave a quick wink in the direction of the person Benjamin assumed was the cute guy Aspen had their eye on. "I promise you it wasn't on Tinder." The group laughed, and the guy in question blushed pink to the tips of his ears. "For those of you I haven't met, I'm Aspen, my pronouns are they/them." He gestured to Benjamin the same way Vanna White presented a letter. "This is Benjamin, he/him. Benjamin and I are going to be your guides today. I know today's hike might be a bigger mountain for you to climb than the three-mile trail we're going to explore, but I want to reassure each and every one of you that Benjamin and I will be with you every step of the way, no matter how long your journey takes."

Benjamin surveyed the group of assembled hikers with a warm smile. Days like today made his daily struggle worth it. Big Dipper Adventures was where his heart was, his baby, and in a few more weeks he'd be able to watch it grow without worrying about his stepmother trying to take it away from him if she found out about it.

The Face Your Fears hike was an easy three-mile trek in the Snoqualmie forest an hour outside of Seattle. The hike was tailored for people who had phobias about nature. Fears about bugs and snakes were the biggest issues with the group.

The young man standing in front of him raised his hand for the third time. He swallowed, his Adam's apple bobbing as he shifted from side to side. "You're sure spiders won't drop down from the trees?"

Benjamin had reviewed the young man's intake form and knew his therapist recommended this hike to help him with his arachnophobia. A couple of the other hikers nodded when the question was asked, clearly sharing the same concern. He exchanged a look with Aspen. They'd been through this routine every time they offered this particular adventure.

"That sounds like it would be frightening, doesn't it?" Benjamin said with a sympathetic smile.

There were more nods.

"Let's try to remember that most woodland creatures are quite shy. They aren't as interested in us as we are in them. Would anyone like to recall what we learned about a spider's vision earlier?"

The hike included an online orientation learning about animal behavior with a focus on specific animals the hikers expressed fear of. Spiders and snakes were always the two they spent most of their time on.

An older woman raised her hand. "Their field of vision is limited. They can't see us very well from far away." She took a shaky breath and added, "From up in the trees, we'd be too far away for them to want to attack us."

Aspen nodded in approval. "That's exactly right, Carol."

"What do you think, should we get started?" Benjamin asked.

"As I said before," Aspen added, "Benjamin and I will be with you every step. We have all day, so if you need to stop and take a break, we can do that. When we get to the end of the trail, there's a beautiful waterfall, and we'll stop for lunch."

"Sorry I'm late."

Benjamin's heart skipped a beat, hearing the familiar voice. His eyes locked with Max Huntington's. What. The. Actual. Fuck.

"Holy shit," Aspen gasped. "It's him, isn't it? The Prince of the Wilderness."

Forget spiders, Benjamin was facing *his* worst fear. He couldn't run away. He'd heard the expression "deer in the headlights," but he'd never known what that really meant until now.

Aspen moved to his side. "What in the world is he doing here?" When Benjamin didn't answer, they gave his arm a little shake. "Benjamin, are you okay? You kind of look like you might pass out."

Benjamin put his hand over his heart and tried to remember how to breathe. He blinked, hoping Max was nothing more than a hallucination he'd conjured with his imagination. But he was very real and standing in front of him. This was an added complication he didn't need.

He glanced down at his tablet to review the names on the list. Only one person hadn't checked in with the rest of the group. He read the name again with an inward groan. Seeing it now, it was so obvious. Maxwell Hunter.

Glancing toward the other hikers, he drew in a shaky breath and forced a smile. He'd have to wait to have a meltdown. "Aspen, why don't you lead our group?" He shot Max an annoyed glare. "I'll walk with Mr. Hunter and get him caught up."

Aspen hesitated, with a worried look.

"Go ahead, I'll be fine," Benjamin said with a nod.

Aspen gave his arm a reassuring squeeze and shot Max a glare before turning toward the rest of the group. Clapping their hands, they announced, "All right, everyone, let's get started."

There was no way out of this. Max knew Benjamin was a part of Big Dipper Adventures. The question was, Did he know he was the owner?

Max was staring at him with a grin on his face. Yeah. He knew.

Chapter Ten

Green shoelaces. Max's gaze went from the emerald-green shoelaces to Benjamin with awe and growing excitement, realization washing over him. The person he'd been searching for all along had been right there in Seattle, within reach. But while Max's heart swelled at the sight of him, Benjamin's clipped, irritated tone made it clear he didn't share the sentiment.

Max tilted his head and flashed a winning smile that never failed him in the boardroom or the bedroom. "What a pleasant surprise." He said, hoping to break the tension.

Benjamin put his hand up. "I-I need a minute. Don't talk to me for the next five minutes."

Max's smile fell. He reached for Benjamin's arm, softening his tone. "I didn't mean to upset you. I swear I didn't know you were a part of Big Dipper Adventures."

Benjamin backed away, turned, and started toward the trail. Max quickly fell into step beside him.

"For right now you are part of the group. My clients depend on me. Don't expect VIP treatment." Benjamin said between clenched teeth. "We need to catch up. There are hikers who legitimately want to be here, and they're my priority."

Shit. This wasn't how he imagined his first meeting with the owner of Big Dipper Adventures would go. He didn't have Benjamin being the elusive owner on his bingo card either. Max kept his mouth shut, concentrating on keeping pace while he frantically tried to come up with a strategy that would salvage the situation. He stayed a few steps behind, giving him a chance to admire Benjamin's calves and toned thighs. For the first time, he noticed the tiny Big Dipper tattoo tucked behind Benjamin's ear. His fingers tingled with the urge to trace the delicate constellation.

At their brisk pace, they caught up to the other hikers right before they turned the first bend and disappeared out of sight.

For the next hour, Max hovered in the background, studying Benjamin at work. Max admired his ability to reassure his clients' fears and encourage them to step outside their comfort zone. He observed every interaction closely, impressed with the way Benjamin paid attention. When one of the hikers lagged behind, he offered gentle words of encouragement and support. The only person Benjamin didn't have any kind words for was Max, still clearly upset at his intrusion.

There were many things that enticed Max about a potential lover. Good looks and sexual attraction were usually enough for the short dalliances he preferred. Benjamin's quiet confidence, intelligence, and compassion mesmerized Max. The force of the magnetic pull he felt toward Benjamin was new and unfamiliar in its intensity.

When they stopped for lunch, Benjamin pointed to a flat rock on the edge of the clearing. "Take your backpack off and sit down. Don't argue," he ordered when Max started to speak.

Max backed away and sat as directed. He slid his backpack off with a sigh of relief and waited while Benjamin checked on the rest of the group, assuring himself everyone was situated with their lunches and that Aspen didn't need any help before he headed toward Max, eyes locked on his, flashing with anger.

Benjamin dropped his backpack at Max's feet, crouched down, and grabbed Max's foot. He unlaced the hiking boot that had been causing Max to limp.

"What are you doing?" Max asked as Benjamin peeled off his sock.

"Your boots don't fit properly. You've been limping for the last mile." Benjamin said, focusing on the blister on Max's heel instead of brushing his thumb over the smooth skin around his ankle, running his hand up his leg, and—Max's fantasy ended abruptly as Benjamin dropped Max's foot and reached into his backpack for his first aid kit. "Do you have a lunch with you? You can eat while I take care of this."

"What about you? You should eat too."

"Don't worry about me. I'll be fine," he snapped, applying antibiotic ointment to Max's blister.

"Benjamin, look at me," Max asked with a quiet urgency. Benjamin's eyes met his. "I'm sorry. I didn't mean to upset you by being here."

"Why are you here?"

"Because I wanted to meet the brilliant person behind Big Dipper Adventures."

"How long have you known?"

"Not until I got here today. The green shoelaces confirmed it. You don't show your face online, but your shoelaces stood out in the Instagram posts."

Benjamin's gaze dropped to his hiking boots. "Dammit."

"Why the green laces?" Max asked.

"My dad wore green laces in his hiking boots." Benjamin fingered the cords. "They were one of the first gifts my mom gave him. They were poor college students. Shoelaces, a compass, a set of mechanical pencils—they gave each other little things since they couldn't afford much more. It wasn't about the value, but the thoughtfulness."

"Your parents sound like they were lovely people."

"They were."

Max heard the love in Benjamin's voice and reached for his hand, gave it a squeeze. "They would be proud of you."

Benjamin pulled out of his grasp. "Not now. I can't have this conversation right now."

"Can we talk after the hike? Do you have anything else planned once you're done?"

"I… Max, you're making this so hard." Benjamin's voice wavered. "I can't afford any mistakes right now. If my stepmother finds out about this, I-I could lose everything. I'm only three weeks away from getting Hyas House. Please, don't ruin this for me."

The pleading in Benjamin's voice pulled at Max's heart. All he wanted to do was wrap Benjamin in his arms and promise to protect him, no matter what.

"What you've built here…. Benjamin, this is something special."

"Thanks," Benjamin said and made quick work of putting a bandage on Max's foot, then handed him back his sock. "Here. I can try to relace your boots so they'll fit a little better." He eyed Max with a wry smile. "I would have thought the Prince of the Wilderness would have better boots."

Max frowned, tugging on his sock. "I didn't have any with me. I had to order these at the last minute."

As soon as he slipped his boot back on, Benjamin crouched down again and adjusted Max's laces, sneaking looks at Max. The sunlight revealed strands of deep auburn in Benjamin's dark curls. Max smiled, noticing the slight tremor in Benjamin's hands as he retied Max's boots. It was nice to know their close proximity affected him as much as it did Max, who ended up grabbing his backpack and pulling it into his lap to hide his body's response at having Benjamin keeling before him.

"All done." Benjamin jumped up and blew out a shaky breath. "Make sure you say something if you're having any trouble on the rest of the hike."

Max nodded and held his hand out without thinking. Benjamin grasped it and pulled him up. Suddenly they were eye to eye. Max took a deep breath, taking in the scent of pine that clung to Benjamin's skin. His gut tightened when Benjamin's tongue peeked out to lick his lips.

"I-I need to get back to the rest of the group," Benjamin mumbled, turning away.

He stopped when Max pulled his backpack on with a wince. Benjamin moved behind him and put his hand on Max's shoulder.

"Wait a minute," he said, slipping two fingers under the shoulder straps. He made a noise of disapproval and started making adjustments.

Max rolled his shoulders. "Thank you, that feels much better."

"Why didn't you check your straps? You should know better."

Max flinched. Benjamin was right. He should. Now wasn't the time to reveal his own secret, but he hoped when he did, Benjamin would understand.

"I forgot," he said, avoiding Benjamin's gaze.

Forty-five minutes later they reached the summit and the spectacular views of the valley below. Max enjoyed watching the other hikers celebrate their accomplishment. Big Dipper Adventures was everything Max hoped it would be and so much more. Benjamin had discovered an untapped market with tremendous potential.

The rest of the hike went well with only one minor panic when a thin little garter snake crossed the trail on their way back down. Thankfully it was a tiny one and went across so quickly half the group didn't see it. Aspen jumped in with a reminder that garter snakes were needed for a healthy ecosystem, saving the day with their quick thinking. A natural performer,

Aspen created an elaborate story about how they'd missed seeing a snake eat a giant spider that was in their path, and wasn't that lucky they had the snake to clear the way. Max bit back a smile while Aspen told their story. Aspen was another one of Big Dipper Adventures' assets.

With a bit of hand-holding and plenty of encouraging words, they managed to push past that challenging point on the trail. When they finally reached the end of the hike, Benjamin congratulated each participant and handed out Big Dipper pins as a reward for overcoming their fears and completing the hike. The pins weren't elaborate, a small oval of cobalt-blue enamel dotted with tiny silver stars in the shape of the Big Dipper. But from the expressions of pride on the participants' faces, you would have thought they'd won the Nobel Prize. Max hovered at the edge of the group, watching Benjamin with admiration.

As the hikers headed back to their cars, Aspen went over and bumped their shoulder against Benjamin's. The two of them whispered out of earshot for a moment before they approached Max.

"Hello, I'm Max Huntington, and I'm sorry I was late and didn't have a chance to introduce myself earlier," he said, holding his hand out to Aspen.

Aspen's lips quirked. "I'm sorry, I thought you were Maxwell Hunter," they said, mimicking Max's upper-class East Coast accent.

"I shouldn't have done that."

"And why did you?" Aspen asked, moving to stand in front of Benjamin and folding their arms in front of them.

"My assistant, Bennett, signed me up. I… we didn't want to cause a stir."

"Oh my." Aspen put their hand over their heart, batting their eyelashes at Max. "Cause a stir? Aren't we fancy."

"Aspen." Benjamin slapped his forehead, shaking his head.

Aspen's eyes narrowed. "Are you going to do anything to scare my best friend?"

Benjamin groaned and gently pushed Aspen so they weren't standing between him and Max. "It's okay, Aspen. I don't think Max came to cause any trouble."

Aspen glared at Max. "He's upsetting you, and I don't like it."

Max liked Benjamin's friend. They had a fiery spirit, and he appreciated the way they defended Benjamin.

He held his hands up. "I can assure you I have no improper intentions toward Benjamin."

Aspen narrowed their eyes, studying him for a minute before they held their hand out. "Okay. Give me your keys."

"What?"

"I'm driving your car back so you can ride with Benjamin." They leaned closer. "I'm doing you a favor," they said in a hushed voice that was still loud enough for Benjamin to hear.

"Stop playing shadchan," Benjamin said.

Max wrinkled his forehead at Aspen. "What's a shad chan?"

"Shadchan." Aspen corrected his pronunciation. "It's a Jewish matchmaker. We met in Hebrew school." Aspen threw their arm around Benjamin's shoulder.

"Okay, enough. You're confusing him," Benjamin said, eyeing Max with a worried frown.

"Fine," Aspen huffed. They held their hand out again. "Keys, please."

Max pulled out his keys and dropped them into Aspen's palm.

"Yay," Aspen shouted. They grabbed their backpack and started running toward Max's Mercedes.

"Please tell me I'm going to get my car back." Max said.

"Um… eventually?"

Max threw his head back and laughed. "Good enough for me."

"We should get going."

Max followed Benjamin to his Jeep.

"Are you hungry?" Benjamin asked as he started the engine. "There's a burger place not too far from here. We could grab some food and have a picnic."

"Sounds good to me."

Max gazed at Benjamin as the Jeep flew down the highway. Benjamin gripped the steering wheel tightly, his jaw clenched.

The wind tousled Max's hair, and the sun's warmth soaked into his skin. Riding in Benjamin's vintage Jeep with the top down was far more fun than driving the finest sports cars Max had access to.

He snuck another glance at Benjamin, sitting with his back straight, his eyes trained on the road.

"Hey," he called out over the wind. "Relax, Benjamin. I promise I don't bite… unless you want me to."

Benjamin's breath came out in a whoosh, and he laughed. "That's the cheesiest line I've ever heard. Does that actually work for you?"

"Truth?"

Benjamin nodded. "Yes, please."

"I've always wanted to try it on someone."

"I suppose I should be honored?"

"As long as you're not offended."

"I have a lot of feelings right now, but offended isn't one of them."

"I'm glad to hear that. I'm blown away by what I saw today. Big Dipper Adventures is a great company."

Benjamin snorted. "I wouldn't call it a company. Right now it's still a dream. I'll be able to grow Big Dipper Adventures into so much more in the future."

"In three more weeks?"

"My twenty-fifth birthday is one I've been counting the days to for a long time."

Benjamin pulled off the freeway and onto a narrow two-lane road, arriving shortly at a classic old-school burger stand. "It's not fancy, but these are the best burgers around."

Max's stomach rumbled at the smell of french fries and grilled meat.

"My treat," Max said.

Benjamin paused. "Are you trying to win me over with a burger?"

"Is there a chance it might work?"

Benjamin smiled. "Maybe."

Chapter Eleven

"This is one of my favorite places." Benjamin said, pulling up to the overlook.

"Wow, this is amazing," Max said, getting out of the Jeep and walking toward the edge of a massive cliffside with a view of a bright blue lake ringed by emerald-green forests below.

Max swept his arm over the scenery. "Who owns all this?"

Leave it to Max Huntington to think of the land as a commodity first.

"We do. This is BLM land."

"It's amazing when you think about it. This is only a small portion of the public land managed by the Bureau of Land Management."

Benjamin busied himself grabbing their burgers and shakes. He'd parked so they could sit on the tailgate and eat their lunch.

Max turned to him with the dazzling smile that made his stomach clench. He walked over and perched on the tailgate, where Benjamin had spread a blanket for them to sit on. He grabbed one of the bags and started rummaging through it. His hand emerged, clutching french fries that he immediately shoved into his mouth.

"Mmm. These are the best fries I think I've ever had," he said around a mouthful.

"I didn't take you for being the kind of guy who is a connoisseur of burger-joint fries," Benjamin said, listening to Max's grunts and groans of satisfaction with amusement.

Max finished chewing and swallowed. Reaching into the bag for another handful, he hesitated for a moment. "Well… I haven't had fries in a while. The chef at Le Bardin got mad at me for making a special request."

"So you're telling me you live in New York City, which has to have about a bazillion burger joints, and you ask a chef at a fancy restaurant to make you french fries?"

Benjamin reached into his bag, pulled out their burgers, and handed one to Max, who opened it and started devouring it with the same gusto as he did the fries. A sudden realization struck Benjamin.

"You don't live the lifestyle that you feature in the Huntington Outfitters advertising, do you?"

Max balled up the empty wrapper from his burger and reached for his milkshake. His lips wrapped around the straw, he sucked in the sugary sweetness while a faint blush stole over his cheeks. Finally, he put the milkshake aside, picked up the wrapper from the straw, and began twisting it between his fingers.

"I didn't want it to be that way. I never wanted to be the poster child, the Prince of the Wilderness. It was my mother's idea, and it got out of hand. Once she put it out there"—his shoulders sagged—"the press grabbed on to it and it just… got out of hand."

"Life doesn't always go the way you'd planned."

"What was your life like before your stepmother came into the picture?"

Benjamin smiled. "We were happy. Always outside, camping and hiking together as a family. My mom would make these big Shabbat dinners, and our house would be filled with their friends."

"Were you religious?"

"Not all that much. My dad wasn't Jewish, but we belonged to a temple that welcomed a lot of interfaith families. I went to Hebrew school and a Jewish summer camp for a few summers before my mother died."

"How old were you?"

"Nine." Benjamin drew in a shaky breath. "She had ovarian cancer. By the time they found it, it was too late. And then it was me and my dad. We spent even more time in the woods. We'd camp under the stars, and Dad would tell the stories of all the constellations."

"Big Dipper Adventures—it makes sense now."

"That was always my favorite story. The Drinking Gourd. We'd lie in our sleeping bags looking up at the stars, and he'd talk about his ancestors in Mississippi and how they followed the Big Dipper, trusting its light to guide them to freedom in the North. Then he'd weave in the African tale of a magical drinking gourd, one that never ran dry and could sustain everyone, no matter their needs. Remembering it now, I think he already knew I was gay. He was giving his support, in his quiet way, that no matter who I was or where life took me, there would always be a place for me, a world big enough to hold me just as I am. That night he pointed to the sky and said, 'See all those stars? Those are your ancestors, and they're shining bright because they are so proud of you. All that brightness is so you can see how much they love you. Always look to the stars. Look closely, and you'll find the answers to many secrets.'"

Max took his hand, weaving their fingers. "You loved him very much."

Benjamin couldn't stop the tear that escaped. "No one could have asked for a better dad."

"You're not angry for him marrying your stepmother?"

"She fooled all of us at first. There was always a reason why they couldn't go camping with us." Benjamin closed his eyes with a shudder. "I think I realized it before my dad did. I came home one day, and the mezuzah on our front door was gone."

Max moved closer, squeezing his hand.

"Don't give me that look. I don't want to be a poster child for having a shitty stepmother. A lot of kids have it way worse than I did. I didn't end up in a foster home. I wasn't rejected for being gay."

"For being Jewish?" Max asked quietly.

"There are a lot of people who are anti-Semitic without thinking they're racist," Benjamin said with a wry smile. "Anti-Semitism is funny that way."

"She took away your Jewish identity along with everything else, didn't she?"

Benjamin nodded, swallowing past the lump in his throat. "Aspen and their Bubbie kept me connected. Shabbat dinners, Passover, and Hanukkah. I've spent them all with them since my dad died."

Even though Benjamin had asked Max not to feel sorry for him, he could still see the shadow of pity in Max's eyes. And for a moment Benjamin felt sorry for himself. He didn't share these details about his life to many people for this exact reason. He hated to see their sympathetic expressions, even though he knew they came from a place of empathy.

"And now you know," he said, trying to sound cavalier.

"Can I ask how you started? What gave you the idea for Big Dipper?" Max asked.

"I was going hiking, and I saw a Black family on the trail. A mom and dad with two little kids. It was pretty obvious they hadn't gone hiking before. They weren't wearing the right shoes and didn't have any gear with them. Another hiker was harassing them, telling them Black folks didn't have any business being in nature. I stepped in, told the other hiker to stop being a racist asshole, and offered to take them hiking with me. As we hiked, I learned that they wanted to take their kids out in nature more but were afraid because of precisely what happened. There's still bias and a stereotype that Black folks don't do outdoor activities. It was part of the reason my dad started his climbing gym and opened it in a predominantly Black neighborhood. Dad wanted Black folks and other minorities to believe they could hike and camp too. When I saw that family, I thought of my dad and wanted to honor his memory. I gave the family my email and offered to help them buy the right gear, and it kind of grew from there."

Max's gaze changed from sorrow to admiration. "That's amazing. You're amazing."

Benjamin's eyes dropped to his lips.

Max unwound their fingers but held on to Benjamin's hand and pressed it to his chest. Could Benjamin feel his heartbeat under his palm? Could he hear Max's heart beating loudly?

"Benjamin." Max's voice dropped low. "I'd really like to kiss you right now."

"Because you feel sorry for me?"

Max shook his head. "No. Because you're the most beautiful man I've ever met, both inside and out. Because you're strong, kind, and—"

Benjamin cut him off, pressing his lips against Max's. It didn't matter what the third reason was—he couldn't resist the temptation anymore. He slipped his tongue inside when Max groaned. His lips were soft and firm; the kiss was salty and sweet from the french fries and milkshakes. Benjamin was usually more timid, but he could sense Max was letting him take the lead, and he did. He devoured Max with each lick, taste, and suck. When Benjamin moved closer, Max wrapped his arms around his waist, and it was his turn. Benjamin whimpered when Max ended the kiss, melted against him, and began to pepper soft kisses along his jaw and his neck. When he returned to Benjamin's mouth, all Benjamin could think was *Ah, there it is*. This is what he needed, what he'd been longing for—a kiss that made every part of him feel complete.

The realization shook him to his core. He dropped his head to Max's shoulder with a shudder.

Max's framed his face with his hands, brushing the wetness Benjamin hadn't realized was there from his cheeks. "What's wrong? What did I do? Whatever it is, I'm—"

"Stop. You didn't do anything wrong. I realized…." He dropped his chin to his chest. "This is embarrassing."

Max grasped his chin and lifted his face so their eyes met again. "I never want you to feel embarrassed with me."

Benjamin tried to look away. "I haven't… no one… I don't get hugs often, that's all."

Max pressed a gentle kiss to his forehead before he wrapped his arms around Benjamin and pulled him into a tight embrace.

"Please don't take this the wrong way, but your timing is the worst. We can't do this. Not until my birthday."

Max kissed the corner of his mouth. Benjamin closed his eyes and shivered when Max's thumb brushed over his cheekbone.

"Okay." Max said.

Okay? That was it? Did that mean Max understood that Benjamin wasn't going to kiss him again no matter how badly he wanted to? If that's what it meant, why was Max cupping the back of his head.

"You said okay. What are you doing?"

"Getting ready to kiss you again."

"But I said—"

Another kiss ended Benjamin's protest. This time Max was the one taking control. As he pulled Benjamin closer, Max shifted his leg and nudged it between Benjamin's thighs. Benjamin opened his mouth, welcoming Max's invasion, and melted into his arms.

"I said we can't," Benjamin murmured in a lust-filled haze.

"I know." Max smiled. "So I'm going to kiss you as much as I can before we leave this place."

By the time they pulled out of the parking lot, Benjamin's lips were swollen, and his body ached for more. In a perfect world they would have stayed until the stars came out and done a lot more than make out like two crazed teenagers. But there was too much to do back home, and he couldn't afford to come home late and incur Rochelle's wrath or suspicion.

"Why were you curious about Big Dipper Adventures?" he asked as they crossed over the floating bridge into the city.

"I thought it would make a better investment than DGD. I was going to try to convince the owner to sell."

Benjamin's jaw ticked. "It's not for sale."

"I admired the business model before I knew it was you. Big Dipper Adventures has so much potential. With the right investment it can be so much more."

Benjamin's grip tightened on the steering wheel. "Do you think I don't know that?"

"Then you should consider what a partnership with Huntington Outfitters could do for you."

"Not interested."

"You haven't even heard my offer."

Benjamin's stomach sank. The perfect afternoon was all a lie.

"I said it's not for sale."

"Maybe it's something you haven't considered before, but—"

Benjamin pulled up to the *Faunus* and slammed on the brakes. "Get out."

"Benjamin, wait. Let's talk."

"I can't be seen with you in my Jeep. Get out."

Max put his hand on the door and hesitated. "We need to talk about this."

"No. We don't. DGD isn't enough. You had to con me to try and get Big Dipper Adventures too. Is my stepmother a part of this? Does she know?" He spat out the questions, his voice shaking with rage. "It doesn't matter. Get the fuck out of my car and my life." When Max stared at him, frozen, he shouted, "Now!"

Max barely got out before Benjamin reached across the seat, yanked the door closed, and peeled away.

"Fuck," he shouted, slamming his palm against the steering wheel. Benjamin bit down on his lip, refusing to let any more tears fall. He went back home to the house that belonged to him but wasn't his and shut himself away. He wouldn't let anyone take anything more from him.

Chapter Twelve

Max couldn't stand it. He prowled his stateroom, frustration and disappointment gnawing at his gut.

It had been two days since he'd kissed Benjamin and then screwed it up by not recognizing how much Big Dipper Adventures meant to him.

Bennett popped his head in. "Are you done kicking yourself yet?"

"No," Max growled.

Bennett opened the door the rest of the way and leaned against the doorjamb. "Well, you can't stay locked up in here forever. It's a beautiful sunny day. Let's get out of here."

"Where are we going?"

"Does it matter?"

"I guess not." Max got up from the sofa. He plucked the sleeve of his sweatshirt. The same sweats he'd worn the day before. "Do I have to change?"

Bennett sniffed the air. "And shower. You're mooning over this man like a lovesick boy."

"Rude," Max grumbled on his way to the shower.

As the water sluiced over his body, Max washed away his self-pity. Bennett was right; lying around kicking himself wasn't going to do him any good. He'd been texting Benjamin since he left—with no answer. It was time to try a different tactic. Showered, teeth brushed, and dressed in a pair of jeans and a heather-gray T-shirt, he slipped his bare feet into a pair of canvas loafers and went in search of Bennett.

His mother caught him on his way to the upper deck.

"There you are. I don't know what's gotten into you since we've been here. You're either not around or locked away in your stateroom."

"I've been busy."

"Please tell me you've been busy meeting someone. Seattle has a lot of young professionals who would be—"

"I don't need to hear you say it again," Max cut her off. "Suitable."

"Well, have you dated anyone since you've been here?"

"I haven't had time for that. I've been digging deeper into the operations at DGD. We need to talk. I have some serious reservations about these acquisitions."

"Yes, yes, I've read the reports Bennett prepared."

"And?"

She pulled her shoulders back; steely determination flashed in her eyes. "Your father and I have been running this company successfully for over thirty years. I've dedicated my life to Huntington Outfitters. I'd appreciate it if you showed a little more respect for my experience."

"Questioning the acquisition isn't disrespecting your experience. I could say the same thing to you. I've earned my position as president of this company, and you don't have any respect for my experience," he said, pounding his chest.

"Sweetheart. You still have a lot to learn. Look at you. You won't even settle down. How can I be sure you'll take your responsibilities seriously?"

Max stopped himself from arguing back. Technically Kathrine was his boss, but she was also his mother. Instead of arguing he pulled her into a hug.

"What… what are you doing?"

"I'm giving my mom a hug. If you don't realize that's what I'm doing then it means I haven't done it enough. I don't want to argue. But I do want to have a meeting with you and Dad to discuss this further."

Her expression softened. "All right."

Max gave her a kiss on the cheek and continued on his way to find Bennett.

"SEE, ISN'T this better?" Bennett said an hour later.

Max bit into a tender morsel of flaky fish fried in a golden batter. They'd come to the Seattle waterfront and walked through the bustle of tourists in Pike Place Market to the new overlook walkway that took them on a curving path down to the water's edge. Max popped another bite of fish in his mouth, admiring the view of a ferry pulling into the dock.

"Amazing, isn't it?"

"It is." Bennett pointed to the mountain range across the sound. "They're so clear you'd almost think you could reach out and touch them."

"Someday I'd like to see them up close," Max said, his gaze distant as he stared out at the horizon.

"Maybe go on a hike with a certain someone?" Bennett teased.

"Maybe… if I don't screw it up again."

"I take it you still haven't heard from Benjamin?"

Max shook his head, his shoulders slumping. "He's not answering my texts," he admitted, his voice tinged with frustration.

"What about his friend?"

Max sat up straighter, a flicker of excitement lighting his face. "Aspen," he said, the name slipping from his lips like a lifeline. A small kernel of hope bloomed in his chest. "I need to find Aspen."

"I was wondering when you'd come to that conclusion. It so happens I know where to find them." Bennett held out his phone.

Max stared at the picture with surprise. "Theresa Hugger?"

Bennett nodded with a grin. "Fancy going out tonight?"

Julia's on Broadway managed to combine steampunk and gentleman's club decor into a cozy space with exposed brick walls, dark wood beams on the ceiling, and plush dark green velvet booths.

Max and Bennett secured a booth close to the stage.

"Well, this is interesting." Bennett tipped his head toward a high-top table at the opposite corner from where they sat.

"And convenient." Max's eyes lit up.

Benjamin and Aspen were sitting at the table, whispering quietly. Max noted the dark circles under Benjamin's eyes were back.

"Should we make our presence known?" Bennett asked.

"I don't think that's an option." Max stiffened when Aspen saw them. Their eyes narrowed and they put a hand on Benjamin's arm, giving it a comforting squeeze before they marched toward their table, eyes blazing.

"What did I say to you about hurting my friend?" Aspen hissed.

"I didn't mean to."

"But you did." Aspen poked Max in the chest. "Did you truly believe you could buy Big Dipper Adventures? I thought you were supposed to be some big-deal businessman." Their gaze landed on Bennett. "What are you, his henchman, bodyguard, or something?"

Bennett sat frozen, staring at Aspen. Max kicked him under the table, and he jerked back. "I'm Bennett," he said as if it were more of a question than a fact.

"Oh Lord, another one with the posh accent. Bennett who? Little Lord Fauntleroy?"

"Bennett Goulding."

Aspen held their hand out. "Shake my hand like a proper gentleman, Bennett."

Bennett shook Aspen's hand while Max took in the scene, amazed by what he was witnessing. He'd never seen his friend so discombobulated before. He was so distracted by their interaction he didn't notice when Benjamin slipped out of the club.

Aspen smirked. "And now my work here is done. You didn't think I was going to let you anywhere near Benjamin, did you?"

"Aspen, I promise—"

"Your little speech about how you don't mean any harm is going to have to wait. I've got to get ready for my set." They considered Max critically for a moment before their expression softened. "If you're still here after the show, we can talk. But—" He waggled his finger. "—you'd better tip well and buy me at least one drink."

Max held out his hand. "Deal."

Aspen shook it and ran off behind the stage. Max watched Bennett, whose gaze was still locked on where Aspen had disappeared.

"Earth to Bennett." He snapped his fingers in Bennett's face.

Bennett blinked as if he was waking from a dream. "What?"

"You seem a little distracted."

"Do I?" Bennett's attention turned back to the stage.

Bennett usually gravitated toward the pretty type. Blond, blue-eyed, the type that wore Savile Row suits.

The first two acts were entertaining enough. One was a Dolly Parton tribute named Busty Bluebell, the other a performer doing an homage to Broadway musicals, changing the lyrics of classic songs with witty double entendres that had Max cracking up more than once.

Then the MC reappeared. "And now, ladies and gentlemen and everything in between, your favorite Girl Scout, park ranger, outdoors queen, dedicated to spreading sparkle in every forest, mountain, and stream. Theresa Hugger!"

Bennett froze, his drink halfway to his lips, when the curtain opened and Aspen appeared. Max was as captivated by his friend's reaction as Aspen's stage presence.

Aspen strutted onto the stage, oozing confidence. The spotlights caught the glitter on the leaves in their costume, creating a shimmering halo around their head. Bennett stiffened, sucking in his breath. His eyes tracked Aspen's movements with a look of awe on his face. Aspen's gaze fell on their table and they froze for a second as well. The artificial blush they'd applied became a bit brighter with the natural one that appeared beneath it. In the blink of an eye, the moment passed, and they fully embraced the music, going into their routine.

Bennett drew in a sharp breath. "They're amazing," he said with awe.

Aspen grabbed the microphone and announced, "Tonight I'm Brittney Bitch," in a low, sexy timbre, sending the crowd into a frenzy of cheers and applause.

The same way they had entertained the group on their hike, Aspen drew the crowd in with their repertoire of '90s pop, a ridiculously sexy version of the Girl Scout pledge that would surely have gotten them kicked out of their troop, and raunchy stories from their hiking and camping adventures. Their act was fantastic, and what impressed Max even more was how beneath all the fun and sparkle, Aspen wove Big Dipper Adventures, its mission, and its message of the outdoors being inclusive for everyone into their act. It was easy to see why Aspen was such a huge hit. Toward the end, they wove their way through the tables with a box of Girl Scout cookies, giving out compliments, trading jokes, and stuffing tips into their Girl Scout uniform.

"Breathe." Max kicked Bennett under the table when Aspen approached their table with a wicked gleam in their hazel eyes, which were accented with glittering green eyeshadow.

"No cookies for you. You've been a very naughty boy," they said, holding their hand out.

Max obliged, placing a crisp hundred-dollar bill into Aspen's palm. "To atone for all my sins."

Aspen didn't respond. Turning to Bennett instead, they cocked their head with a cheeky smile. "You I'm not so sure about." They reached up with long glittering green nails to tickle Bennett's shoulder. "I see a devil on one shoulder—" They reached around to tickle the other side. "—and an angel on this one." They stood back. "I haven't decided yet which one I wanna sleep with." With a saucy wink, they turned and strutted away.

With a shaky hand, Bennett grabbed his drink and drained it in one go that left him coughing and sputtering. "It's not funny," he wheezed, glaring at Max.

"It's not every day when I see my best friend speechless," Max said with a mischievous smile. "I am totally going to mark this on my calendar and send you a card next year."

"And will you be happily ensconced with your celestial lover in some kind of wooded love nest by then?" Bennett snapped, returning to his usual sarcastic self.

"I—"

"Left my performance and thought it was the most amazing thing you've ever seen?" Aspen said, appearing at their table in a jewel-green kimono robe decorated with pink-and-white peonies. They slid into the booth next to Bennett, whose calm demeanor had disappeared as quickly as it had returned. He sat stiffly, staring at Aspen. Their wig gone, they appeared even more stunning with pixie-cut hair, the tips cobalt blue, and still wearing a face full of makeup.

"What can we get you to drink?" Max asked.

Aspen waved a hand. "Tonic water. I think for this conversation it's best that I stay completely sober."

Max flagged down a waiter and ordered two more whiskeys, neat, and a tonic water.

"Your act is fantastic. How often do you perform here?" Max asked.

Aspen looked around the room with an affectionate smile. "Not often. Maybe once a month."

"Helping Benjamin with Big Dipper Adventures must keep you busy," Max said.

Aspen's smile faded. Their eyes narrowing, their expression morphed into one that was all business. "What I do for Big Dipper Adventures is none of your business."

Their drinks arrived, and Max took advantage of the moment to consider his strategy. Meanwhile Bennett continued to stare at Aspen like a deer in the headlights.

"Aspen." Max took a deep breath. "I want you to know I have no intention of causing Benjamin any trouble. I've been following the Big Dipper Adventures Instagram account for quite some time, and I think what he's done is amazing. It's the kind of business that I've been trying to get Huntington Outfitters involved in since I became president."

"And yet here you are, buying a tacky, overpriced athletic-wear company with fake gyms that are more like a sad pickup market for tech bros and women trying to get their ass to match the size of their lip filler."

Bennett choked on his drink. Aspen reached over, thumping his back while continuing to glare at Max.

"That wasn't my choice. My parents are insisting on this deal. It's not what I want."

Aspen cocked their head. "I thought you were the president. We have a real president who acts like a dictator now. Why can't you... dictate?"

"It's complicated. My parents—mainly my mother—aren't ready to give up control of the company. Mother has certain... requirements she wants me to meet before she's convinced I'm ready to take over Huntington Outfitters."

Aspen studied him for a moment before turning to Bennett. "You're his best friend?" Bennett nodded.

Aspen turned back to Max. "You may go," they said with a dismissive wave of their hand. "This is the one I want to talk to. Don't worry, I promise I'll bring him back to you in one piece," they said with a wink.

Did he have any other choice? Max knew Aspen was the Guardian of the Gates when it came to Benjamin. His fate lay in the hands of a very overprotective, slightly twinkish drag queen.

CHAPTER THIRTEEN

"Do you want to hear what happened last night, or would you like me to keep it a secret like the formula for the orange face paint the president uses? I mean, seriously, what is that stuff?" Aspen perched on the corner of Benjamin's desk.

He glanced up from his spreadsheet. Aspen was doing that thing they did when they were sitting on a piece of gossip they were dying to share. Returning his attention to the screen, Benjamin frowned. No amount of massaging would make the numbers look better than they were. Preparing for the Huntingtons' visit created an even bigger deficit in the monthly budget. And no matter how much he wanted to, he couldn't stop thinking about Max. He was dying to know what happened at Julia's last night, but stubbornness kept him from asking outright.

With a disgusted grunt he pushed away from his desk and folded his arms in front of himself. "Okay, spill it. Did Bennett fall for those googly eyes you were giving him?"

Aspen lifted their chin. "Those were not googly eyes. They were my moon eyes. Honestly, Benjamin, I'd think you'd know the difference by now."

Benjamin waved his hand in a circle. "You're getting distracted."

"You're the one asking about googly eyes and not what Max said." Aspen leaned across the desk. "Did you know Max Huntington's extremely handsome assistant Bennett Goulding is royalty? Well, practically royalty. He's like *Downton Abbey* royalty. Either way, he's got these shoulders that are so…." They inhaled with a dreamy expression. "And his eyes. Did I tell you about his eyes? They're brown but not ordinary brown. They're this deep brown, and they match his hair, only his hair has shades of brown like…." Aspen snapped their fingers. "Remember that gorgeous MAC eyeshadow I bought last year?"

Benjamin waved his hands in front of his friend. "Stop. Can we back up to the part where you talked to Max?"

"Oh, you know, he said all the right things. He respects you. He thinks Big Dipper Adventures is great blah, blah, blah. I didn't get the good stuff from Max, but I managed to loosen Bennett's tongue," Aspen said with a little shoulder shimmy.

Benjamin let out a frustrated groan. "Aspen, I love you, but I need you to focus and finish telling me what happened without getting distracted."

Before his friend could continue, Monaco and Milan waltzed into the building.

"Too late," he muttered under his breath.

Aspen jumped off his desk and blew him a kiss. "I'll fill you in later," they said before turning to the twins. "Well, if it isn't Tweedledee and Tweedledumb," they said with a Cheshire cat grin. Aspen leaned in and whispered. "Don't worry, Alice, the Red Queen isn't going to rule for much longer."

Monaco flipped her hair over her shoulder and walked past Aspen with her nose in the air. Today she'd paired her workout outfit with a pair of red-and-gold leopard sneakers that made it appear as if someone had murdered a big cat and walked through the crime scene. The jungle theme continued with a pair of leggings from last summer's collection. Tropical leaves covered her legs, and thanks to her less-than-stellar design skills, the pattern was placed so that anyone walking behind her would think there were two leaves grabbing her ass.

Milan had already started taking selfies, ignoring Aspen. If Benjamin had to come up with a description of his outfit, it would be a Pepto Bismol explosion with layers of pink on pink on pink. Somehow Milan had managed to pick three distinct shades of pink that did not complement one another.

Aspen rolled their eyes and made a face behind their backs on their way out the door. Benjamin schooled his expression, keeping his eyes trained on his laptop, trying not to laugh.

Monaco tossed an envelope on Benjamin's desk. "This month's receipts," she said, continuing on her way to her office.

Benjamin picked up the envelope as if he were handling one of her dirty thongs. As he pulled out the stack of receipts, a dull pounding started behind his eyes. A headache was better than a heart attack, Benjamin thought. This must've been how his father felt trying to keep up with Rochelle's spending habits. He quickly sorted through the expense reports, entering them into a spreadsheet and then attaching them to the monthly budget report. Realizing this would be the last time he would have to do this, Benjamin smiled as he added it to the top of the pile of paperwork he'd put together earlier. Grabbing his tablet, he headed toward his stepmother's office. In the beginning the DGD offices were a hub of activity, full of talented and enthusiastic people from diverse backgrounds. As he walked down the hallway past the empty cubicles and desks, the latest exodus only exaggerated the silence.

Benjamin noted the full garbage cans that would need to be emptied as he made his way down the hall. Part of Rochelle's cost-cutting measures included getting rid of janitorial services a couple of years ago. Considering they could barely afford the lease on the building, paying someone to empty the garbage and clean the bathrooms was out of the question. Those became some of Benjamin's tasks, along with so many other duties that facilitated the day-to-day operation of the company. Rochelle may have thought she was punishing Benjamin by adding HR and accounting to Benjamin's job description, but those responsibilities gave Benjamin an opportunity to gain the skills he needed to run Big Dipper Adventures. He'd added classes in project management, accounting, and human resources to his course load. Drive, determination, and good grades, combined with a strong desire for independence, helped Benjamin earn enough scholarships to pay for the majority of his education. Going away to college was out of the question. Rochelle made that clear, and Benjamin didn't want to leave anyway, afraid of what she would do to his home in his absence. Online college courses gave him the flexibility he needed.

All you have to do is hold out a little longer.

Benjamin would never know why his dad decided he needed to be twenty-five to receive his trust fund. Trust fund. In her case, the phrase was an oxymoron. His father trusted Rochelle to take care of Benjamin's trust. There wouldn't be a big party when he turned twenty-five. Those celebrations ended when his dad died. At first Benjamin recreated their annual birthday campout in the backyard. On his sixteenth birthday, he took his dad's Jeep, which had sat unused in the garage, and drove it over to Aspen and Bubbie's house. The fact he'd been able to keep the Jeep at all was a small miracle, only made possible because his father specifically left it to Benjamin in his will. Bubbie had given both Aspen and Benjamin driving lessons, and that day she drove Benjamin to the DMV. By that afternoon he had a driver's license. On that birthday he camped under the stars at one of his dad's favorite spots.

Staring at the Big Dipper that night, he'd tried to imagine his dad was with him, watching for shooting stars. On his eighteenth birthday he celebrated by getting his Big Dipper tattoo. Now his twenty-fifth birthday was within sight. It didn't matter if the money was gone. The only thing Benjamin wanted was the deed to his parents' house.

He steeled himself and knocked on his stepmom's door.

"Enter."

Rochelle flicked her wrist to glance at the rhinestone-encrusted Apple watch on her wrist. "You have five minutes. I have a luncheon at the Seattle Club for Women in Business Leadership this afternoon."

Without responding, Benjamin moved to her desk and placed the files on the corner, then held the stylus poised over his tablet and waited. Early on he learned that the fewer words he exchanged with his stepmother the better. Rochelle liked to dictate when it came to her interactions with Benjamin, not converse.

"The Huntingtons have invited us to their yacht for dinner tomorrow night." Benjamin must have allowed a spark of interest to show because Rochelle continued, "Not you. Monaco, Milan, and me of course. I want the latest trend reports for outerwear in my inbox before end of day. Monaco and Milan will need color forecasts and some talking points on sustainable clothing as well." She narrowed her eyes. "Max Huntington was talking to you last time he was here. I shouldn't have to remind you to stay away from the Huntingtons. They're interested in DGD as a Black-owned company. Obviously we need to keep your connection to the company limited."

Benjamin gripped the stylus so tightly he thought it would snap. "He was asking for directions, nothing more."

"Make sure that's the only thing he asks you for, understood?"

"Yes."

"Is there anything else?"

Benjamin read the running list of issues that would eat away at what little free time he had. "No."

"Good." Rochelle stood from her desk and ran her hands over her hips, smoothing away the wrinkles on her deep red Michael Kors suit. She gathered her black patent crocodile Coach handbag. "Take care of whatever you put on my desk," she said, brushing past Benjamin on her way out the door.

Once the distinct clip of stilettos faded away, Benjamin let his shoulders slump. He stepped onto the balcony outside Rochelle's office to retreat from the cloying scent of her perfume and inhaled a deep breath of city summer air. The odor of car fumes mingled with the faint smell of urine from the alley below was still better than the smell of two-hundred-dollar-a-bottle perfume.

Leaning against the railing, he contemplated the scene in front of him, taking in the activity around South Lake Union. The DGD offices offered a view of both the lake and Puget Sound. His gaze strayed to the smaller body of water and the yacht.

It wasn't good that Rochelle caught Max talking to him. He'd have to be even more careful, and make sure Max understood that he couldn't pay attention to him when his stepmother was around.

"What are you doing out here? I've been calling for you for the last ten minutes." Monaco said as she came out on the deck.

"Making sure everything is tidy," he said, taking one last look toward the *Faunus.*

"Sarah says she's quitting," Monaco whined.

Benjamin moved back inside, grabbed his tablet, and made his way back toward his desk. "I told you, you can't keep expecting your assistants to break in your shoes for you."

"I can't get blisters. And then there's this." She held out her phone. "Who is doing this?"

Benjamin bit the inside of his cheek trying to keep a straight face as he read the latest post from BirchBitch206.

I bought these $200 "revolutionary, performance-enhancing" leggings expecting them to turn me into an Olympic-level athlete or, at the very least, a more dignified version of myself at yoga class. Spoiler alert: THEY DID NOT.

The leggings are so sheer I bent down to tie my shoe and accidentally gave everyone behind me a live-action anatomy lesson.

Benjamin schooled his expression. "Why does it matter? The sale of DGD is almost closed."

Monaco smirked. "You haven't heard?"

Benjamin's breath caught. Was the sale not going through? "What happened?"

"Mommy renegotiated our agreement." Monaco folded her arms across her chest in what Benjamin called her girl-boss pose. "Milan and I stay on as designers, and Mommy will still be president."

Benjamin found himself questioning how the Huntingtons had achieved so much success and yet were making such a bad decision buying DGD. How could they not see how badly the company had been managed? He wanted to ask Max, but that would mean talking to Max, and he was still too upset with him. What would Max do now that he knew about Big Dipper Adventures?

Reluctantly he pulled out his phone.

We need to talk, he texted.

In less than a second after he hit Send, his phone pinged.

Where? When? Tell me and I'll be there.

Track. Tomorrow 7:00 a.m.

I'll be there.

Benjamin blew out a shaky breath and went back to his desk. At the end of the day, he packed up his gear and went to Aspen's house.

"Tell me what happened with Max?" Benjamin asked when Aspen opened the door.

Aspen grabbed his hand and pulled him inside. "Forget Max. We've got a bigger problem."

Chapter Fourteen

Max blew out a sigh of relief when he saw Benjamin's text. He was getting another chance, and this time he wasn't going to mess it up.

His heart quickened at the thought of seeing Benjamin again. One kiss—well, several kisses—with the right person could change your entire life.

Leaning against the railing on the bow of the *Faunus*, Max let his thoughts drift. He'd always believed he'd be content as a bachelor. It wasn't out of stubbornness that he'd rejected his mother's matchmaking attempts. Staying untethered gave him freedom, and he never understood why anyone would choose to be tied to one person. Why settle, he'd always thought, when you could move on to something or someone new the moment things got boring? But what if you met someone who you never got tired of waking up to? A person who you couldn't wait to see every day? The first person you wanted to share good news with or commiserate with when things went wrong? Life would be anything but boring; every day would be a new adventure.

"What a nice surprise. I didn't think you were on board," Max's dad said, joining him against the railing. "It's beautiful here, isn't it? I wouldn't mind coming back here someday."

Max looked at his father, genuinely looked at him. He'd aged without Max noticing. His dark hair was now heavily threaded with silver. His frame was still lean and athletic, but his shoulders stooped more, and the lines around his eyes were deeper. Their wealth could buy a lot of things, but it couldn't buy time.

"Where's Mom?"

"Your mother was invited to attend a luncheon with Rochelle Tremaine."

Max nodded, watching the clouds reflected in the water.

"Dad, can we talk?"

"Of course. Feels like it's been a long time since you and I have had a chance to talk when it's the two of us."

Max gestured to a couple of deck chairs.

"You already know about my concerns with the DGD acquisition," he said after they sat.

"I do, and some of them are valid. But there's nothing we can't fix. I don't care about the gyms or the apparel." He gave Max a tight smile. "We will be hiring competent designers to work with Monaco and Milan. The real value lies in the patents for adaptive equipment."

Max frowned. He agreed with his dad. Buying DGD was all about acquiring the patents. It should have been a straightforward deal, and now his mother had informed him this morning that she'd renegotiated the terms. Instead of buying the company outright, DGD would become a subsidiary. Rochelle would continue running the company, and the twins would stay in their roles as designers.

"I agree the patents are what's important, but these last-minute changes to the sale are—" Max pressed his mouth into a flat line, shaking his head.

"Son. You're doing an amazing job, and I'm proud of you. You're going to be the right person to run Huntington Outfitters when it's your time. But your mother and I have the experience. You need to follow our lead on this."

"How long am I going to be following your lead? At what point are you going to let me do my job?"

"Your mother feels—"

Max jumped up and started pacing, rubbing the back of his neck. "Please, don't. I don't want to hear about how I need to be settled down with the right person. That doesn't impact my ability to do my job."

"No, but it shows stability."

Max stopped. "And I haven't shown that already? When have I missed a day of work? When have I not done everything you've asked me to do?"

His father's expression grew thoughtful. "No one could ask for a more dutiful son."

"What about a son who's happy?"

"Of course we want you to be happy. All parents want their children to find a partner who will support them in their hopes and dreams."

Max pictured sitting next to Benjamin in his battered Jeep, a smile on his face while they sped down the highway. It was difficult to picture him in a Savile Row suit.

"And what if the partner I found doesn't fit your image of who you think that partner should be?" he asked.

His dad's eyebrows rose. "Have you found someone?"

Max sat back down. "I don't know. Maybe. But I do know that I wanna see where this could go. I've met someone who shares my goals and my interests. He makes me feel…. It's hard to describe. He gives me purpose."

"I see. And this person is a he?"

"Does it matter?"

"No, of course not. Your mother and I accept that you have attraction to both sexes. You have to have that connection that's deeper than gender. That's something special. I respect that."

"So you can respect that, but not my opinions about the business?" Max asked quietly.

His dad sighed. "Let me talk to your mother."

"I'm not asking you to fight my battles for me."

"Okay. But perhaps I can smooth the way for you a bit."

"I appreciate it."

Some of the tightness in his chest eased when his conversation ended with his dad. Still, that night Max tossed and turned, anticipation keeping sleep at bay. He'd rehearsed his apology again and again. With a frustrated groan he flopped over on his back and stared at the ceiling. All he could think about was when he could kiss Benjamin again. Did he imagine the spark between them? Would Benjamin want more as much as he did? Would he let Max touch him the way he wanted to?

MAX ARRIVED at the track early after a restless night picturing Benjamin naked and writhing under him. Shouting his name when Max coaxed another orgasm from him.

He forced himself not to rush forward and pull Benjamin into a hug when he arrived. The grim expression on Benjamin's face made his stomach drop.

"Thank you for agreeing to talk to me."

Benjamin shook his head sadly. "I can't talk. Something came up. I have to go."

"What's wrong?"

"I…." He hesitated. "It has to do with Big Dipper Adventures. I'm still not sure… you've got me feeling…." He blew out a shaky breath. "Aspen says I should try to keep an open mind. Bennett must have made a good impression on them. So I'm going to tell you something."

Max took a step closer. "You can tell me anything."

"I started a pilot program last year. Offering a Big Dipper Adventures accreditation for campgrounds. I reached out to three campgrounds in the area. The campground went through a training program Aspen and I put together. At the end they received a plaque to display. The idea is if you're a minority and you see the plaque, you know that campground is a safe place. You can camp without any kind of harassment."

"I never thought—I didn't know."

"I don't have time to educate you on prejudice in the outdoors. Aspen had a call yesterday from one of our campers. There was an incident at a campground we certified. There's a new manager, and I need to see for myself. I'll only be gone overnight. We can talk when I get back."

"Can't you send someone else?"

"It's my responsibility. I don't have hundreds of people on my payroll, Max. It's me and Aspen and a few volunteers."

"Let me come with you."

The request startled him. Max wasn't being serious, was he? Benjamin found the offer tempting, but it wasn't realistic. "I have to leave now. I already have all my gear packed."

"I'll follow you. Tell me where you're going and I'll meet you there."

"You don't have to do this, Max."

He reached for Benjamin's hand. "I've been trying to talk to you for days. I've missed you, Benjamin."

Benjamin's shoulders dropped. "I've thought about you too." He looked at Max with a little smile. "I'm mad at you for that. I don't want to think about you all the time the way I do."

Max brushed his thumb over Benjamin's knuckles. "So, you've been thinking about me all the time?"

"Don't get cocky."

"Let me come with you," Max asked again.

"You could help," Benjamin hedged.

Max grinned. "What do you need me to do?" When Benjamin finished explaining his idea, Max nodded. "I can do that."

"Do you have any camping equipment?

"Of course," he lied.

Benjamin put the address of the campground into his phone. "I've got to get going. I don't want any other campers to have a bad experience."

"Can I do one thing before you go?"

"What?"

Max put his arms around him and pulled him into a tight hug.

"What was that for?" Benjamin asked when Max let him go.

Max reached up and cupped his cheek. "You should be hugged every day."

Benjamin's face heated under his palm. "I didn't tell you that because I wanted you to feel sorry for me."

"I don't. I think you're amazing. I admire you."

"Don't," Benjamin said in a shaky whisper. "Don't say all the right things and make me believe… not right now."

Max leaned in to gently graze Benjamin's lips. "Okay."

Benjamin took in a deep breath and nodded. He pulled himself out of Max's arms and got back into his Jeep. "Call me if you change your mind and can't make it."

Nothing would change his mind. Max called Bennett as he pulled out of the parking lot. "I need a tent and a sleeping bag." He rattled off a list of additional equipment.

"Are we going camping?"

"I am. I'll explain when I'm back at the *Faunus*. I need that equipment in the next hour."

"Got it."

"WHAT DO you want me to tell your parents?" Bennett asked when Max explained what he was doing.

Max muttered an expletive, throwing a T-shirt and a pair of jeans into the backpack he'd used for the Big Dipper hike.

"I can tell them you decided to make a surprise visit to one of our stores in Vancouver," Bennett suggested.

Max shot him a grateful look. "Thanks."

"Benjamin continues to surprise us, doesn't he?"

"Yes, he does," Max said with a soft smile.

"Maxwell Huntington, you are smitten."

"And you're not?" Max raised an eyebrow. "You came back from your evening with Aspen with a love bite on your neck."

Bennett rubbed the now-faded spot. "Aspen is… intriguing."

"This trip hasn't turned out the way I thought it would."

"Definitely not."

Max slung his backpack over his shoulder. "It's better." He clapped Bennett on the shoulder on his way out. "Thanks for covering for me."

Max headed north and then east, this time over a narrow two-lane pass-through with scenery that rivaled the Swiss Alps. Three hours after leaving Seattle, he arrived at the campground, grinning when he saw the cobalt-blue metal Big Dipper sign posted at the entrance. He followed Benjamin's directions, repeating what he'd told Max to say at the camp manager's office when he checked in.

"Well, the MAGA hat the campground manager was wearing wasn't a good sign," he announced when he arrived at his spot.

Benjamin glanced up from his book at his site next door to Max's. His lips quirked. "Thanks for the confirmation. Glad you made it."

He shook his head when Max started toward him. "We don't know each other, remember?"

"Got it."

"Go ahead and start setting up your camp." Benjamin said, turning his attention back to his book.

Max opened the trunk of his car and started sorting through the gear Bennett had packed for him. He stared at the tent with dread. He glanced over his shoulder at Benjamin's campsite, which could have been a Huntington Outfitters catalog spread.

With a resigned sigh, he reached for the tent. The sound of a utility vehicle approaching stopped him. The campground manager pulled up to Max's spot with a big smile, followed by a scowl for Benjamin.

"Wanted to bring you some firewood," he said, pulling a bundle from the back of his Gator. He eyed Benjamin's campsite again with a scowl. "Are you sure I can't put you in a better spot?"

"My friends who sent me here were right. The view of the lake is beautiful here. I'll stay, but thanks for the offer."

The campground manager tipped his head toward Benjamin. "Let me know if this one gives you any trouble."

"Sure thing," Max said, fighting to keep the bitterness out of his voice.

It took all of his willpower not to strangle the man when he drove his Gator the few feet between camps and got out again, but not before making a show of putting a holstered gun on the dash. Max stood by helplessly as the manager approached Benjamin without the friendly smile he'd had for Max.

"I run a clean campground here. I don't want to hear any of that loud gangbanger music, and if I get one whiff of drugs from you, I'll have you in handcuffs in the back of the sheriff's car before you can blink."

Benjamin stood tall, looking the man in the eye. "Yes, sir. I understand."

They locked eyes for a moment before the manager pulled his red hat low over his eyes and got back in the Gator.

Benjamin stood ramrod straight, watching until the Gator was out of sight. Max rushed over and grabbed his shoulders.

"Are you okay?"

"I'm good." He smiled. "And I have a witness. Thank you."

Max blew out a shaky breath and dropped his forehead to Benjamin's. "I don't ever want to see you put yourself in a situation like that again. I was scared to death."

"We're not quite done yet. I thought we'd spend the night, but now that I know how bad the situation is, we're going to leave now. It's early enough, and there's another campsite about an hour from here we can go to, or we can go back to Seattle if you want."

"Let's get out of here. I don't want to be here another minute more than we have to be. If there's another campground we can go to, I'd still like to spend time with you."

"I need to call Aspen. Do you mind helping me break camp?"

"I'll take care of it."

He moved quickly, listening with one ear while Benjamin called Aspen and told them what had happened. When all of Benjamin's gear was packed in his Jeep, Benjamin grabbed Max before he got in his car.

"I'm going to stop at the managers station on the way out. You can go on to the main road, and I'll meet you there."

Max shook his head. "You know I can't leave you behind with that asshole."

"You have to stop with the whole 'handsome prince slash knight in shining armor' schtick. It makes it hard to be mad at you."

"Knight in shining armor schtick?" Max's mouth twitched.

"You and I both know it's all an act. Especially when the Prince of the Wilderness doesn't know how to take down a tent."

"Dammit. I thought you wouldn't notice."

"I notice everything, Max," Benjamin said with tenderness in his voice. "Come on, it's time to go back to reality."

Chapter Fifteen

Benjamin stopped at the manager's station at the entrance of the campground. He took a deep breath, grounding himself before he faced the man again. He took the toolbox he'd placed on the passenger seat with him and got out.

Max pulled up behind him. He leaned against his car door and folded his arms in front of him, waiting and watching. Benjamin gave him a reassuring smile as he walked past. He knew Max wanted to be by his side. He wasn't afraid of facing the manager, but knowing he had Max there, his confidence in Benjamin clear in his eyes, bolstered his own.

Benjamin put his toolbox on the hood of his car, opened it, and grabbed a large screwdriver. He went over to the Big Dipper sign and started taking out the screws holding it to the signpost.

"What the hell do you think you're doing?" The campground manager burst out the office and came barreling toward him.

"I'm removing your Big Dipper accreditation," Benjamin said, continuing to take out screws.

"You don't have the right to do that!"

Benjamin turned to the man, his face mottled with anger. "Yes, I do. I own Big Dipper Adventures. We've received several complaints about this campground since you took over as the new manager, and I came to investigate personally." As he spoke, other campers with Big Dipper stickers on their windshields and bumpers started to leave the campground. There were honks and waves with approving nods as they went by. Benjamin turned back to the manager, who gaped wide-eyed at the scene with his mouth hanging open. "An announcement went out on all Big Dipper social media a minute ago and was posted on our website. Our members know that you've been charging minority campers double the regular fee, and the campground owner has agreed to refund anyone who has been charged erroneously since you took over. My assistant is making arrangements to rebook any of our members who have reservations with you."

"That's half the reservations for this weekend alone," he sputtered.

"Yes, it is, because diversity is good for business. You should have thought of that before you decided to—" Benjamin pointed at his red hat. "—Make America Great Again."

"You can't do this," the manager growled, taking a step toward Benjamin.

"I can and I have."

Max moved toward them, his hands balled into fists and an absolutely murderous expression on his face.

Benjamin pointed at him. "Do not take another step," he ordered.

Max froze, then with a frustrated grunt went back to his car.

Benjamin finished taking the sign off the post as the manager's phone rang. He pulled it out of his pocket and answered.

"Yes, sir. No, sir. But I—" the color drained from the managers face and he hung up. "I hope you're happy. I've been fired," he spat out.

"I'm not happy. I don't take pleasure in seeing someone lose their job. What's happening here makes me sad. You made a choice. Let me give you some advice, even though I doubt you'll take it. Hate isn't the key to success. You can bully and bluster trying to prove you're somehow superior, and maybe you'll succeed for a while, but in the end, you're going to end up alone." Benjamin pointed to another wave of campers driving out of the campground. "Everyone deserves to be happy and secure. Even you. But you won't find happiness through hate."

"You arrogant—" He started toward Benjamin with his hand fisted.

Benjamin stepped back, his tone low. "I should warn you I have a black belt in Krav Maga."

The man swallowed and took a step back, confirming Benjamin's instinct that he was all bluster.

The manager's eyes flickered toward his office.

"If you're thinking about getting your gun, you're going to have a hard time claiming self-defense when I've been recording all of this," Max said casually, still leaning against his car.

The man worked his jaw for a minute before he stormed back into the office.

"Get in and drive away now," Max said between clenched teeth. "I don't trust him not to try something."

Benjamin got in, and Max followed him so closely they were almost bumper to bumper.

For the next hour Benjamin led them through steep mountain roads while he fielded frantic calls from the campground owner and Aspen. The campground owner was furious at losing their accreditation. Benjamin felt sorry for the position the campground manager put the owner in. They would have to go repeat the training before they could apply for accreditation again. Aspen was already revising the training now that they'd identified a weak point in the program. Any changes in campground ownership or management would put a pause on recommending the campground to their membership until another round of training was completed.

At the end of a narrow road, they arrived at their next destination.

Max parked next to Benjamin in front of the small modern cabin.

"This is—" Before he could finish, Max grabbed him and pushed him against the side of his Jeep. His hand fisted in Benjamin's T-shirt as he crushed their mouths together. It was a kiss that claimed him, taking possession of Benjamin completely. "You can't scare me like that again," he said, his voice low and gruff when he tore his mouth from Benjamin's.

"It's my responsibility to make it right," he explained.

"I know." Max exhaled, stepping back. "But that was… intense."

"I didn't think he was going to back down. Thank you for filming. That may have been what got him to walk away."

"I don't want to think about what would have happened if he hadn't."

"I'm sorry this trip hasn't gotten off to a great start. Let me try to make it up to you."

"This isn't exactly roughing it," Max said.

"It belongs to my friend Noah's boyfriend, Gideon. We aren't staying here." Benjamin held up a finger. "Give me a sec."

He jogged around the side of the cabin and entered the code Noah had given him into the key box. Keys in hand, he opened the storage shed. A minute later he drove an ATV with a small trailer attached out of the shed toward Max.

"Gideon and Noah built a camping spot on their property. We're staying there tonight. Let's load everything up. Even with these long summer days, we'll lose daylight a little earlier in the woods."

Benjamin added his gear and a cooler of food and drinks to Max's overpriced camping supplies with the tags still on it. He got on and patted the seat behind him. "Climb on."

Max got on, wrapping his arms around Benjamin's waist when he took off into the woods.

"It's not too far," Benjamin shouted as they sped uphill through the trees. Twenty minutes later Benjamin drove through the trees onto a bluff.

"Wow," Max breathed as he got off the ATV and walked toward the edge of the bluff.

"It's a spectacular view, isn't it?" Benjamin followed his gaze toward the ribbon of water winding its way through the valley below.

"What's that town down there?" Max asked, pointing to a small cluster of buildings clinging to the river bank.

"That's Blink. We can grab breakfast at the Wishful Café in the morning. Ed makes the best french toast in the state."

Max turned to him, his hazel eyes lighting up. "Sounds perfect."

"The sooner we get camp set up, the sooner we can have dinner."

Max circled the fire pit in the center of the camp. "This is almost glamping," he said, poking his head into the outdoor shower.

"Gideon likes his creature comforts." Benjamin laughed. "He insisted on a bathroom and a shower."

"Gideon sounds like my kind of guy. I like the way he designed the bathroom with the vintage trough sink on the outside."

"It does double duty as a kitchen sink."

"How did you meet?" Max asked as they unloaded their supplies.

"I went to summer camp with Gideon's boyfriend, Noah."

Did you go to camp every summer?"

"For a few years." Benjamin avoided Max's gaze as he finished putting up his tent. When he turned around, he clapped his hand over his mouth, but a snort escape, anyway.

"It's not funny," Max growled.

Benjamin schooled his expression. "I'm sorry, I don't understand how the Prince of the Wilderness doesn't know how to put a tent together."

Max threw the tent pole he'd snapped in two onto the crumpled mound of nylon at his feet and ran his hands through his hair with a huff of frustration. "I haven't been camping since I was eight, okay?"

"Did you go with your mom and dad?"

"No, with my granddad. It was my great-grandfather who started the company in the forties, after the war. He loved camping and the outdoors. He took my granddad camping, hunting, and fishing," he said with a wistful smile. "Grandad kept the company going and passed it down to my parents. That love-of-the-outdoors gene didn't pass down to my dad, and my mother was a debutante from a family that thought being outdoorsy was having dinner on the patio. But… they knew a good business opportunity when they saw it." Max nudged the mess he'd made with the toe of his hiking boot. "This is humiliating."

"Okay, here's what's going to happen. I'll share my tent with you. But—" He held up a finger when a slow smile spread over Max's face. "—you're going to have to figure out how to keep warm tonight, because you've brought a junior-size sleeping bag and that mattress pad has terrible reviews."

Max's smile fell. "Shit. I wanted to impress you."

They were so close Max must have been able to feel how hard Benjamin's heart was beating. He stared into Benjamin's eyes—which were searching his, asking a silent question—before he leaned in, his lips brushing against Benjamin's temple before he whispered in Benjamin's ear. "Because I like you, and I want you to like me too."

"I don't get it. Why me? I'm nothing special."

Max reached for his hand and pressed it to his chest. "Benjamin, I can't begin to tell you all the ways you're wrong about that."

Benjamin tried to step back, but Max held him in his place. "Benjamin, please don't shut yourself away," Max said, his voice low and pleading.

Benjamin took a ragged breath. "I'm not shutting myself away. I'm doing my best to hold on to what little I have."

"I don't want to take anything from you."

"Except Big Dipper Adventures."

"I didn't understand how much the company meant to you. Even today I didn't realize how much you are a part of the company until I saw what happened at the campground. I'd like to partner with you—" Max put his finger on Benjamin's lips when he protested. "—someday. If there's an opportunity. If there isn't, then I'll happily stand on the sidelines and be your biggest cheerleader."

Benjamin looked down at Max's palm pressed against his chest, warm and solid, the heat sinking through his shirt. He wanted to believe what Max was saying. But doubt began to creep in, and Benjamin took a step back, creating a little distance between them. "I can't risk it, Max. My stepmother is ruthless. She'll cut me off at the knees if she even suspects I'm trying to take anything back for myself." A rush of emotions surged through Benjamin: hope, fear, a glimmer of excitement. Could he trust Max? Could he allow himself to rely on someone else, especially someone from a world so different from his?

"I want…." He put his hand over Max's, looking into his eyes. "I know you're going to sail away soon. And it's reckless and maybe selfish, but I want… more with you while you're here."

Max ran his thumb along Benjamin's jawline. "I'm selfish," he whispered against his lips. "I want everything." Their lips met in a greedy kiss. Max's hand slipped under the hem of his T-shirt, his fingers digging into Benjamin's waist to draw him closer.

Benjamin wound an arm around Max's shoulder, cupping the back of his head and fusing their bodies together. The list of men Benjamin had ever kissed was short, a couple of guys in high school and one disastrous blind date Aspen set him up on that they both swore they would never speak of again. None of those kisses kept him up at night longing for more. Every kiss with Max imprinted on his soul. Every night since that first kiss, Benjamin fell asleep longing for more kisses. Wondering how it would feel to have the freedom to explore more than Max's mouth.

He shivered when they broke apart. Max wrapped his hand around his neck. His lips curled into a smile. "Please tell me you've changed your mind and we can share a sleeping bag tonight."

Benjamin leaned forward and nipped at Max's plump bottom lip. "I'm counting on it."

Chapter Sixteen

They finished getting the camp set up, with breaks for kisses. Their bodies were constantly gravitating toward each other, with brief touches and longing looks. As they worked, the warmth between them grew, solidifying the fragile bond that had sparked in brief glances and passionate kisses. The force of his possessive feelings toward Benjamin took Max completely off-kilter. For the first time he could remember, Max wanted more than a no-strings-attached relationship. He wanted to be tied up in Benjamin.

Before long the campfire crackled cheerfully with wood stacked high, casting glowing embers into the evening sky. Benjamin was right; the sunlight faded quickly this high in the mountains. As soon as the sun dropped behind the mountains surrounding them, the air around them cooled. The trees loomed larger in the night sky.

They sat side by side on a large log bench next to the fire pit, basking in the glow and in each other.

"You know, it's nights like this I miss the most," Benjamin said, pressing his shoulder against Max's, glancing contemplatively up at the blanket of stars. "Sitting by a fire after a long day in nature…. It reminds me of my dad and our camping trips."

Max brushed the back of Benjamin's neck with his fingertips. "Tell me more about him."

Benjamin hesitated for only a moment. "My dad believed in connection—to nature, to others, to yourself. Every star told a story, and every hike we took was about finding ourselves in the world around us. He would say to me, 'Always turn to the stars, son. Look closely and you'll find they hold the answers to many secrets.'"

Max moved a little closer. "And what do you see in that connection now?"

"I've spent so long trying to fight for my space. Being a biracial kid with a complicated family history made it tough. But with Big Dipper Adventures… I was able to keep my connection to my dad. It's the same way with Hyas House. Even though I'm living in the garage, I feel connected to my mom there."

Max closed the space between them a fraction more, their thighs brushing. The warmth of proximity felt more comforting with each moment that passed.

"And that connection? I want to help others find theirs too. That's what it's all about," Benjamin continued. "I want everyone to feel like they belong in the outdoors."

Max nodded. "You have a rare gift, Benjamin, to bring people together. I've seen it firsthand, and I admire it about you."

He pulled Benjamin in for another kiss. In the glow of the campfire, their kiss deepened, and Max's hand found its way to Benjamin's cheek, caressing it softly as they explored each other's mouths. The taste of him was intoxicating, a mix of the outdoors and a natural sweetness that was purely Benjamin.

Max pulled away slightly, breathless. "Is this okay?" he asked, his voice husky with desire.

Benjamin nodded, his eyes dark with need. "More than okay," he confirmed, his voice barely above a whisper.

Their hands began to roam, tentatively at first, then with growing confidence. Max traced the contours of Benjamin's chest through his shirt, causing him to gasp with pleasure. In response, Benjamin's hand slipped under Max's shirt, and his fingertips skimmed over the toned muscles of his abdomen.

"I want to feel you," Max murmured, tugging at the hem of Benjamin's shirt.

With a nod of agreement, Benjamin lifted his arms, allowing Max to pull the garment over his head, revealing his slender, toned torso. Max took a moment to appreciate the sight before leaning in to press a trail of kisses along Benjamin's collarbone.

Max grabbed Benjamin's hand and pulled him into his arms. They stumbled toward Benjamin's tent, touching and kissing. Their movements became more urgent the moment they tumbled into the tent. They grappled with belts and zippers, shedding their clothes until they were both naked in the cool night air. Max's gaze lingered on Benjamin's cock, thick and hard, a bead of precum glistening at the tip. The sight of it sent a jolt of arousal coursing through him. Without a word, he sank to his knees in front of Benjamin, silently seeking permission, which was granted with a single nod.

Max took Benjamin's cock in his hand, stroking it gently before circling the head with his tongue, eliciting a ragged moan from Benjamin. Encouraged by the sound, Max took him deeper into his mouth, his lips and tongue working in unison to bring Benjamin ever closer to the edge.

"Wait," Benjamin gasped, pulling back slightly. "Condoms. In my bag."

Max released him with a reluctant groan, rummaged through Benjamin's backpack, and quickly found the condoms and a small bottle of lube. His eyes met Benjamin's with a cheeky grin. "Let me guess, you were also a Boy Scout."

"Be prepared."

Max sheathed quickly, then coated his fingers with the slick liquid.

As Max prepared himself, he paid close attention to Benjamin, his eyes dark with desire and wonder. Reassured he wanted this as much as Max did. His hands trembled. After all the tension and uncertainty, they were finally going to be together in the most intimate way possible.

As Max laid Benjamin on the sleeping bag, their cocks brushed against each other. The sensation was electrifying, and Benjamin rocked his hips as if seeking more friction.

"Are you ready for me?" Max asked, his voice strained with need.

Yes," Benjamin breathed, digging his fingers into Max's back.

Max sank in slowly, both of them groaning as Max filled him. He framed Benjamin's face, peppering him with kisses as he thrust into him. Their bodies moved in perfect sync, as if they'd known each other since the stars were born. Max gripped Benjamin's hips, guiding but never forcing, always mindful of his comfort.

"You feel incredible." Max groaned, his eyes locked on Benjamin's.

"So do you." Benjamin panted, leaning up to capture Max's lips in a searing kiss.

Their climaxes built slowly, each wave of pleasure cresting higher than the last. Benjamin reached down to stroke himself in time with Max's movements.

"I'm going to come," Max gritted out, his body tensing.

"Take me with you," Benjamin gasped.

With a final thrust, Max tipped over the edge, his orgasm washing over him as he cried out Benjamin's name. Benjamin came with him, his cock spurting thick ropes of cum onto Max's chest.

They stayed locked together for a long moment, both panting and covered in a sheen of sweat. Max pulled his softening cock from Benjamin's body and collapsed onto the sleeping bag beside him. Max disposed of the condom and then pulled Benjamin into his arms, their bodies fitting together perfectly. They lay in silence, the only sounds the crackling of the fire and their mingled breaths gradually slowing to a normal rhythm.

"That was… incredible," Max whispered into Benjamin's hair.

Benjamin hummed agreement and snuggled closer to Max. Max had never thought of himself as a cuddler, but he relished the warmth of Benjamin's body and the steady thump of his heartbeat.

Eventually they roused and showered under the stars, exploring each other's bodies until they ended up jerking each other off. They collapsed in Benjamin's tent, their legs wound around each other's in the soft down of the sleeping bag. As sleep began to overtake him, Max felt a sense of contentment he hadn't experienced in a long time. Maybe ever.

THE MORNING sun cast a golden hue over the campsite as Max took his time packing their gear, reluctant to leave. The previous night had been a revelation for him. He'd shared more of himself with Benjamin than he had with any other lover. But as they rolled up sleeping bags and disassembled the tent, reality began to seep back in. He could tell Benjamin's mind was racing with doubts and questions, and he had plenty of his own. What did this mean for them? He glanced at Benjamin out of the corner of his eye, the playful banter from the night before replaced by quiet contemplation.

"A penny for your thoughts," Max said, breaking the silence as he tossed his backpack into the trailer attached to the ATV.

Benjamin offered a half smile, his hands pausing on the zipper of his duffel bag. "I'm thinking about what happens next."

Max stepped closer, his voice low and sincere. "I know things are complicated, but I meant what I said last night. I'm not going anywhere, Benjamin. I want to be there for you, whatever that means for you, in whatever way you need."

"Max, you live in New York. Your life is there, and mine is here. How can we possibly make this work?"

Max reached out, brushing his fingers through the curls that caressed Benjamin's ear. "We'll find a way to see each other. Distance is nothing more than a detail. What we have, this connection, it's worth exploring more, don't you think?"

Benjamin nodded. The hope and sincerity in his eyes were undeniable. As they finished packing and extinguished the remnants of their campfire, the weight of the unknown pressed heavily on his shoulders.

They took the serene landscape in one more time before hopping onto the ATV. "We'll take it one step at a time, okay?" Max said.

"That's what I've been doing since my dad died," Benjamin said with quiet resignation.

"That's part of what draws me to you," Max said softly. "You care so much about what you do and where you come from. That passion? It's attractive."

Benjamin's cheeks flushed at his compliment. "It's more than a passion, Max. It's survival. I'm fighting to reclaim what's mine and keep my family's legacy alive."

Max nodded, understanding the weight of Benjamin's words. "You don't have to be alone in this. Let me help. I want to work with you. I can help bolster the visibility of Big Dipper Adventures."

Benjamin bit his lip as if considering his options. "And what do you get out of this? Another business deal for you to add to your portfolio?"

"Maybe it's as simple as wanting to support the man who's made an impression on me," Max countered earnestly.

Max saw the moment Benjamin's defenses kicked in again. "I want to trust you, Max, but I…." He blew out a shaky breath. "For a long time now, I've had to rely on myself, take care of myself. I can't trust anyone will take care of me as well as I can take care of myself."

Benjamin's words hurt, but Max understood where they were coming from. "If you're willing to give me a chance, I promise I won't let you down. You mean too much to me now." The weight of his words hung in the air between them.

"Then let's take it slow," Benjamin said at last.

Relief washed over him as Benjamin trusted him enough to open his heart despite all of the doubts clearly crowding his mind.

"I'll start drafting some ideas tonight," Max said, capturing Benjamin's gaze. "We could have a brainstorming session over dinner tomorrow."

Benjamin's smile fell. "I don't think we can do that. I can't be seen with you, remember?"

"No. Unacceptable. I'll figure it out."

Benjamin's smile returned. Hesitant but hopeful. "Good."

The air in between them felt charged, with a sense of promise lingering. Separating to drive back to Seattle in their own cars left Max feeling frustrated and angry. He called Benjamin and put him on speaker phone. The drive back to Seattle was filled with a mix of comfortable silence and light conversation, each moment a delicate balance between the present and an uncertain future.

Max arrived back at the *Faunus* and handed the keys to a crew member who rushed to greet him. He boarded his family's yacht with greater awareness of the opulence that surrounded him than he'd ever had before. Benjamin would be unpacking his bags and sleeping in a room behind a garage while Max was waited on hand and foot.

Max couldn't find Bennett in any of his usual haunts on board, and he wasn't answering any of Max's texts.

"Aren't you dressed a little too casually for making corporate visits?"

Max's mother waylaid him on the way to his cabin, taking in his rumpled shorts and T-shirt with a critical eye.

"I wanted to go undercover. That way I'd have an unfiltered view."

"I see. And how are things looking?"

"Good. Fine."

"Perhaps you'd like to give us a report at our meeting with DGD this afternoon. I'm sure Rochelle and her team would be interested in learning more about our Canadian business."

It wasn't a question. It was a request and a test.

"Of course. I'd be happy to." Max forced a smile.

He escaped to his cabin and sent Bennett another text. "Damn it, Bennett. Where are you?" he muttered under his breath. He straightened his shoulders, grabbed his laptop, and began preparing for the meeting. This was a test he couldn't fail. He would do whatever it took to keep his promises to Benjamin.

Chapter Seventeen

"STOP QUESTIONING me."

Benjamin eyed Aspen over the rim of his coffee cup, his lips curling into a smile. "I didn't say anything."

"You're questioning me with your eyes," Aspen said.

"Okay, fine." Benjamin leaned across the kitchen table. "I cannot believe I caught you and Bennett Goulding making out like it was the last slow dance at prom."

Benjamin had stopped by Aspen's house on his way home from his overnight with Max to give an update and make sure their campers were taken care of. His thank-you died on his lips when he walked into the kitchen and found Aspen on the counter, Bennett wedged between their knees and their tongue stuck down Bennett's throat.

Aspen's cheeks flushed bright pink. "It was—I was having a moment, okay?"

"A Cinderella moment where the handsome prince sweeps you off your feet?"

"He's not a prince."

"But he is kind of royalty, isn't he?"

"Second son of an earl."

"Maybe there's a trip to England in your future. We've had a few inquiries from campgrounds in the UK who are interested in getting Big Dipper certification. Maybe you should be the one to vet them."

Aspen rolled their eyes. "We don't believe in fairy tales, remember? And you have no business lecturing me when you've been busy doing naughty tent things in the woods with Max."

Now it was Benjamin's turn to blush.

"Ooh." Aspen's eyes gleamed with curious excitement. They leaned forward and rested their chin in their hands. "Tell me everything."

"I'm not telling you everything. Yes, we hooked up. Yes, it was amazing. And nothing is going to come of it. Max will go back to New York when the DGD sale is finalized. There's nothing for him here."

"Nothing?" Aspen arched their brow.

"Come on, Aspen. You know this isn't going to go anywhere."

"Never say never." Aspen waved their fork with a piece of french toast on the tip around as if it were a magic wand.

"Right now I want to focus on the campground accreditation program." Benjamin ignored Aspen's statement. His emotions were too raw and close to the surface. He wasn't willing to let the small spark of hope that kept growing the closer he got to his birthday to burn any brighter for now. "We didn't account for staffing turnover—that was a mistake."

"Agreed." Aspen opened their laptop. "I've started revising the contract with a requirement that any new camp owners and managers will have to take the training course to keep the accreditation. I've also updated the website."

"This looks great. Thank you." Benjamin nodded with approval at the changes Aspen had made. "I hope this didn't take away from any of your other jobs."

Aspen waved their hand. "Not a problem."

"I've been thinking about expanding. After my birthday, when I'm not chained to DGD anymore, I'll finally be able to work on Big Dipper Adventures full-time. I thought I would make the lower level of Hyas House an office… for both of us. What do you think? I can't pay you much right now, but as soon as—Ow!" Benjamin rubbed his shoulder where Aspen's fist landed. "What was that for?"

"Of course I'm going to come work for you. I can keep taking freelance jobs. Don't worry about paying me." Aspen waggled their fingers. "Once I put these magic fingers to work, you'll have enough to pay me and grow the business."

Aspen wasn't boasting. Coding and drag weren't their only talents. Aspen's analytical mind also made them a natural at finance. Every spare dollar Benjamin could scrape together, Aspen carefully funneled into an investment account. It wasn't much, but it was a start, a foundation Benjamin could use to grow Big Dipper Adventures. With time he'd have the resources to expand: better marketing, upgraded campground signs, and polished informational materials. One day, he even dreamed of launching a line of adaptive outdoor clothing. But all of it required capital, money he didn't have. Not yet.

Benjamin inhaled deeply. There it was again. That stubborn spark of hope, flickering to life. He pressed a hand to his chest, as if he could keep it from taking root. "What are you smiling at?" Benjamin asked when he noticed Aspen watching him with their chin resting on their palm and a wistful smile.

"I don't see you like this very often," they said, quietly.

"Like what?"

"Excited, happy, like you finally believe you have something to look forward to."

Benjamin bit his lip, squirming in his seat, wrestling with the truth of what Aspen said to him. As the days grew closer to his birthday, so much of the apprehension he'd been feeling seemed to be slipping away. But the reality of his current situation couldn't be ignored. When his phone pinged with another text, he pressed his lips into a hard line, reading the messages. With a groan he got up and quickly started gathering his things.

"I've gotta go. I'm never gonna get through my to-do list."

Aspen gave him a sympathetic pat on the shoulder. "They're piling it on, aren't they?"

Benjamin rolled his eyes in response.

"THERE YOU are." Milan snatched the dry-cleaning bag out of Benjamin's hand as soon as he returned to the house "I needed this an hour ago. I won't have enough time to get ready."

"What about me?" Monaco pouted.

Milan rolled his eyes. "I told you, you're wearing too much mascara to appeal to a man who runs an outdoor company. He's going to want someone with a more natural presence."

Benjamin froze. "Are you meeting with the Huntingtons?" he asked, trying to sound like he didn't care.

Milan gave him a Cheshire cat grin. "I have a date with the prince."

"No, you don't." Monaco snapped. "We've all been invited to a party on the Huntingtons' yacht."

"Yes, but Mommy said I'm the one he was excited about seeing."

Benjamin began to turn away, leaving his stepsiblings to argue between themselves. His gaze drifted to the dark burgundy walls of what had once been his bedroom. The black-velvet-upholstered headboard and the black-lace-accented furniture gave the room the appearance of a modern Italian bordello. His bedroom set was long gone, along with the rest of the furniture his parents had decorated the house with. The white walls that made the house feel so light and bright were gone too. Rochelle couldn't make any major changes to the house, but she made sure to impose her style with paint and furniture that made Benjamin nauseous.

"Take those with you on your way out." Milan pointed to a file folder on the corner of his dresser. "Make sure the design team has them first thing in the morning and they've started on the CAD drawings."

Benjamin picked up the file, gave a curt nod, and left as the twins restarted their argument over which one of them would earn Max's attention at the party.

On his way back downstairs, he opened the file folder. His jaw ticked when he saw what was inside. This wasn't the first time the twins—who were supposed to be such brilliant designers—found their inspiration in someone else's work.

Rochelle waylaid him on his way out. "The house needs cleaning. Since we'll be gone tonight, you'll be able to clean and not be in our way. I expect everything to be dusted and polished." She gave him one of her trademark withering glances. "This is your home, Benjamin, I'd think you'd take more pride in it."

Benjamin mumbled an apology and scurried out the door. The temptation to snap back grew with every day his birthday drew closer.

Back in his room behind the garage, he closed the door and leaned against it with a sigh. After a few heartbeats, he tucked the file of copied designs into his messenger bag.

Along with the growing spark of hope, a new feeling took up residence in his heart. For the first time he could ever remember, he was jealous of Monaco and Milan. They would drink champagne and fancy cocktails on the *Faunus* tonight. That part didn't bother him. He wasn't a fancy champagne kind of guy. But a part of him longed to dress up and stand on the bow of Max's elegant yacht and watch the stars with their arms around each other.

BENJAMIN BOBBED in the water, listening to the sounds of the party drift down toward him. Every once in a while, a high-pitched peal of laughter he recognized as Monaco's echoed in the air.

What he had done was completely reckless. As soon as his stepfamily left for the party, Benjamin raced through his cleaning duties, took a quick shower, changed, and jumped in his kayak. He couldn't risk driving over and having his mother or stepsiblings recognize his Jeep, but in the dark waters, he could watch the party without being noticed.

For the first time in a long while, he wanted to belong. He remembered a brief period when his dad first married Rochelle. Benjamin and his new stepsiblings would sit upstairs, peeking through the railings. They'd spy on their parents and their friends, all dressed to the nines, drinking and laughing as the smooth sounds of Jeff Bradshaw, Branford Marsalis, and Incognito drifted through the speakers, filling the house with warmth and rhythm.

Those days were short-lived. When his dad passed away, Monaco and Milan were invited to the party, while Benjamin was relegated to the kitchen to help the caterers. Rochelle and his stepsiblings went to other people's elegant homes for parties, and Benjamin was never invited. At first he was sad, then disappointed, but then he became grateful not to have to watch the spectacle Monaco and Milan made of themselves. It was better to be invisible than vain, ignorant, and beautiful.

Benjamin froze, his paddle hovering right above the water, when the face he'd been longing to see appeared along the railing. His eyes locked with Max's for a moment. He held up a finger when Benjamin started to dip his paddle in the water and turn away. Then he disappeared. Benjamin kept his focus on the space on the railing, expecting him to return, when a few minutes later a quiet splash caught his attention. He turned toward the sound, and his eyes grew wide at the sight of Max—in a tuxedo, barefoot, with his pant legs rolled up above his ankles—coming toward him on a stand-up paddleboard.

"You look ridiculous," he said with a quiet laugh.

"I prefer to think of myself as dignified."

Max aligned his paddleboard with his kayak and carefully lowered himself to sit cross-legged on the board facing Benjamin.

The smile Max greeted Benjamin with fell. "I was standing on the bow, wishing you were here. I saw you, and for a second I thought I was dreaming."

Another ripple of laughter floated toward them.

"It sounds like you're having fun."

They spoke in hushed voices, moving a little farther away from the party, both of them wanting to move out of earshot and away from any prying eyes.

Max tilted his head toward the sound of laughter. The lights from the vessel cast a warm glow over his face. "I think our guests are having a nice time."

"And you're not?"

"I'd be having more fun if you were there. I made sure your name was on the invitation. You're here, but why didn't you come to the party?"

"My name hasn't been counted on any invitation my stepmother receives since my dad died. I didn't know I was invited."

"But you came anyway."

"You're a bad influence, Max. You make me do things that I know I'm going to get in trouble for later."

Max's nostrils flared. "I can't stand how Rochelle and her spawn treat you."

Benjamin's lips quirked when Max referred to his stepsiblings as spawn.

"It doesn't matter, Max. My birthday is a little over a week away now. And then I'm done. I'll never be at Rochelle's or my stepsiblings beck and call again."

"Any big plans for your birthday?"

"No." Benjamin shook his head.

"What do you usually do?"

Benjamin shrugged. "Nothing."

Max frowned. "What did you used to do when you were little."

"My mom and dad and I would go hiking and have a picnic. After my mom died, my dad and I would go camping, but then when he got married again, he… was too busy."

"And after he died?" Max asked softly.

"If I can get away, Bubbie, Aspen's grandma, makes me a chocolate cake."

Max stared at him for so long he started to squirm before he confessed, "If I'd known you, I would have made sure we had a picnic every year."

The care in his voice brought tears to his eyes. Benjamin drew in a shaky breath.

"Thank you, Max."

A posh voice drifted toward them. "Darling, have you seen Max?"

"Mother," Max muttered under his breath.

"You'd better get back to the party."

Max leaned over, careful to keep his paddleboard steady, and gave Benjamin a quick kiss before he stood up gracefully, handsome in his tuxedo. He looked down at Benjamin with a smile, and Benjamin's heart did a little flip-flop. Every time Max smiled at him, Benjamin felt seen. He'd become so used to being ignored, the attention from Max made his stomach flutter like the ripples on the water. At first Benjamin thought he'd feel that way from any man who flirted or smiled at him, made him feel seen. But now he knew only Max made him feel that way.

"Are you going running tomorrow?" Max asked with a hopeful glint in his eyes.

"I…." The lawn needed to be mowed and the front yard weeded, and that was before Benjamin was supposed to be at the gym. "I'll be there."

Benjamin bobbed on the gentle waves as Max paddled back to the dock. A crew member stood by, waiting to take care of the paddleboard when Max returned. He waited, his gaze trained on the railing where Max had made his appearance before. A minute later his face appeared, but his smile faded, and he gestured Benjamin away. As he turned the kayak around, he heard his stepbrother, Milan.

"There you are. I've been looking for you everywhere. What are you looking at? There's nothing out there but water. I can think of much better things for you to pay attention to."

Benjamin dug his paddle into the water, moving away from Milan's cloying voice as swiftly as possible.

CHAPTER EIGHTEEN

MAX TOOK another sip of coffee, the warmth spreading through him as he leaned against the hood of his car, waiting for Benjamin to show up at the track. He had arrived so early the sun was beginning to crest over the mountains, its rays burning away the lingering chill of the night and coloring the sky in hues of pink and orange.

A smile tugged at his lips as he spotted Benjamin pulling in earlier than expected. After setting his cup aside, Max pushed off the hood and walked over to meet him at the drivers-side door.

"You kind of have a thing for pulling me out of my car and kissing me," Benjamin said when their lips parted.

Max made a low possessive sound in the back of his throat. "I definitely have a thing for you."

This idea of seeing Benjamin had Max so keyed up he'd hardly slept that night. He'd been waiting at the track for thirty minutes before Benjamin arrived.

Benjamin let his forehead fall against his. "Why? You live in a world surrounded by glamorous people. You live in Manhattan, probably in a fancy penthouse." Benjamin tugged at the hem of his running shorts. "I wear clothes from the clearance rack."

"I haven't seen you wear anything from DGD."

"Would you?"

Max barked a laugh. "Definitely not my style."

"Neither is this," Benjamin said, gesturing toward the empty track. "I don't know anything about your life beyond the *Faunus*. Do you travel that way often?"

They started around the track, their arms brushing occasionally, fingers intertwining and slipping apart in a gentle unspoken rhythm.

"Not often. It can be stifling. If I take a vacation, it's usually to ski in Switzerland or go to our vacation house in the Hamptons."

Benjamin bumped his shoulder. "You do know you kind of sound like a pretentious asshole right now."

Yeah." Max sighed. "I could hear it as I was saying it out loud."

"I shouldn't tease. It's a nice life, and your family has worked hard to earn it."

"Lately I haven't been feeling that way."

"Do you want to share why?"

"I'm not sure I can without sounding like an entitled ass again."

"I shouldn't have said the pretentious asshole thing. If you want to talk it out, I'm here to listen."

Max took a deep breath. "I've worked my way up the company ladder." He gave Benjamin a wry smile. "Yes, probably faster than most. But I started in the warehouse and learned every job in the company I could. I'm president of a company with a revenue of two billion dollars a year, and I can't get the CEOs of the company to listen to me."

"By CEOs you mean your parents."

Max nodded.

Benjamin gave him a sympathetic smile. "I think it must be hard, working with family. I'm sure if I'd joined the company when my dad was alive, we would have had some horrible fights."

"That's part of the problem," he said, frustration threading through his voice. "My parents and I don't fight. Some of that's my fault. I've had the dutiful son role drilled into me. Even when I try to stand my ground, they… it's like a wall goes up, and they ignore everything I'm saying." He ran a hand through his hair. "It's happening now with the DGD sale. I've tried to share my concerns with them, and they keep dismissing me. I don't have to tell you there are some serious issues with DGD."

"No, you don't," Benjamin frowned. "I-I hope you know I'm not involved. I mean… I don't approve of anything Rochelle and my stepsiblings do."

Max threaded his fingers with Benjamin's again. "You're nothing like them."

The coil of tension in Max eased as he shared his worries with Benjamin. He didn't dismiss Max's concerns, listening and understanding instead.

Benjamin smiled at him, giving his hand a squeeze, then asked another question. "What do you like to do when you're not working?"

Max paused. The question should have been an easy one to answer. "I…."

Benjamin stopped. He turned to Max and searched his face. "Max?"

"My entire life is Huntington Outfitters. When I do go to parties, it's usually a benefit or a gala. I'm there to represent the company."

"What about friends?"

Max shrugged. "Bennett is my best friend."

Benjamin brushed the back of his hand against Max's cheek. "Now I know what we have in common. We're both lonely people."

There was kissing and then there was kissing Benjamin. His lips were warm and soft, and it felt like the most natural thing in the world. Max delved into his mouth. He wanted to claim Benjamin, ruin him from kissing any other man. Each sweep of his tongue drew Max deeper under his spell. Benjamin's hands skimmed his arms until they wrapped around his shoulders. He shuddered when Benjamin's fingers brushed against the hair at the nape of his neck. Max shifted so that one of his legs rested between Benjamin's, fusing their bodies together.

"Max." Benjamin broke their kiss; his eyes darted around nervously. "We can't do this here."

"I need another night with you," Max said.

I need a hundred more nights with you, and it still won't be enough.

His gaze dropped to Benjamin's lips, and he brushed his thumb over them before he let him go.

They started walking again. Max ached to pull him back to his side, but they'd already put on enough of a public display. Besides, if he touched Benjamin in any way, he didn't know if he could stop at kissing.

The air grew warmer and the sun higher in the sky.

"I have to go," Benjamin said.

They'd returned to their cars, where they continued to talk, stopping for brief frenzied kisses and longing touches.

Max cupped Benjamin's face and brushed his thumb over Benjamin's cheek. "I'm going to take you on a date."

"Max," Benjamin sighed his name. "You know we can't."

"I'm going to figure out a way."

They indulged in one last kiss before saying goodbye.

"How was your morning?" Bennett said with a knowing smirk.

"Are you telling me you didn't sneak away for your own morning treat?" Max asked, tugging the collar away from Bennett's neck. "You've got another love bite."

"Dammit." Bennett slapped his hand on his neck, his cheeks turning a deep pink.

Max could count on one hand the times he'd seen Bennett flustered or blushing before this trip. Since he crossed paths with Aspen, he'd been thrown off-kilter, and it entertained Max to no end.

"If I can figure it out, I'm going on a date tonight. So you can get another hickey to match that one." He laughed.

"Asshole," Bennett muttered, glowering at him.

"Hey." Max dropped his teasing tone. "I'm happy for you. Aspen has been a good friend to Benjamin. That gets them my approval."

Bennett's eyes lit up. "Aspen is… I've never met anyone like them. They're absolutely brilliant. Did you know they have degrees in both finance and computer science? They do contract work for Ryan Blackstone. Ryan's even tried to hire them full-time, but Aspen's holding out to work with Benjamin when he's ready to expand Big Dipper Adventures."

Max paused, absorbing Bennett's words. All the conversations he'd had with Benjamin—none of them had included his long-term plans for Big Dipper Adventures. Now Max's mind buzzed with ideas about how Huntington Outfitters could partner with Benjamin. More than anything, Max wanted to be part of Benjamin's vision for the future. Not for his own benefit but because of the satisfaction he knew he'd feel watching Benjamin finally have a chance to follow his dreams.

Bennett's expression clouded. "It's going to be difficult when it's over."

Max frowned. "What do you mean?"

"We're going to be leaving next week. You've got meetings in New York. Your mother submitted a proposal for another acquisition this morning. We're going to be slammed when this trip is over."

Max's gut tightened. He hadn't thought beyond the next time he could see Benjamin. Never before had he pushed away his responsibilities or had been blinded to everything else going on around him. What would happen when he went back to New York? Could he make a long-distance relationship with Benjamin work? Would Benjamin be willing to come and visit him in the city? Would he want to? He ignored the rational part of his brain that whispered no. He would figure out a way to make it work. The family jet would get a little more use than usual. No, that wouldn't work. He'd be constantly fighting with his parents over scheduling.

"Bennett, I'm going to buy a jet. Can you call our pilot and find out what she suggests, please?"

Bennett raised an eyebrow.

"It doesn't make sense to keep sharing with my parents."

"Of course." Bennett kept his expression blank. But Max knew by his skeptical tone he didn't believe the lie.

"You can use it too, you know."

"Even if it's back and forth to England?" Bennett said with a grim smile. 'Troubles at home?"

"When aren't there troubles at home?" Bennett snapped, his tone sharp. He let out a heavy sigh, lowering his head. "I'm sorry. It's not your fault I'm the only sensible one in my family."

"Have you told Aspen about them yet?"

"They know I'm the younger son, the spare. The one who doesn't matter in the grand scheme of things."

Max's chest tightened. He hated when Bennett talked about himself like that. The rejection Bennett faced because of his sexual identity ran deeper than he let on, but it was there, plain as day, in the haunted shadow in his eyes every time the subject came up.

Max placed a hand on Bennett's shoulder. "I'm sorry. We'll figure something out, Bennett. There's got to be a way—"

Bennett let out an exasperated groan, cutting him off. "Could you not?"

"Not what?"

"You always have to fix things. Sometimes you can't. You need to understand that, Max. You can't always get what you want."

Max smirked and waggled a finger at him. "Ah, but if you try sometimes, you just might find you get what you need."

"Bugger off." Bennett shoved him playfully, a ghost of a smile tugging at his lips. "The Stones are British, mate. You can't use them against me." Bennett checked his watch. "Playtime is over. We have calls with the team back in New York on the schedule."

"Let me jump in the shower, and I have one quick call I need to make."

"Ticktock." Bennett tapped his watch.

Bennett was wrong. He could have everything he wanted. Including seeing Benjamin again. Max smiled and dialed Ryan Blackstone's number.

"Hi, Ryan, it's Max. I need a favor...."

Chapter Nineteen

Benjamin read the text from Dylan. Earlier he'd been disappointed when Max messaged to say an unexpected meeting had come up, forcing them to postpone their date. The change had left Benjamin feeling at loose ends, unsure of how to spend the unexpected evening off.

He'd considered heading over to Aspen's, but his friend was busy with Bennett tonight. Instead he'd gotten the lawn mowed and worked in the yard for a couple of hours, doing his best to make it picture-perfect. The finished product was far from impeccable but reasonably good. When the house was his and he had enough money, Benjamin planned to hire a gardener to help prune the plants properly and replace the plants that had withered away beyond saving through the years. The yard work finished, Benjamin's restlessness returned. That was when Dylan's text came through, inviting him over for dinner and putting a smile to Benjamin's lips.

He texted back yes and hurried to put his tools away and take a quick shower before he walked over to Dylan and Ryan's house.

Go around to the back. We're having a picnic in the back yard, the note on Ryan and Dylan's front door said, with an arrow and a little smiley face under the message. Benjamin went around to the path on the side of the house that led to their backyard. Unlike Hyas House, Ryan and Dylan's backyard was taken care of like it should've been in a gardening magazine. A large patio took visitors down a wide staircase to a massive expanse of lawn, lush and green, framed by maple trees, rhododendrons, and hydrangea bushes. Benjamin continued on the path beyond the guest house by the pool, where Ryan and Dylan's housekeeper—who was so much more, a surrogate mother and honored grandmother to their children—Mrs. Lieu, lived. Lately the lights in the guest house weren't on as often as usual. To everyone's surprise, after Brian and Dylan moved in, Mrs. Lieu and one of their neighbors, a man everyone considered the neighborhood curmudgeon, formed a friendship that had both of them smiling more, with a twinkle in their eyes.

The sun had almost dropped below the mountains and treetops, bathing the yard in shadows.

"I put up the tent myself," Max called out to him.

Benjamin's step hitched as he took in the sight of Max standing by a small dome tent set up at the bottom of the yard where the lawn met the shoreline. A lantern nestled in the grass next to the tent provided a beacon to guide Benjamin to him.

Max shoved his hands in the pockets of his jeans, his bare feet shifting nervously from one to the other while watching Benjamin approach with hungry eyes. It was the most romantic gesture Benjamin had ever experienced. As soon as he was within arm's reach, Max pulled him into a hug, whispering in his ear, "Has anyone hugged you today?"

Benjamin accepted the invitation, wrapping his arms around Max's neck.

"This is a creative ruse to get me over here. I'm impressed," Benjamin said when Max let go.

"How does a picnic on the dock sound?"

"Perfect. I'm starving." Benjamin took his phone out of his back pocket. "Let me send a quick text first," he said, glancing back at the house.

You are a good liar. Thank you.

Benjamin added a wink emoji and sent the text to Dylan, who replied with a kiss emoji.

"I didn't realize you knew Ryan and Dylan," Benjamin said, pocketing his phone.

"Ryan and I met at an executive roundtable a few years ago." Max picked up the lantern at his feet and took Benjamin's hand, nudging him toward the dock.

A picnic basket Benjamin hadn't noticed before was waiting for them at the end of the dock.

Max set the lantern down and pulled Benjamin to sit with him on the edge, their feet dangling over the water.

"Mrs. Lieu is a goddess. She packed fried chicken, potato salad, lemon bars for dessert, and…," Max said, rummaging through the basket to pull out plates, silverware, and two wineglasses. "And this." He held up a bottle of wine with a grin.

"Wow, how did you manage to get your hands on a bottle of Brothers in Arms? This is one of the most sought-after wines in the state."

"Ryan let me raid his wine cellar." Max produced a corkscrew from the basket, opened the bottle, and poured the pinot blanc.

Max held his glass up. "Here's to our first date."

"So far it's the best date I've ever been on." Benjamin clinked his glass against his.

"If things were different, I would have taken you to a nice restaurant. We would have dinner, maybe find a rooftop bar and have a drink after."

"And then what would happen?" Benjamin asked.

Max's voice took on a deep, sultry tone. "Then I would take you back to my apartment and spend the rest of the night worshipping every inch of your body."

Benjamin shivered. "I'm not a fancy restaurant kind of guy."

"Then I'm glad we're having a picnic." Max leaned closer, wrapped his hand around the back of his neck, and whispered against Benjamin's lips. "And I have every intention of worshipping every inch of you in that tent tonight."

Benjamin closed his eyes when Max ghosted his lips over his. His body was already straining with desire.

"Finish your dinner so we can get to dessert." Max said, moving away.

Later Benjamin looked up at the stars, taking the last sip of wine from his glass. They'd finished their picnic and packed the dishes and silverware back in the basket. Benjamin put his empty glass down. He leaned back on his hands and craned his neck, admiring the canopy of light overhead.

"I only know the Big Dipper." Max said.

"That one that's like a chair is Cassiopeia. And that one—"

"The one that's supposed to be like a bear?" Max followed where he was pointing.

"Yup, that one is Ursa Major."

"I've never paid attention before. The Big Dipper is a part of it. It's all connected, almost as if there are worlds within worlds."

Benjamin nodded with a wistful smile. "Always turn to the stars. Look closely and you'll find they hold the answers to many secrets."

"The quote from your dad, right?"

Benjamin turned to sit, mirroring Max. "You remembered."

Max took Benjamin's hands in his, then rubbed his thumb over Benjamin's knuckles. "Is that your favorite memory of your dad?"

"One of them. The thing I miss the most are the Friday night dinners my parents would host. The house would be filled with friends.

Both my parents were only children. My dad's parents died before I was born. My mom was raised by a single mother, who passed away when I was a baby. My parents' friends became their chosen family. Mom would bake challah and light the candles. The house was filled with light and laughter."

Benjamin didn't realize a tear had escaped until Max reached up and brushed it from his cheek, his fingers gently trailing against Benjamin's face until his hand fell away.

"Sorry, I didn't mean to get so sentimental."

"It's a beautiful memory, Benjamin. Thank you for sharing it with me."

Their eyes locked, and once again they gravitated toward each other like two stars on a collision course. Max stood up, pulling Benjamin up with him. They kissed and stumbled across the yard and into the tent.

"I picked the Stargazer," Max tugged at the hem of Benjamin's T-shirt. "I wanted to make love to you under the stars."

Benjamin glanced through the mesh top of the tent before he returned his attention to Max, where the stars above were reflected in his eyes. Max peeled off Benjamin's T-shirt, his hands skimming over the light smattering of hair on his chest.

Benjamin did the same, pulling Max's shirt over his head. He ran his hands over Max's shoulders, solid and tan from the summer sun. Max made a sexy, growly noise, bringing them chest-to-chest, then fusing their mouths together. His tongue ran over Benjamin's lips, sending a jolt of heat through him. Max dug the fingers of one hand into Benjamin's hip and dipped the other into the waistband of his jeans to squeeze his ass.

"You're going to make me come before you've even gotten all my clothes off," Benjamin said, panting.

Max pushed him back on the sleeping bag, tackled him, and jerked his pants and briefs down together. His eyes glittered when Benjamin's cock sprang free. When he started to reach for him, though, Benjamin shook his head.

"Not until you're naked."

Max smirked and popped the button on his waistband. In seconds he was naked and on top of Benjamin.

"Better?" he asked.

"Much," Benjamin said, cupping the back of his head and pressing their lips together again. Benjamin could spend all of his days kissing Max, and it still wouldn't be enough. When Max kissed him, he felt desired, wanted in a way that was both tender and demanding. It made him dizzy knowing he had the power to make Max want more.

When Max pulled back, his lips were pink and swollen, his pupils large, darkened with lust. Benjamin wrapped his arm around his waist and rolled them over. He pressed his hand over Max's heart.

"Is this okay?"

"It's kind of what I hoped for when I planned for tonight. I have condoms, I've been tested, and I want you so bad I haven't been able to think about anything else since our first time."

Benjamin kissed him, at the same time running his hand down the length of Max's body to wrap his fingers around his cock. "I've wanted this. Wanted you. I haven't been with anyone for years before the other night. I've been tested too. Do… do you want me to… would you let me…?" Benjamin fumbled for the right words, fighting against the creeping insecurity his inexperience gave him.

"Yes," Max said, thrusting his pelvis against Benjamin's. "I want you to fuck me."

Benjamin swallowed, nodding. Everything around him disappeared. Only Max existed. Their kisses—some soft, others hot, openmouthed. Their touches—some a gentle caress, others possessive, with fingers digging into skin almost to the point of pain. Benjamin licked and sucked at Max's neck, his mouth, until he panted beneath him, his hips thrusting forward, begging him for more.

Max arched, calling out his name when their bodies joined. He dug his fingers into Benjamin's arm.

"Max," Benjamin breathed his name. He was ruined now. He'd never share his body with any other man again.

"More," Max breathed, lifting his hips, urging Benjamin deeper.

Benjamin lost himself in Max's body. His thrusts, tentative at first, afraid of hurting Max, became harder, his rhythm erratic as the pressure began to build, his legs beginning to shake as his body drew taut.

Max grabbed his face between his hands. "Come with me, baby," he begged.

They came together. Max's hot cum coated Benjamin's hand where it wrapped around his cock at the same time as he filled Max with his.

He collapsed on Max, their chests heaving in unison as Benjamin tried to catch his breath. He sighed. "I don't want to crush you," he said, lifting away.

Max banded his arms around him and wrapped his legs around Benjamin's, trapping him. "Don't move," he breathed, kissing the side of Benjamin's neck. "Stay with me a little longer."

Their caresses became slow and languid as their heartbeats returned to normal, remaining in sync.

Benjamin propped himself on one arm and searched Max's face for any sign of discomfort. "Are you okay?"

"Better than okay." Max smiled and hauled Benjamin back down for another kiss.

Eventually they used the washcloth and water bottle Max had stashed in the tent to clean themselves up before climbing into the sleeping bag.

"I think you may have earned your first Boy Scout badge." Benjamin kissed the top of Max's head where it lay on his chest.

Max's lips curled against him. "Be prepared."

Benjamin stilled, the reality of what had happened washing over him. This was more than sex. He'd developed feelings for the man in his arms.

"We're in trouble, Max," he whispered.

Max pulled himself up, his body draped half over Benjamin's. Worry clouded his eyes. "What do you mean?"

"I don't think I can pretend this is something casual between us. I-I care about you, Max."

"We passed casual a while ago. Even though I'm going back to New York, that doesn't mean this has to end. We can make it work, Benjamin."

Benjamin wanted to believe in the fairy tale, in happily ever afters. Could they make it work? "I've never been to New York."

"Tent sex is fun, but wait until I get you in my king-size bed," Max said with a wolfish grin.

Benjamin's body heated again at the picture Max painted, whispering all the things he planned for him in New York, none of which were about sightseeing. He was so caught up in his fantasy he didn't register what Max said right away.

"My parents are having a party to celebrate the deal with DGD on Friday. Will you come? I want to introduce them to you properly as my boyfriend before we leave."

Benjamin chuckled, shaking his head. "Friday's my birthday."

Max kissed him. "That's perfect. There won't be any reason to hide anymore." He kissed Benjamin again, coaxing, teasing at first, then hot and possessive. "Come with me?" he asked again.

Defenseless against his kisses, Benjamin pressed his forehead against Max's. "I'll come with you."

They spent the rest of the night lost in each other's arms. Whispering secrets and promises until dawn.

Chapter Twenty

Max matched his pace to Benjamin's slower gait. Reluctant to leave each other again, Max coaxed Benjamin into going on a morning run with him before their time together ended. This morning Max was able to weasel stories from his childhood out of Benjamin, revealing happy ones from before his father remarried. He didn't believe Joe Colton meant to neglect his son. From what Benjamin told him, Max had the impression his dad was a pleaser, willing to sacrifice his own needs to make the people he loved happy. Joe assumed Rochelle would love his son as much as he did. He prioritized making his wife happy, trusting his wife was making his son happy. The memories Benjamin shared from the years since his father passed were tinged with heartache. Those were the times Max struggled to keep running and not stop to gather Benjamin into his arms and kiss every bad memory away.

They made their way around the track side by side, enjoying the peaceful summer morning and the cooler temperature before it became too warm. After their sixth lap around the track, Benjamin stopped. Panting, he rested his hands on his knees.

When he caught his breath, he straightened with a smile. "It's been nice having company on my morning runs."

Max stared into his big brown eyes, taking in the hint of sadness in their depths. The reality of Max's eventual departure had stayed unspoken between them. He reached up to brush his fingers over Benjamin's tattoo, and somehow that unlocked Benjamin's reticence.

"You're not going to be here for much longer," Benjamin said with a slight tremor in his voice.

"I can come back. I want to come back."

"My birthday is almost here. I should be excited, but I'm also…. What do you do when you get the thing that you've been clinging to, the thing that's been giving you hope? What happens after that?"

Max wrapped his arms around Benjamin, hugging him tight. "You get to live your life and be happy. You have as many wishes as you want, Benjamin."

If I could, I would make them all come true.

Benjamin cupped his cheek, searching his face with an unreadable expression. "Tell me something about you no one else knows."

There was an urgency in his voice, a desperation that caught Max by surprise. Max saw the need for reassurance for what it was. They'd started walking hand in hand, their pace unhurried.

"I'll give you three things, since that's how many questions you gave me," Max said, bumping Benjamin's shoulder.

"I was kind of an ass that day," Benjamin muttered with a sheepish smile.

"You didn't know if you could trust me yet. Now let me see. Three things no one else knows about me. That might be a challenge. You should know, Bennett knows all my secrets."

Benjamin's step hitched. "Were you and Bennett ever—"

"Good God, no." Max shuddered. "It would be like kissing my brother. Plus, he's not my type. You have to understand that when you're away from home at boarding school, well… it's hard to keep secrets from your roommate. And if you're both keeping the same secret, you create a bond that's impossible to break."

"When did you come out?"

Max smiled. "When I brought Bennett on a family skiing trip in Switzerland. I didn't have a conversation where I shared my sexuality with my parents. My mother took one look at the two of us and said, 'Oh, for heaven's sake, both of you?'" Max laughed and then sobered. "I was lucky. My experience with my parents was much better than Bennett's." He kicked a piece of the crumbling track. "Then when I told my mother I was bi, she was surprisingly enthusiastic. It took me a while to realize she was thrilled to have twice as many opportunities to marry me off."

"Th-that's just—"

"Gross?" Max finished for him.

"Sorry, but yeah."

"Nothing to be sorry for. You're right." He squeezed Benjamin's hand. "You already know my biggest secret."

"I do? What is it?"

"That I'm a fraud."

Benjamin stopped, and his grip tightened on Max's hand. "What are you talking about?"

"I don't live the lifestyle we promote. I don't know how to put up a tent. I don't go hiking or camping. The pictures of me in our company catalog are all staged."

"What happened? How did you end up being the head of a wilderness company who has never been camping?"

"My parents were more into the business than the lifestyle. And I was too. Until—" He wrapped his arm around Benjamin's waist. "—I met a guy who showed me what I've been missing." His lips curled into a sly grin. "I do have one more secret. One that Bennett doesn't know." Max leaned in and caressed the shell of Benjamin's ear as he whispered. "I've recently developed a thing for tent sex."

Max caught Benjamin's laugh with a kiss. Their eyes remained locked when their lips finally parted.

"You may be a fake Prince of the Wilderness," Benjamin pressed his forehead to his. "But you're a very real Prince Charming to me."

"NICE NIGHT?" Bennett smiled at Max over the rim of his coffee cup.

"I could ask you the same thing." Max said, joining him at the dining room table.

Bennett set his cup down and leveled Max with a serious gaze. "What are we doing, Max? This is all going to end in a few days."

"Maybe it doesn't have to." Max leaned forward, his hands clasped tightly on the table. "I'm going to talk to my parents. I want to tell them about Big Dipper Adventures. I want to invest in Benjamin's company."

The lines bracketing Bennett's mouth deepened with a frown. "Benjamin has guarded his identity and his involvement with Big Dipper Adventures for a reason. What does he think about this?"

"I haven't told him yet. We've been talking about what Big Dipper Adventures could be like in the future."

Been raised in eyebrow. "You've had time to talk?"

"Don't be an ass. Yes, we've been talking. A partnership with Big Dipper Adventures has the potential to be much more lucrative than anything DGD could bring to the table."

"How so?" Phillip Huntington asked, walking into the dining room with mild interest in his eyes.

Bennett glanced at Max with alarm. Max was intending on going to his father at some point today to make his pitch. He figured his dad would be more receptive and could possibly help him sell the concept to his mother.

"Where's Mom?" Max tried to sound casual.

"She and Rochelle are having a spa day," Phillip said, doctoring his coffee. "Have you discovered who the owner of Big Dipper Adventures is?" he asked, joining them at the table.

"I have." Since his mother wasn't on board and he didn't have to worry about her overhearing their conversation, now was as good a time as any to talk to his dad.

"I'd like you to keep this between us for now and not tell Mom yet. I want to wait until the party for her to meet Benjamin first. Really meet him this time."

Confusion clouded his father's eyes. "Benjamin? The assistant?"

Max balled one hand into a fist. "He's much more than that."

Bennett got up and excused himself from the table, understanding that what Max was about to tell his father was a private conversation between father and son.

His father studied him for a moment. "What's going on, son?"

"Benjamin Colton is the man behind Big Dipper Adventures."

"Why all the secrecy?"

Max chose his words carefully. There was no way his father would betray his trust, but at the same time Max calculated now wasn't the right time to share everything.

"Benjamin is a guarded and private person. His relationship with his stepmother is strained, and he doesn't want Big Dipper Adventures to be tied to DGD. It's a separate company and his alone."

"Tell me more about the company."

"First. I'm telling you first. I know Mother will reject any idea I bring to the table. It seems to be standard form these days. I want you to hear me out first, and if you think my gut is right that Benjamin has created something special, I hope we can approach Mother as a united front. Your endorsement of my proposal will at least get her to listen."

"Your mother isn't rejecting all your ideas. She's worked tirelessly, we both have, to get Huntington Outfitters to where it is today. Give your mother time, Max. She'll come around."

"Will you hear me out?" Max asked, ignoring his father's excuse for his mother's unwillingness to let Max take the lead.

"Of course, son."

For the next hour, Max shared what he had learned about Big Dipper Adventures and Benjamin's plans for expanding the company. When he finished, his father sat back, nodding. "This is intriguing. Big Dipper Adventures would be an excellent fit with Huntington Outfitters. Good work, son."

Max released the breath he had been holding. He was on the right track. Working with Benjamin would mean he would have an excuse to make frequent trips to Seattle.

"And what about the young man you're seeing?" his father asked.

Should he tell him it was Benjamin? No, not yet. He wanted to wait for the party and introduce Benjamin to both his parents as his partner in both business and life.

Max ended up spending the rest of the day working with his dad, something he hadn't done in a long time without his mother's presence. They reviewed other business proposals, stores, expansion plans, and new products that were in development.

"I can't wait to get my hands on those DGD patents," his father said. "I'm amazed. Rochelle is ignoring her company's greatest asset."

"I asked Milan about that at the party. He said his mother's vision has always been to focus on the fashion. He said the gyms were a leftover from Benjamin's father's time, and long-term their plan was to phase them out and open boutiques instead."

"What do you think of that?"

"I have to agree the gyms aren't profitable. With the right investment and partnership that we are going to offer, the clothing brand can expand. Milan proposed working with more Black creatives on design, and I think that is a good direction to go in."

Max had been surprised by his conversation with Milan at their party. Once Milan finished peppering him with questions about the celebrities he knew, they had managed to have a decent conversation about DGD's branding. Monaco and Milan were still far too self-involved for Max. And of course he couldn't stand the way they spoke about their stepbrother, as if he were nothing more than an employee.

"Good to know," his father said with a note of approval in his voice. "Send me all your notes and start drafting a proposal."

"It's already done."

"Send me everything, then, and we'll plan our pitch to your mother."

That night, Max sent Benjamin a text.

Did anyone hug you today?

It took a minute before the three dots rippled for a second at the bottom of his screen.

I didn't see you today.

Max leaned against his pillows with a soft groan, tempted to drive over, find Benjamin, and make sure he ended his day with a hug.

Chapter Twenty-One

THE STACK of papers on his desk was piled so high it obscured Benjamin's view, and he didn't realize Max, his parents, and Bennett had arrived until Max's mother cleared her throat with a pointed look.

"Excuse me." Benjamin jumped up, knocking one of the piles of file folders askew. Max reached out a split second before it toppled over. "I didn't see you there."

"Clearly," Mrs. Huntington snapped, earning an angry glance from Max. "We have a lunch date with Mrs. Tremaine."

"Of course." Benjamin fumbled for the phone. "Feel free to go in, and I'll let her know you're here."

Max turned to his mother. "You go ahead. Bennett and I need to get a few more reports while we're here."

"Bennett can take care of it. The Tremaines are waiting for us. Milan wants to show you some of his new designs."

Benjamin watched Max's jaw as he wavered for a moment. "Of course."

Benjamin called to announce the Huntingtons while Bennett waited. As soon as the doors separating the lobby from the office closed behind Max and his parents, he smiled at Benjamin. "Sorry. I told Max that excuse wasn't going to work."

Benjamin dropped back down in his seat. "Why is he so stubborn?"

"He likes to get his way. He's an only child who grew up with privilege." Bennett's voice dropped to a low, serious tone. "Are you prepared for that?"

"Prepared how?

"If your relationship continues. Which I think both of you want. Are you going to be able to handle it when Max is always used to getting his way? I'm not asking because I don't approve. I'm asking because Max may be my best friend, but I like you, Benjamin, and I don't want to see you get hurt."

"I could say the same thing to you about Aspen. They're more than a friend, they're family. Maybe not by blood, but they are family. What are your intentions with my Aspen?"

Bennett pulled his shoulders back at the forcefulness of Benjamin's words.

"I… it is not my intention to hurt Aspen. Aspen is a very special person."

The office door opened. Bennett straightened, snatched a folder from a random pile, and clutched it.

"Did you get everything you need?" Max asked, eyeing Benjamin as he clapped Bennett on the shoulder.

Bennett tapped the folder. "Yes, right here."

Max gave Benjamin a longing glance over his shoulder as he was swept out of the building with Milan's arm wrapped around his. His stepmother and Max's mom followed, chatting as if they were lifelong friends. As soon as the door closed behind the group, Benjamin dropped his head in his hands.

The closer he got to his birthday, the more anxious and off-kilter he felt. One minute he was excited about the party—to be able to be the one standing with Max's arm wrapped around his—and the next doubt would creep in, and he wanted to tell Max he'd changed his mind. He'd put himself in the shadows for so long, it wasn't easy to come out into the light. If he wanted to grow Big Dipper Adventures, he needed to stop hiding.

Rochelle returned from lunch alone. "Benjamin, a word." She crooked her finger for him to follow on her way to her office.

He grabbed his tablet and trailed behind her. She took her seat behind her desk, crossed her legs, and folded her hands on her desk.

"Benjamin. Since your birthday is a couple of days away, I thought we should discuss your future."

Benjamin froze, the stylus in his hand hovering over his tablet, her statement catching him off guard.

"As you know, the terms of the sale of DGD have changed," Rochelle began, her voice cool and precise. "Instead of being incorporated into Huntington Outfitters, DGD will remain a subsidiary. I will continue to run the company, and Monaco and Milan will stay in their roles as designers. It occurred to me that you won't have any means to support yourself once this transition is complete. I'm offering you the opportunity to continue in your position here."

Benjamin bit down on his lip, suppressing the urge to laugh at the sheer absurdity of her offer. Of course she had no idea about Big Dipper Adventures and the life that awaited him as soon as he was unshackled from her control as trustee.

Clearing his throat, he forced his expression into something neutral, professional. "Thank you for your offer," he said carefully. "However, I think it's time for me to pursue other opportunities."

Rochelle's manicured nails tapped an irritated rhythm on the glossy surface of the desk. Her thinly veiled annoyance rippled through the room, sharpening the air between them. Was she delusional enough to think he would continue working under her thumb?

"I see," she said, her words clipped. Then, after a pause, her eyes narrowed slightly. "And do you have any specific opportunities in mind?"

There was something in her tone, an edge, a calculated curiosity that made the hair on the back of Benjamin's neck prickle. Her question wasn't innocent; it felt like a probe, a subtle attempt to extract information.

Benjamin met her gaze evenly, his pulse steady despite the unease creeping into his chest. "A few," he replied with a polite smile.

Rochelle's lips pressed into a thin line, but she said nothing, her tapping nails falling silent. Benjamin resisted the urge to smirk. She wasn't going to get anything more out of him today.

He cleared his throat, his voice steady. "Since you brought up my birthday, we should talk about the house."

Rochelle shifted her attention to her laptop, dismissing the conversation before it had even begun. "The trust ends on your birthday, Benjamin. There's nothing I can do about that," she said briskly, her tone laced with impatience. "I hope you can appreciate how busy I am with the merger."

Benjamin's first instinct was to walk away—it's what he'd always done. She'd taught him to retreat, to yield, because he'd never had the leverage to stand his ground. But not this time.

He planted his feet firmly, his voice unwavering. "I'd appreciate it if you could be out of the house by Friday."

Rochelle froze for a split second, her fingers pausing over the keyboard before resuming their steady typing. She didn't meet his eyes, but the tension in her posture spoke volumes. This time, Benjamin wasn't backing down.

Her fingers paused over the keyboard for a moment before she acknowledged him, her eyes glittering with thinly veiled annoyance. "Since the party celebrating the partnership is on Friday, I would appreciate it if you could extend me the courtesy of an extra day to move."

She'd never extended Benjamin any courtesy since his father died. The irony of her request made his stomach churn. The calculating gleam in her gaze sent a ripple of unease through him. He wanted his house back, wanted Rochelle out of his life for good. He could say no, draw a line. But was one more day worth the fight?

He clenched his jaw, weighing his options before giving a curt nod. "That's fine."

Her smile was quick, polished, and insincere. It didn't touch her eyes. "Thank you, Benjamin," she said smoothly.

He returned to his desk, his eyes sweeping over the piles of files, reports, and invoices that no longer held any significance. The thought liberated him, making it effortless to power through his duties. With each completed task, a weight lifted, leaving him feeling lighter, knowing this was his final time doing them. By the end of the week, he would walk out of DGD's doors forever and never go back.

The restless feeling that had been gnawing at him lately surged back, sharper than ever. He wanted to see Max, not only to feel the reassuring warmth of his presence, but to talk to him, to be able to see his face and hear his voice. To know Max would wrap his arms around him and give him a hug. Benjamin pressed the heel of his hands against his eyes. Damn Max for getting him so used to getting hugged. He wanted to share the tangled mess of his uncertainty and excitement about the future, to tell him about Rochelle's offer, knowing he'd laugh at the absurdity of it with him. More than anything, he missed him, the sound of his voice, his confident smile, his confidence that everything would be okay.

He wasn't able to connect with him until later that night. He grinned when he read his text.

Did anyone hug you today?

I miss you.

Miss you too.

Benjamin snorted a laugh when Max texted, *Did you know your stepsister can tie a cherry stem with her tongue?*

Is it crazy to miss someone so much that you saw a few hours ago? I'm nervous about the party but I'm excited to see you there.

I wish I could see you before the party, but I'm slammed with meetings and going over the final details for the merger.

Benjamin told Max about his stepmother's job offer, his feelings a mix of excitement and apprehension.

Max's response came as a string of laughing emojis, making Benjamin huff out a quiet laugh despite himself.

His phone vibrated, and Max's name flashed on his screen.

"Ever have phone sex?" Max asked when he answered, his tone dropping into a teasing, sexy drawl that sent a spark racing through Benjamin's chest, which his hand was already skimming in anticipation.

"Not yet," he said in a breathy whisper.

"Take a breath, Benjamin," Max ordered and preceded to whisper dirty things in his ear.

"Definitely a fan of phone sex," Benjamin said once they finished. He lay panting, spent on his bed, his stomach sticky with his release.

Max chuckled low and deep in his ear. "See, I told you we'd be able to make things work when I go back to New York."

Benjamin blinked rapidly, his chest tightening with an unspoken plea. He wanted to ask Max to stay, the words trembling on the edge of his tongue, but fear held them back. How could he ask Max to give up his position in New York? Huntington Outfitters was his family legacy. As much a part of him as Big Dipper Adventures was a part of Benjamin. Whatever this thing was between them, it was too new, too fragile to ask for such a big sacrifice.

"Get some sleep, Benjamin," Max whispered. "I'll be waiting at the *Faunus* to wish you a happy birthday."

His body sated, Benjamin's chest still felt heavy as he drifted off to sleep, the unspoken words still weighing on his mind. His dreams pulled him back onto his kayak, bobbing gently on the water below the *Faunus*. On the deck above, Max stood at the bow, his face turned toward the open sea. His light brown hair was highlighted gold by the sun and ruffled by the breeze, and his laughter echoed faintly toward Benjamin.

Benjamin tried to call out, but his voice refused to cooperate, the words stuck like stones in his throat. The waves grew bigger as the engines of the *Faunus* churned the water.

"Max!" He managed a strangled shout, his voice breaking with the force of his panic.

Max turned, but his expression was unreadable, distant. Instead of answering, he simply waved—a casual, fleeting gesture that cut Benjamin deeper than he expected. The *Faunus* pulled away from the dock, moving faster and faster. Benjamin dipped his paddle into the water but couldn't move, and with each stroke the *Faunus* pulled farther away.

He jolted awake, his heart pounding and his hands clutching at the sheets. The room was dark and quiet, but his pulse roared in his ears, the image of Max's retreating figure still vivid in his mind.

He sat up, running a hand over his face, his fingers trembling. "I can't lose him," he whispered into the silence, the words as raw and fragile as the fear still clinging to him.

Chapter Twenty-Two

Another seaplane traced a wide arc above the water before beginning its descent. Max shifted his attention back to the backlog of emails. Since arriving in Seattle, his focus and drive had waned. He smiled, knowing the reason why. He never imagined he'd start longing for nights spent in a tent, cuddled up in a sleeping bag.

"What has you smiling this morning?" His mother stood in front of him, watching him with her own slight smile. He'd been so caught up in his daydreams he hadn't even noticed she was there. "I expected you'd be working at the DGD offices today." She scrutinized him with narrowed eyes, taking in his cargo shorts and T-shirt. "You've gotten so sloppy since we got here."

"We own an outdoor lifestyle company," Max said. "There's nothing wrong with dressing this way. I decided to work out here and enjoy the view." He pointed toward another seaplane descending over the water.

"Have you read the email I sent? I want to review the guest list for the party."

Max pulled up the email he'd been planning on ignoring. The party was all he'd heard about for the last week. Socializing with Rochelle and party planning had taken precedence over finalizing contracts and double-checking numbers.

"I don't care, Mother. Invite whoever you want."

She shook her head with an exasperated sigh. "You keep telling me how you're ready to take over, and yet you don't pay attention to the details."

"I am paying attention to the details. Have you read the DGD's staffing report?"

"Seattle is a competitive job market."

That still didn't explain the numbers in the latest report. The company had been reduced to a skeleton crew. From the fear etched in the employees' eyes whenever Rochelle Tremaine walked through the office, it was clear the high turnover wasn't due to a competitive job market but to poor management practices. He'd started noticing the same pattern emerging at Huntington Outfitters as soon as his mother arrived. A toxic work environment was bad for business. Max made a mental note to add improving corporate culture to the ever-growing list of changes he wanted to make when he had control. For now he scrolled through the list, searching for one name he already knew wouldn't be there.

With a decisive click, he shut his laptop and rested his folded hands in his lap. "I have someone I'd like to add to the guest list."

"Of course, dear. Who do you have in mind?"

"Benjamin Colton."

Kathrine's smile faltered, becoming tight and forced. "And why would you want to invite him?"

"Benjamin Colton is the son of the founder of DGD. Don't you think it would be appropriate for him to be there?"

"Rochelle said he's shy and doesn't like parties."

He locked eyes with his mother. "I want him there anyway."

She crossed her arms in front of her and cocked her head, studying him.

"It's good business, Mother. There are a lot of people who admired Benjamin's father. His presence will show he approves of the merger." He made up the excuse on the fly.

"I suppose so."

An experienced negotiator knows when to play their hand, and now wasn't the moment to tell his mother about his relationship with Benjamin. Max planned to introduce Benjamin as his boyfriend at the party—though part of him had toyed with the idea of saying fiancé, because that's what he hoped Benjamin would become someday.

Finally his mother smoothed a hand over her sleek bob, her expression a mix of impatience and indifference, as if the conversation had already worn thin. "Rochelle, Monaco, and Milan will be there, and that's what matters."

Max stared at his mother. He'd always dismissed his parents' snobbery as a quirk of their generation, assuming they were playing along for appearances. He didn't think they truly believed any of it. But now a sick feeling churned in the pit of his stomach.

"Benjamin is coming to the party as my guest. It's not open for negotiation," he said in a steely voice.

"I'll make sure he's added to the list."

I believe Bennett has a plus-one as well. I'll check with him and get you that name."

"Fine." His mother's voice was clipped, her annoyance clear. "Make sure Benjamin dresses appropriately for the party. It's black-tie."

Max reopened his laptop and focused on the screen. "I have work to do, Mother."

When she walked away, Max rose to his feet, pacing the deck as he raked his hands through his hair. Frustration clawed at him, sharp and relentless. The merger and the party couldn't come soon enough. He was tired of the tension, the scrutiny, the constant pressure. For a fleeting moment, the thought of walking away from it all crossed his mind, but he dismissed it almost instantly. He was an only child, the heir to an empire. Walking away wasn't an option. Besides, he loved the company his family had built; it was in his blood, a part of who he was.

"Well, this is fun." Bennett approached, looking down at his phone with a wry smile.

"What?"

Bennett paused. "Snappish today?" he said with a raised eyebrow.

"Tired of... everything today."

"Then you may not want to see this."

"What is it?"

"Our friend BirchBitch206 is at it again."

Max groaned. "Oh God, what now?" he said, taking Bennett's phone.

If frustration had a physical form, it would be the DGD Designs sports bra. This glorified elastic band is less about support and more about crushing your soul—and your rib cage. It's marketed as "high impact," but the only impact it has is on your self-esteem when you try to get it on. I don't know whose titties they think they're supporting, but it ain't mine and probably won't be yours either. The padding shifts around like it's trying to escape a bad relationship, and the straps, well... are they straps or rubber bands with some lace glued over the top? Speaking of lace, why? Who puts gold lace on a sports bra? Was it designed for Melania Trump? By the time you've wrestled it on, you've already had your workout, and taking it off feels like auditioning for Cirque du Soleil. Or in this case, Cirque du Don't.

Max clapped his hand over his mouth, his shoulders shaking with laughter.

"Whoever this is, they have a gift with words and an impressive vocabulary. I must say I've started looking forward to their reviews."

Max tried to school his expression. "We should be taking this seriously—" he began, but the words barely left his mouth before laughter bubbled up again, ruining any attempt at composure. "Before I forget," he said when he finally got his laughter under control, "I spoke to my mother about the guest list for the party."

"Ah, hence the frustration I encountered."

"I demanded Benjamin be added to the guest list and told her you might have a plus-one. I'm assuming you might want to bring Aspen with you."

Bennett's expression became apprehensive. "I would."

"That's great, but why do you have a look on your face like that's bad news?"

"It means I'm going public with my relationship with them."

"Do you think your parents will act on their threat?"

"And disown me? Yes, I absolutely believe they will. They've made it clear they'd rather have a drunk, degenerate son than a gay one."

"I'm sorry, Bennett." Max clapped him on the shoulder. "I know there's nothing I can say that will make the sting less sharp."

Bennett's jaw ticked. "He's going to ruin generations of hard work and preservation. Goulding Hall will end up being sold to some tech billionaire asshole."

"If it comes to that, I'll buy it and give it back to you."

Bennett answered with an exasperated sigh. "You can't solve all your problems with money, Max. Someday there's going to be a problem that you can't buy your way out of. A situation where you can't send your assistant to buy whatever you need to fix the problem."

Bennett's words were a punch in the gut and the resentment in his eyes a revelation.

"Bennett, I-I apologize if I ever made you feel like nothing more than my assistant. You are much more than that to me. You're my best friend and confidant. You're essential not only to me but to Huntington Outfitters as well."

Bennett's expression softened. "Thank you for saying that. I'm angry and frustrated about a situation that you haven't caused. I'm angry at my parents, at the world, and frustrated with myself for not having the courage to tell my parents to go ahead and disown me. I'm tired of living with that anvil over my head. Wondering, will they or won't they? Keeping my relationships a secret so I don't incur their wrath." He pinched his brow. "How can I ask Aspen not to shine so brightly?"

Max put his arm around his friend's shoulder. "You'll figure something out."

"What about you? You certainly smile a lot more since you've met Benjamin."

Max glanced over his shoulder, making sure they wouldn't be overheard.

"I think I'm going to ask him to marry me," he confessed.

Bennett drew back. "Careful, Max. Are you prepared to go against your parents and marry someone they don't approve of?"

"They don't know him yet. Once they've spent time with Benjamin, they'll realize how remarkable he is."

"Are you sure about that, Max? Absolutely sure?"

He ignored the doubt he felt. "Absolutely. We'll figure out a way to make it work."

Bennett sighed. "Do you realize how many times a day you say that?"

"Say what?"

"That you'll figure something out. You can't always bend the universe to your will, Max. Some forces in this world are out of your control. You can't always get what you want."

"But if you try—"

"Maximillian Huntington, I swear if you quote the Rolling Stones to me again, I'm going to toss you overboard," Bennett said, giving him a playful shove.

Max sobered as his mother's earlier comment about his clothing resurfaced in his mind. He compared his outfit to Bennett's, who had also adopted a more casual style—trading in his usual trousers for chinos and pairing them with untucked Oxford shirts. The thought of returning to the formality of suits and ties felt stifling.

"I didn't expect it," Max said, gesturing between himself and Bennett, "but this trip has been good for us. Even with all the extra work this messy merger is going to bring, we've both found something special here."

"We have. So what happens next?"

"We'll dance the night away with Aspen and Benjamin and figure out the rest later." Even as the words left his lips, Max knew the dance ahead wouldn't be a simple one. He might be able to sway his father into accepting Benjamin as his partner, but his mother....

Would she follow through on her threats if Max refused to marry someone she didn't consider suitable? He rejected the idea his parents could be as heartless as Bennett's.

"Let's get back to work. I'm scared of what BirchBitch206 would say if she were the one writing our performance review."

Chapter Twenty-Three

"Benjamin, what's wrong?" Aspen asked. "You've been moody all day."

Benjamin put the last of his gear away after their hike.

"Max invited me to the party on the *Faunus*."

Aspen nodded. "To celebrate the DGD partnership. Bennett invited me."

"It's not exactly how I hoped to spend my twenty-fifth birthday."

"True. But you'll be with Max. It's your birthday. It won't matter if Rochelle sees you together. Hyas House will be yours. You can do whatever you want."

Benjamin considered what Aspen said as he pulled out of the trailhead parking lot. "True. I… I don't know. It will be fancy and… I don't have anything to wear, okay?"

Aspen grinned at him. "I can fix that."

"I can't afford to spend a ton of money on a tuxedo that I'm never going to wear again. I suppose I could rent one."

Aspen gasped. "Over my dead body. We can do better than that."

Instead of going back to their place, Aspen directed Benjamin to Capitol Hill and a little vintage clothing store tucked away on a side street away from the hustle and bustle of Broadway.

A little bell chimed over the doorway as they walked in. "I overheard some of the other queens talking about this place at my last show, and I've been dying to come here. I'm sure we can find something for you." Aspen went straight over to a rack on the wall and started flipping through the vintage blazers.

The little store overflowed with colorful clothes, shoes, hats, and vintage accessories.

A man dressed like a 1920s page boy with bright pink suspenders and a pink-and-brown paisley bow tie came through a doorway concealed behind a heavy, deep forest-green velvet drape.

"Can I help you?"

"My friend needs a suit for—"

Before Aspen could finish, the man looked at Benjamin and gasped. "It can't be."

Benjamin and Aspen exchanged confused looks. The man came forward, staring at Benjamin. "You're Lucy's son, aren't you?"

"How… how do you know that?"

He took one of Benjamin's hands, sandwiching it between his own. "Your mother was my best friend. I remember the day you were born. Able," the man called, "come out here."

A tall Black man, bald, with rich dark skin and warm brown eyes, came through the curtains, wearing a pair of deep red silk pajamas and red satin pumps.

"What is it, Charlie?"

He stopped when he saw Benjamin. His hand, with long red painted nails, flew to his mouth.

"I can't believe it," the man, Charlie, said, continuing to stare at him in awe.

"I'm sorry, do I know you?"

"You're too young to remember."

The other man, Able, moved behind the one named Charlie and rested his hands on his shoulders. "You're scaring the child," he said, smiling at Benjamin.

"Oh, sweet boy, where are my manners? I'm Charles Horowitz, and this is my husband, Able."

Aspen reached for Benjamin's hand and gave it a comforting squeeze.

"Let me make you some tea," Able said. He paused at the green velvet curtain. "Miss Theresa Hugger, why don't you come with me, and we'll let Charlie and Benjamin catch up."

Aspen let go of Benjamin's hand and walked toward Able. They looked up at the older man with wonder. "I love you," they blurted out.

Able threw his head back and laughed. "Of course you do, child. Fabulous recognizes fabulous." He draped his arm around Aspen's shoulder as they disappeared behind the curtain.

"Come sit with me," Charlie said, gesturing him toward a vintage love seat covered in navy-blue velvet.

"Your mother and I met at Hillel our first week of college," Charlie began as soon as they sat down. "It was like meeting someone and knowing you'd found a kindred spirit." He laughed, shaking his head. "Lord, we had fun. We'd listen to Depeche Mode, Scritti Politti, and of course the fabulous Ms. Jackson. We would have dance parties in our dorm." He shook his head with a wistful smile. "I remember the first day

I met your mother and the last day I spent with her before that horrible cancer took her away from me." He reached over and patted Benjamin's knee. "I remember you running around at the Shabbat dinners your parents used to have."

Benjamin gasped, his heart tipped over as if it were going over a waterfall. "You were there. I-I wish I remembered."

"You were just a little boy, a sweet child with his mother's eyes." The light dimmed in Charlie's eyes. "Lucy in the sky with diamonds. Your mama shined so bright, like the stars in the sky your daddy loved so much. She was the brightest one of all, and he loved her so—" He pressed his lips together and turned away, blinking back tears. Benjamin pressed his hand to his heart, fighting back his own tears. Charlie's love for his mother was palpable.

Aspen returned with tea for four in vintage teacups, with saucers, on a small silver tray, followed by Able with a plate of cookies. "Presentation is everything," he said, setting the plate on the small coffee table in front of the settee and adjusting it until he nodded with satisfaction.

"What brings you into our shop today?" Charlie asked.

"Benjamin needs a suit for a fancy party," Aspen said to Able. They both studied Benjamin, tapping their lips.

Able snapped his fingers. "Come with me, my young padawan," he said to Aspen.

The two of them went over to another section of the store, chatting as if they were old friends.

"I'm afraid Able isn't going to be a good influence on him," Charlie said with a sigh.

Benjamin chuckled. "Aspen uses they/them. And it's going to be a competition to see who corrupts whom."

Aspen and Able returned. Aspen held up a suit, their eyes sparkling with excitement. "It's perfect." Able nodded in agreement, and they promptly ushered Benjamin into the dressing room.

"It fits like it was made for you." Able walked around him, smoothing the navy-blue jacquard fabric over his shoulders.

"The pants don't even need to be hemmed," Aspen said.

Based on the slim cut of the suit and pants, it must have been from the '60s. Able and Aspen were right. The suit fit like it had been made for him. The pants skimmed his ankles, which, according to Aspen, made them the perfect length to wear loafers without socks.

Able produced a pair of navy-blue velvet Ferragamo loafers with gold buckles and slipped them on Benjamin's feet. "Perfect."

Able and Aspen engaged in a spirited debate about a tie or no tie. Charlie finally put his foot down and ended the debate, siding with Aspen on no tie and earning an angry pout from his husband.

"It's not formal enough," Able insisted.

"This is Seattle, remember? People show up at black-tie events in jeans and their—" Aspen curled his fingers into quotes. "—good flannel."

Able's lips twitched into a wry smile. "Fair point. I'm trying to educate these heathens as best I can. I still can't believe people don't use shoe bags when they travel. I mean, it's what makes us a civilized society."

"Oh my God, yes." Aspen nodded emphatically.

"Good Lord, do not get him started on shoe bags." Charlie rolled his eyes. But his voice was loving when he stood on tiptoes and kissed Able's cheek. "Darling, you've done a wonderful job. Benjamin will be the star of the party." He patted Benjamin's shoulder. "There's one more thing you need." He went behind the curtain and returned a few moments later with a small red leather case in his hand.

"Your mother gave me these for graduation," he said, holding the box out to Benjamin.

Benjamin's chin quivered when he opened the container. Sitting on the cream silk lining were a pair of gold cuff links. The Big Dipper, made of tiny diamonds, dotted their gold oval surfaces.

"Charlie, I can't—"

Charlie wrapped his hand around Benjamin's. "You can and you must. These are meant for you."

When another customer walked in, they found Benjamin and the other three hugging and crying.

"Don't mind us." Charlie sniffed and waved his hand toward the racks. "Help yourself."

THE NEXT couple of days were a whirlwind of preparations for the party. It turned out Able was a hairdresser, and he insisted on cutting Benjamin's hair while Charlie fussed over him like a mother hen.

Benjamin was slightly overwhelmed by all the attention, unused to being in the spotlight. His anxiety grew as his birthday and the day of the party approached. And then….

"Happy birthday!" Aspen shouted as they burst into the guest room. Gwen had firmly insisted that Benjamin stay with them, determined he wouldn't wake up alone in his room behind the garage on his birthday.

Benjamin jerked awake and sat up in bed. It took him a moment to register what was happening. Gwen followed Aspen, holding a stack of pancakes with candles on top, singing "Happy Birthday." Aspen joined in, and Benjamin fought back tears.

"Come on." Aspen grabbed Benjamin's hand and dragged him from the bed. "Breakfast, then prezzies, and then we have to get ready for the party."

"Aspen, we have all day. The party is not until tonight."

Aspen gave him an exasperated look. "It might not take *you* that long. But this…." They gestured to themself. They were wearing a pair of silk pajamas, similar to the ones Able wore when Aspen first met him. "Being fabulous takes time, care, and attention to detail," Aspen said, parroting Able.

Benjamin sat at the kitchen table while Bubbie fussed around him, stopping every few minutes to pepper his cheeks with kisses.

His phone pinged, and he rolled his eyes at the message.

"What is it?"

Benjamin turned his phone around to show Aspen his screen.

"You've got to be fucking kidding me. Are they seriously that clueless? Not today, bitches," Aspen said, waving their hand as if they were shooing a fly. "And that color lipstick is hideous and doesn't look good on anyone."

"What's going on, honey?" Bubbie peered over his shoulder, squinting at the words on the screen.

Where are you?! I need you to run to the tailor with my pants. They aren't fitting right. Monaco needs you to stop at MAC and get her more mascara and another frost lipstick in High Strung.

NOW!!!

Benjamin sighed and started to get up. "I should—"

Bubbie's hands landed on his shoulders, holding him in his seat. "Absolutely not. You will sit here and eat your breakfast pancakes." She moved him around gently to face her and cupped his chin. "Sweetheart, it's your birthday. You don't have to do what they tell you anymore."

Benjamin swallowed the lump in his throat, realizing how special today was. Gwen was right. Today was the first day he could let go and just breathe.

Charlie and Able descended on the house after breakfast, arriving in a flurry of garment bags and presents.

"You're spoiling me," Benjamin said, holding a book about Benjamin McAdoo in his hands.

"My dear boy—" Charlie patted his hand. "—you should be spoiled, especially today of all days."

The floor was littered with wrapping paper, and Benjamin sat on the sofa, surrounded by everyone's thoughtfulness. There were more books from Charlie and Able and a generous gift certificate to a store that sold mid-century modern furniture to help him redecorate the house.

Aspen gave him a pair of new hiking boots, already relaced with sparkly emerald-green shoelaces.

It was Bubbie's gift that had him fighting back tears, though. The challah plate, kiddush cup, and candlesticks were ceramic, glazed in shades of dark blue that swirled like clouds against the night sky and dotted with gold and silver stars.

"I figured you'd want to start having Shabbat dinners when you get settled in."

Benjamin threw his arms around her. "Thank you, Bubbie."

Once all the presents were opened, Gwen and Charlie disappeared into the kitchen to make lunch, and Benjamin was left to the mercy of Aspen and Able's party preparations.

"You are both a vision," Able said with pride as he continued to tug at and adjust their outfits. He stood in front of them as if he were a field marshal about to give directions to his troops. "Now I want both of you to walk in there, shoulders back, heads held high, sparkling like the stars you are."

They left the house to blown kisses, waves, and shouts of last-minute advice.

Aspen laughed as they got into the Jeep. "This is so much better than Cinderella going to the ball. The only thing we're missing is if someone could've turned this Jeep into a McLaren."

Benjamin patted the dash. "Don't be mean to Estrella. She may not be fancy, but she'll get us to the ball."

He started the engine and took off. A mixture of hope and excitement took over from worry. It was his birthday, and tonight he'd be by Max's side, looking up at the stars.

Chapter Twenty-Four

"Stop fiddling. You look amazing," Aspen said.

Benjamin tugged on the cuff of his jacket one more time. They stood on the walkway of the *Faunus*, the hull looming above them. The yacht sparkled with lights, and the sounds of laughter and music drifted toward them.

Benjamin repeated Able's instructions under his breath as they boarded the *Faunus*. *Shoulders back, head up, smile. Sparkle like the star you are.*

"Are you okay?" Aspen asked. "You look a little green, and the boat's not even moving."

"I don't know when I've ever felt so out of place." Benjamin said, taking in their opulent surroundings. A steward passed by with a tray of champagne flutes. Aspen grabbed two and handed one to Benjamin.

"It's going to be fine. It's your birthday. It's time to celebrate."

Max and Bennett appeared, coming toward them with big smiles.

"Happy birthday." Bennett shook his hand.

"Happy birthday." Max leaned forward and pressed a kiss to his cheek.

Benjamin took in the sight of Max with hungry eyes. He'd never had any doubt that Max would look dashing in a tuxedo. Butterflies flittered in his stomach, seeing him in the perfectly tailored deep navy, almost black, tux. His hair was trimmed and tamed, and instead of being clean-shaven he had a close-cropped beard, golden and soft-looking, that Benjamin wanted to reach out and touch.

"Thank you. So do you."

"Don't be nervous," Max said, taking his hand and leading him into the crowd while Bennett did the same with Aspen.

"I'm trying not to be, but I can't help it. I've been waiting so long for this day, and now that it's finally here, I'm having a hard time believing it's real."

"It's very real." Max's voice dropped low. "Like my plans for you after this party is over." Max leaned forward to grasp Benjamin's waist. His lips grazed Benjamin's ear. "As handsome as you are in that suit, I can't wait to get you out of it."

"I wish I could spend the night at Hyas House with you tonight."

"Why can't we?"

"I gave Rochelle and the twins an extra day to move out."

"You're too generous, Benjamin. It doesn't matter. Besides, I thought we'd go camping again. You've gotten me addicted to tent sex."

Benjamin laughed softly. "That sounds like a perfect way to celebrate my birthday."

"Then you won't mind that my car is packed with camping gear and we can leave as soon as the party is over?"

"As long as you packed a full-size sleeping bag this time."

"I made sure this one is big enough for two."

Max's fingers caressed the back of Benjamin's neck where his curls met the collar of his shirt.

As they mingled with the other guests, Benjamin began to enjoy himself. Even though there was no reason to hide when he saw his stepmother, he quickly pulled his hand out of Max's warm grasp. He wasn't sure when they were going to tell Max's parents about the relationship. Knowing it would be that night, Benjamin struggled to completely relax.

"Excuse me, Max." Rochelle came toward them. "Your mother is asking to speak to you."

"Of course." The back of his hand brushed against Benjamin's before he walked away.

As soon as Max was out of earshot, Rochelle turned on Benjamin, her eyes glittering with pure hate. She grabbed his arm, her fingers digging painfully into his flesh as she dragged him farther away from the crowd.

"Let go of me." Benjamin pulled out of her grasp. "You don't get to order me around anymore. I've put up with everything you've done to me, waiting for today. Hyas House is finally mine. After tomorrow I never want to see you again."

Rochelle's smile sent a chill down his spine.

"I planned on telling you this in the morning, but since you've decided to worm your way into getting an invitation to this party, I should tell you now before the announcement is made." She took a deep breath, clasping her hands in front of her as if she were about to sing. "As your trustee, I had no choice but to file a lien against the house." Her sad pout didn't reach eyes that glittered with malice. "You were lucky a buyer came along right away. When I shared your troubles with the Huntingtons, they were happy to purchase the house as an engagement present for their son."

"You can't sell the house. It's mine."

"Oh dear, I've been so busy I haven't had a chance to tell you," Rochelle said with a fake pout. "I'm afraid you owe me so much as executor, I simply had to put a lien on the house. I sold it to Kathrine to pay off your debts. It was in your best interests, dear."

"You spiteful bitch." Benjamin fisted his hands at his sides.

Rochelle grinned a brittle smile filled with triumph.

"You think you've won, don't you? You think you've finally beaten me down. It must make you feel good to know you've destroyed someone who only ever wanted to be a good stepson to you, to love you. I was so happy when you married Dad. You fooled me too, at first. You never wanted to be a mother to me."

"You weren't important. As long as I convinced your father I cared, that's all that mattered." Rochelle snapped at him, her face a mask of hate directed at Benjamin. "Oh, and thanks to Max sharing your brilliant idea for Big Dipper Adventures, DGD will be launching its own platform for curated outdoor events and campground accreditations in partnership with Huntington Outfitters. With the Huntington money, we will be able to expand our reach far beyond what you've done."

Numb, Benjamin stared at his stepmother. Max said he would never hurt him. But he'd gone beyond that. He'd destroyed him. Benjamin's gaze flew to the upper deck where Max was smiling down at the guests. His mother and father stood on one side of him while Monaco pressed against his other side, her arm coiled around his.

"You'll have to excuse me. I need to head up for the announcement," Rochelle said with a malicious smile.

She walked away, leaving Benjamin numb from what she'd told him. Hyas House was gone. Everything he'd worked for had been taken from him.

The party became a blur of noise and sound. Benjamin pressed his hand against his chest. His heart beat so heavily it hurt. He fought to get air into his lungs. In a panic he searched the crowd, desperate to find Aspen. He found them with Bennett, the two of them talking and laughing, their faces so close they were about to kiss. They were having their magical moment. The one he'd hoped to share with Max. Benjamin wanted to call out for Aspen, but his throat closed up.

His gaze flew back to the upper deck when Kathrine Huntington picked up a champagne glass from the tray a steward held for her and clinked on the glass.

"Ladies and gentleman. Thank you for joining us tonight as we celebrate the partnership between Huntington Outfitters and DGD." The guests surged forward, clapping. Kathrine turned toward Max. "Tonight we are also celebrating another partnership. I'm thrilled to announce my son, Max, and Monaco Tremaine are engaged. Their marriage will be the start of a new age at Huntington Outfitters as I turn over the reins to Max."

There were shocked gasps and oohs and ahhs. Unable to bear listening to any more, Benjamin pushed his way through the crowd. He didn't move fast enough.

"And as a special surprise," Max's father chimed in, "Kathrine and I are giving Hyas House to the happy couple as a wedding present."

A sob escaped, but then Benjamin swallowed hard, determined not to let anyone see him break.

"Benjamin!" Aspen rushed toward him.

He couldn't feel Aspen's hand holding his.

"Let me go, Aspen. I've got to get out of here."

"I'll come with you."

"No," he cried out. "Leave me alone, Aspen." He grabbed the lapel of Aspen's jacket. "Please. I can't talk to anyone right now."

Aspen nodded, their eyes bright with unshed tears.

Chapter Twenty-Five

Max ripped his tie undone. "Don't make a scene, darling," his mother said through clenched teeth, her manicured nails digging into his arm like talons, stopping him from going after Benjamin.

The applause in the background was drowned out by the roaring in Max's ears. His pulse thundered, each beat a jarring reminder of how out of control everything had become. He jerked his arm free from Monaco's grasp, ignoring her gasp of indignation, and headed for the railing. He scanned the crowd frantically, searching for Benjamin. His stomach churned when he didn't see him, or Bennett and Aspen, among the well-dressed guests milling about the deck.

Gritting his teeth, Max pushed away from the railing and strode toward the stairway leading to the main deck. His breath came in shallow bursts, and he barely registered the people grabbing at him, calling his name, congratulating him.

"Max, stop making a fool of yourself this instant!" His mother's sharp voice rang out behind him as she grabbed his arm.

He turned and yanked his sleeve out of her grasp. "Is that what I'm doing? Making a fool of myself? How dare you pull a stunt like this!" he hissed.

His mother's face flushed, her composure slipping. "You told your father you'd met someone special."

"I meant Benjamin."

Kathrine drew back as if he'd slapped her. "That boy isn't suitable for you. No. Monaco is the right match. Max, if you won't do what needs to be done for your own good, then I will. I'm your mother—"

"Then act like it," he snapped.

His father appeared at the top of the stairs, his tie loosened and his expression uneasy. "Son, now isn't the time."

Max's laugh was hollow. "I don't care. I don't care about anything other than finding Benjamin."

"He's gone." Bennett said, walking toward them, anger radiating from him.

Rochelle descended the stairs one careful step at a time, her hand clutching the railing as she wobbled on sky-high stilettos.

Max's jaw tightened. "Where is he?"

"Does it matter?" Rochelle shrugged, her perfectly coiffed hair swaying with the motion. "He shouldn't have been here in the first place."

"Why do you hate him so much?" Max demanded, his voice trembling with anger.

"Because he doesn't have any class," Rochelle said, her tone as dismissive as ever. Monaco and Milan joined their mother, their identical smirks only fueling Max's fury.

"And you think you do?" he asked, his voice sharp.

"Well, duh. I mean, look at us," Monaco said, gesturing to herself and Milan with a self-satisfied grin.

Max shook his head, a bitter laugh escaping his lips. "I have looked at you—both of you. And all I see are two of the most vain, vapid people I've ever met."

Rochelle's expression darkened. "How dare you talk to my children that way!"

"Why not? It's no different than how you've talked to Benjamin for years," Max shot back.

"He deserved it," Rochelle said, crossing her arms.

Max's hands balled into fists at his sides. "What did he ever do to deserve it? He was a little boy who only wanted to be loved, to be part of a family."

"He got plenty of love from his father," Rochelle snapped.

Max stared at her, the depths of her cruelty leaving him cold.

Rochelle's carefully curated mask of sophistication cracked, revealing the bitterness beneath. "Marrying Joe was my chance at happiness. I clawed my way out of a rundown house in Detroit, taking care of everything because my parents were too drunk or high to do it themselves. My first husband turned out to be like my father—abusive, lazy, and he did a damn good job of hiding his cocaine habit until I had a ring on my finger." She fingered the diamond Benjamin's father gave her. "Even that was fake," she spat out with disgust. "When I met Joe, I thought I'd finally found someone who would love me. But no, Benjamin came first. He always came first. The world is a ruthless place. I had to take what I wanted because I learned no one was ever going to give it to me." Her voice shook with fury. "I had to play along and pretend that I actually liked raising a mixed kid. He was an embarrassment—not even truly Black. It was bad enough he was Jewish." She spat the word out as if it left a bad taste in her mouth. "Thank God Joe died and I didn't have to pretend anymore. Joe put his son first, and now I've made sure to put my children first."

Max kept staring at her, disgust mixing with a flicker of pity. "If you're expecting me to feel sorry for you, I do. I'm sorry that you let your pain and bitterness turn you into this." He gestured to her, his tone growing colder. "I feel sorry for you because you'll never know how amazing Benjamin is. How smart, caring, and loving he is. But I'm not sorry that you'll spend the rest of your life wondering why you're so miserable."

Rochelle's face twisted with hatred, her poised façade shattered revealing the ugliness inside.

"Maximillian," his mother hissed, her voice a sharp warning.

Max turned on his mother. "Are you going to tell me you're okay with this?"

"Max, Rochelle is a mother trying to protect her children." Kathrine said.

Max reared back as if his mother had slapped him. "I can't believe I'm hearing this."

"How could you be so obtuse?" Bennett's voice cut through the chaos like a knife.

"Max, you are risking your position at this company. If you refuse this marriage, then I cannot put you in charge of Huntington Outfitters."

Max froze. He watched his dad, standing motionless at his mother's side, and waited for him to object. Phillip's face remained an unreadable mask.

Kathrine lifted her chin, the challenge clear in her eyes. She'd set a trap and was confident it had worked. He'd spent his whole life working toward taking over Huntington Outfitters. It was all he'd ever wanted. How could he give that dream up now?

"I need time to think."

"What the hell are you doing?" Bennett demanded. "You're going to reject this madness."

His gaze flew to Bennett. "I-I need time to figure this out."

Bennett's shoulders sagged as he exhaled deeply. "I'm resigning. I'm giving you two weeks' notice."

"What?" Max stared at him, blindsided.

"I can't believe you're being disloyal to this family." Kathrine said.

"I'm not the one who is being disloyal," Bennett said, looking at Max.

Max blinked, his friend's words striking him like a blow to the chest. "I'll accept your resignation," Max said after a long pause, his voice raw.

Bennett turned his back on him and walked away.

Max faced his mother. "My heart is not a company asset. It's not something you can negotiate away. You've negotiated a deal that may end up damaging Huntington Outfitters and destroying our family."

Kathrine lifted her chin, defiance in her eyes. "I am not destroying our family."

"How can you stand there and not say anything?" Max asked his dad, incredulous at his silence.

"I...." His father pressed his lips together and hung his head, defeated.

"Enjoy the rest of your party." Max turned on his heel and walked out.

He went straight to his cabin, closed the door behind him, and leaned against it, squeezing his eyes shut, trying to make sense of what happened, of how the evening went so horribly wrong. Benjamin's birthday was ruined. Instead of celebrating his freedom, Max was now the one who was ensnared in a trap. He never imagined his mother would go so far to get her way. He couldn't accept the marriage. There was no way. But could he accept losing his position at Huntington Outfitters, of not being a part of his family business? For the first time in his life, Max felt utterly alone. This must've been how Benjamin felt, he thought. His hands shook as he picked up his phone. He hesitated, trying to figure out what to say.

Where are you?

Can we talk?

We need to talk.

Please let me know you're okay.

I love you.

The screen became blurry when he typed the last text. An hour later his mother walked into his cabin without bothering to knock.

"The party's over. What an absolute disaster. I can't believe you embarrassed us like this."

Max jumped up. "I embarrassed you? What you did tonight was—I don't even know how to begin to describe what you did tonight. Disrespectful for a start."

"Disrespectful to who?"

"To me, Mother." Max pounded his chest.

"I can't be disrespectful to you. I'm your mother," Kathrine scoffed.

"And yet you treated me like I was another acquisition. How in the world did you think that I would agree to a marriage with Monaco under any circumstances?"

"You told your father you had met someone special, someone who shared your interests. I assumed—"

"No." Max cut her off. "You wanted. You got so caught up in your vision and what you wanted, you didn't stop to think. You didn't even talk to me about this."

Kathrine stared him down with steely determination. "I meant what I said, Max. I'm not turning over Huntington Outfitters to you until I know you're ready for the responsibility."

"And that means doing whatever you tell me to do? In both my personal and business life? That's what it is, isn't it? You'll always know better. That's the disrespect. You don't even believe I'm capable of knowing what's best for myself." Max took a deep breath and squared his shoulders. "You've given me a lot to think about. I'll let you know my decision in the morning."

Kathrine hesitated for a moment. "Max, I love you. I only have your best interests at heart."

Max didn't answer. When she moved closer and put her hand on his back, he flinched and moved away. The silence hung heavy between them. It wasn't until he heard the cabin door close behind her that he exhaled.

It was late when his phone pinged with a text from Benjamin. He stared at the screen, reading the short message over and over again. Max went to Bennett's cabin next door and knocked.

"Benjamin sent me a text." He flashed his screen at Bennett when he answered the door. "I'd like you to be at the meeting."

Bennett sighed, leaning his head against the doorframe. "I gave two weeks' notice. Of course I'll be there."

"Thank you."

Bennett answered by closing the door in his face. Max went back to his cabin with a heavy heart. He spent a sleepless night trying to figure out how to keep his position at Huntington Outfitters and get Benjamin back. There had to be a way—he hadn't figured it out yet, but he would, he always did. He sent his parents separate messages letting them know about the meeting Benjamin had requested. His mother sent a brief, terse response. His father acknowledged the message, asking if Max wanted to ride with them to the DGD offices. Max declined the offer, hoping he'd be able to have time with Benjamin alone to talk after the meeting.

The next morning, he arrived at the dining room with dark circles under his eyes. He blew out a sigh of relief when it was his father sitting alone at the table.

He poured himself a cup of coffee from the buffet set up on the sideboard and sat down across from his father.

"Son, I—"

"I don't want to have this conversation right now. We can talk after the meeting."

Max couldn't bear to hear any more excuses for what happened last night. During the long sleepless night, Max had considered his options with the company. If worse came to worse, he could challenge his parents for control. His mother's past missteps would help convince the board. It would be a last resort. He hoped he could reason with his parents and it wouldn't come to that.

His dad sighed, looking dejected.

"I didn't mean to snap at you," Max said. "It's been a long night."

"I understand."

"I wish I believed that you do," Max said quietly.

His father pushed away from the table. "I'll see you at the meeting. We'll talk more after."

His coffee tasted like cardboard, and his stomach was already in too many knots to eat. With a mixture of hope, fear, and worry, he dressed for the meeting, his hands trembling as he buttoned his crisp white shirt. He had to make Benjamin see that he was on his side, to make his mother understand she couldn't keep dangling control of Huntington Outfitters like a sword over his head. As he adjusted his tie in the mirror, his reflection stared back, determined but with a hint of fear in his eyes. What if he couldn't do either? He rejected the possibility as he got into the car, with Bennett silent at his side, and left for the DGD offices.

Chapter Twenty-Six

Benjamin ignored the text notifications and Max's name on his screen. He shut the ringer off and focused on the road, wiping tears from his eyes.

He arrived home, a sob breaking from him as he pulled up to Hyas House. He dropped his head to the steering wheel, fighting to breathe. After a few minutes he lifted his head and stared at the starry canopy above. There were no shooting stars to wish on. The North Star couldn't guide him home.

He went straight to his room and with shaking hands tore off his suit jacket and toed off his shoes. He quickly changed into a pair of jeans, a T-shirt, and his hiking boots, tying the green laces as tears continued to roll down his cheeks. He took one more look around the room that had been his home for the last ten years. There wasn't much to take with him. He shoved a few items of clothing he had into his backpack. He threw his camping gear into his Jeep, then went back to his room for one last thing.

Under his bed, tucked away in the corner and hidden behind a floorboard, he pulled out a book and a small box. Benjamin clutched the book to his chest with one hand, holding the box tight in his grip with the other. He hadn't taken them out of their hiding place for years.

His dad gave him the book the day after Benjamin won their constellation contest. *A Guide to the Constellations*, by Samuel G. Barton and Wm. H. Barton. The edition was printed in 1928 and was one of his dad's prized possessions.

"Did you know, Dad?" Benjamin whispered. "Did you know you were gonna leave me and that's why you gave me this?"

His dad's words when he handed Benjamin the book—along with an antique telescope in a mahogany box nestled in dark blue velvet embroidered with gold stars—came back to him.

Always turn to the stars, son. Look closely and you'll find they hold the answers to all the secrets.

He put the book aside and opened the telescope box. The instrument was made of brass, with a mahogany grip. Benjamin's dad explained that Benjamin's grandfather had traded for it with a British officer after World War II.

He'd kept the book and the telescope hidden away and had been afraid to even take it out, fearing his stepmother or stepsiblings would see it and want to claim it as their own or think it had some value and try to sell it. His fingers trembled as he lifted the telescope from the box. Not much bigger than the width of a piece of paper, it still gleamed with the fresh polish his father must've given it before he gave it to Benjamin. When his father died and Benjamin had to pack up his room and move to the garage, it was the only thing he cared about making sure he took with him. He held the telescope in his hand and turned it around, admiring the craftsmanship. He had meant for it to sit on the mantle in Hyas House when it was restored.

He settled the telescope back into its velvet-lined nest, but something crinkled beneath the fabric. His brow furrowed as he noticed a slim strip of white peeking out. He lifted the telescope again and pulled back a corner of the velvet, revealing an envelope.

Slowly he peeled away the rest of the fabric, his breath catching when he saw his name scrawled across the front in his father's handwriting. His fingers trembled as he took it from the box and opened it.

It took him a moment to comprehend what he was reading, but when he realized what he held in his hands, he couldn't hold back his tears. The Huntingtons could buy DGD, and Rochelle could take all the profits, but it didn't matter anymore. He held his father's legacy in his hands.

His heart shattered as he left Hyas House for the last time, what little he owned packed in the back of his Jeep. He drove past Jason and Joy's house. As he started to pass Dylan and Ryan's house, he slowed and then stopped instead of continuing out of the neighborhood. He turned down their driveway.

Mrs. Lieu, their housekeeper, answered the door. "Benjamin, what a nice surprise."

"Can I come in?" he asked, his voice shaky.

Her face immediately morphed into a concerned, motherly expression. "Of course, of course, come in." She urged him inside instinctively, clearly knowing he needed the support and comfort of her hand threaded through his arm. It didn't take long for Dylan and Ryan to return home from the disastrous party on the *Faunus*. When they did, they found him in the kitchen with their son, Leo, in his lap, reading a story, a cup of tea and a bowl of Mrs. Lieu's delicious pho on the counter in front of him.

"Benjamin," Dylan exclaimed, rushing toward him and giving him a fierce hug, even though he still had Leo in his lap.

Mrs. Lieu spoke a few quick hushed words with Ryan and then took Leo and his baby sister out of the room.

"Oh my God, Benjamin, that was…. It was horrible. I don't know what to say. I'm so glad you came here," Dylan said.

Benjamin could only nod, his emotions too overwhelming to allow him to speak. Ryan went over to a cabinet and pulled out a cut-crystal glass and poured some whiskey into it, then slid it across the island countertop toward Benjamin. "Here, I think you need this."

Benjamin took a sip, forcing the smoky amber liquid past the lump in his throat. Dylan coaxed him into the living room and sat next to him on the couch while Ryan pulled a chair close and sat facing Benjamin. "What do you need?" he asked.

"Give me a minute." Benjamin went to his backpack he'd left by the front door and returned with the box that held the telescope. Dylan let out a small gasp when Benjamin opened the box, peeled away the lining, and held the envelope out to Ryan with trembling fingers. "I found this when I was packing after, after—" His voice broke, and he shook his head, squeezing his eyes shut.

Dylan grabbed his hand in silent support. They both watched Ryan read through the paperwork.

"I know you're not a lawyer," Benjamin said, "but you get finance stuff. I thought…." He shrugged, uncertain what he should ask for.

Ryan nodded. "I'm glad you came to us." He stood and pulled his phone out of his pocket. "I need to make a few calls," he said, walking out of the room.

As he left, Benjamin's own phone blew up again, the buzzing of the silent calls and texts incessant.

"Do you want me to take care of that for you?" Dylan asked.

"No." He blew out a shaky breath. "This is my problem. It's my fault for being reckless and thinking I could trust Max." Benjamin looked at his friend. "I have to leave. I can't stay here knowing that my house, my home," he choked out, "is gone."

"You don't have to go," Dylan said with urgency in his voice. "You can stay here with Ryan and me, or Aspen and their Bubbie, or Jason and Joy, or Noah and Gideon. We all have a place for you, not just in our homes but in our hearts. Benjamin, please don't go."

Overwhelmed, Benjamin buried his face in his hands. "I can't be here, not after what was taken from me."

Ryan returned. "My friend Gina is coming over. She's a corporate attorney with knowledge of patent law." He sat down with a grim smile. "And she is a shark."

Dylan let out a low whistle. "You called out the big dog."

"Thank you," Benjamin said in a shaky whisper.

Within the hour, Benjamin was reviewing the patents for his father's designs with Gina.

"Your father was a brilliant man," she said, with approval and a note of admiration in her voice while her fingers flew across the keyboard, taking notes.

For so long the love for his father and his mother had given Benjamin hope. It was the catalyst for so much of what he did. Now that love was a heavy weight in his heart. "I wish he had loved me enough that I didn't have to live the way I have for all these years."

Gina gave him a sympathetic look. As she opened a new document on her laptop, she turned to him with a shrewd gleam in her eye. "Let's talk about that."

By the time they finished, Benjamin's fingers were fumbling, even as he typed one more message. The emotional exhaustion had become physical exhaustion, and he struggled with the final task he needed to complete before the night was over. The last thing he wanted to do was send a text to Max. Gina, Ryan, and Dylan gave their input, making sure every word of the brief text was what he needed. It was a simple request for a meeting at the DGD offices with Max and his parents. Of course Max responded immediately. Benjamin couldn't bear to read what he said, handing the phone blindly to Dylan.

"He'll be there," Dylan said quietly.

Gina took the phone from him, reached for Benjamin's arm, and gave it a comforting squeeze. "I'll send the next one. We've already worked out what to say." She sent a text to Rochelle, explaining to Benjamin that his stepmother would likely reject a face-to-face meeting. The text said Benjamin wanted to meet her at the office to make sure he handed over all of his files, an apparent capitulation that would please Rochelle no end and ensure the meeting.

BENJAMIN DIDN'T remember climbing into bed in Ryan and Dylan's guest room, too exhausted to brush his teeth or cry any more after he completely broke down when Gina left. His eyes were gritty and dry when he peeled them open the next morning. A long hot shower didn't do anything to relieve his aching body. Mrs. Lieu fussed over him, insisting he eat a good breakfast to prepare for the day ahead.

"Aspen called," Dylan said, taking a seat next to Benjamin at the kitchen table. "They're frantic, Benjamin. Both they and Gwen."

"I don't know how to tell them that I'm leaving. I know I'm going to hurt them, but I'm too broken to stay. If I see them—I can't see that look in their eyes."

"What do you want to do?"

"I'll text them when this is all over."

Dylan nodded with a heavy sigh, his disapproval of Benjamin's plan etched on his face.

Ryan came into the room, dressed in a dark suit. "Ready?"

Benjamin looked down at his own clothes. Fresh tears pricked at his eyes. "Look at me. I am Cinderella dressed in rags. Only in my story there is no happily ever after."

Dylan pulled him into a fierce hug as he left. "Don't give up," he whispered before he let go.

Ryan followed Benjamin to the DGD offices. Benjamin planned on leaving as soon as the meeting was over. He didn't want to be in Seattle for a minute longer than he had to be. He didn't know where he would go as long as it was far away. Gina pulled into the parking lot right behind them. She was dressed in a sleek black pantsuit, her blond hair cut into a short hairstyle with a punk edge, shaved on the sides to reveal tiny diamond hoops lining her earlobes.

She came with her assistant, who she introduced to Benjamin. Staring intently at Benjamin, she asked, "Are you ready?"

He blew out a shaky breath. "I am." He wasn't, though. How could he ever be prepared to face Max again?

CHAPTER TWENTY-SEVEN

MAX JUMPED up from the boardroom table the minute Benjamin walked in. He looked at the two women and Ryan behind Benjamin but dismissed them in favor of approaching Benjamin, only to have him hold his hands up.

"Don't come near me, Max. Don't forget I'm a black belt, and I will fight you to the ground."

"How dare you threaten my son?" Kathrine Huntington stood from the table, pressing her hands against the smooth, polished surface and glaring at him.

One of the women with Benjamin stepped in front of him. "Those are the last words you'll be saying to my client. Any further communication will go through me." She turned to Benjamin and in a furious whisper said, "Sit down."

Rochelle was in her usual place at the head of the table. Monaco and Milan rushed to take seats on either side of her.

Monaco leaned close to her mother and in a loud whisper said. "Mommy, what is going on?"

Rochelle shushed her daughter.

Max took a seat at the other end of the table next to Bennett and his parents.

Benjamin took his seat at the middle of the conference table. The woman who'd admonished Benjamin sat next to him and the other woman next to her. The latter reached into her briefcase, pulled out a laptop, and began to type. Ryan sat on the other side of Benjamin, with a withering look of disappointment in Max's direction.

"I'm Gina Burke," the first woman said. "I'm representing Benjamin Colton in this matter."

"What matter?" Max asked, directing his question to Benjamin.

"You have acquired DGD with the understanding that that acquisition includes the patents for the original designs my client's father created. That is false." Gina nodded to her assistant, who jumped up and started passing out papers around the table. "As you can see, Benjamin

Colton is the rightful owner of all patents filed by his father." She turned to Rochelle with a malicious gleam in her eye. "It has come to my attention that DGD has been operating in noncompliance with Washington state employment laws. In addition, the designs that Monaco and Milan Tremaine have claimed are original were stolen from students at the school of design. The state has been notified of this noncompliance, and the students of the school have also been notified. I'm offering free legal representation to any student who would like to pursue compensation."

Max froze. For the first time, Benjamin's eyes met his, unwavering, his expression haunted, grim, and resolute. He leaned over and whispered something to Gina and then to Ryan. They both nodded, and he got up and left the table.

Max jumped up, calling out for him. Benjamin's step hitched, but then he squared his shoulders and continued walking away without looking back.

His mother grabbed his arm, looking at him in a panic. "What are we going to do about this?"

He looked down at her. "I'm not going to do anything. You ignored my warnings. You tried to manipulate my life. I'm done. You can take this as my official resignation from Huntington Outfitters."

His mother's face became mottled and red. "You can't do this to us… to me. I'm your mother. I know what's best."

"If you knew what was best for me, you never would've done this." Max looked at his dad, who was reading through the papers that had been passed out, his hands shaking, his face pale. He looked at Max with a grim expression. "I'm sorry, Dad," Max said.

His father, whose presence had always seemed so imposing, looked smaller, his shoulders slumped. "I'm sorry too, son."

Rochelle jumped up from her seat and stared at Gina, her head still held high but a look of absolute terror in her eyes. Kathrine was now shouting across the table that they were going to sue Rochelle for fraud. Monaco and Milan were yelling at each other, their voices growing higher pitched and more panicked with each passing moment.

"I told you it was a bad idea." Milan wailed.

"It's your fault you couldn't bring us a rich husband," Monaco screamed while mascara streaked down her cheeks.

Bennett got up and moved to stand next to Max, a silent question being asked in his raised eyebrow. Max nodded. There was no reason to stay. There was nothing for him here, not now that Benjamin was gone.

"Do you know where he went?" Max asked Ryan.

Ryan's jaw ticked. "If I did, I don't think that's information I would share with you. Look at what happened here. This doesn't impact Benjamin alone. Aspen and Gwen, Dylan and me, an entire community of Big Dipper hikers and campers that Benjamin has cared for and worked so hard for. Rochelle did most of the damage, but your family played their part. Honestly, Max, how could you have been so reckless?"

Every one of Ryan's words was a blow, only adding to the self-loathing that he felt. Between arguing with his parents, Bennett's outrage, and his own anger at himself, Max hadn't slept or eaten since last night. And now he'd lost the respect of someone he considered a friend, someone he admired.

"I know it's not enough. I know it doesn't even begin to make a difference, but I'm sorry. You're right. I assumed. I shouldn't have told my parents about Big Dipper Adventures." Max glanced over his shoulder where his parents were on their phones speaking in panicked tones. "They're my parents. I thought I could trust them. I was wrong."

"You were selfish," Ryan shot back. "You wanted to have it all. Benjamin and the business. Why did you hesitate last night?"

"I needed time to think."

"About what? You wanted to be able to have everything go your way without making any compromises or sacrifices. Like I said. Selfish."

"That's a bit harsh, don't you think, Ryan?" Bennett put a steadying hand on Max's shoulder.

"He's right," Max said. "You didn't hesitate when your family tried to get Dylan out of your life and take Leo away from you."

Ryan shook his head. "Not even once."

"We're done here," Gina snapped, breaking into their conversation.

Max and Bennett walked out with them, leaving Rochelle, her hysterical children, and his parents behind.

In the parking lot Gina handed him her card. "Mr. Huntington, I'm sure your lawyers will be in touch. I want you to know Benjamin's claim is rock solid. And I'm making it my personal mission to return Hyas House to its rightful owner."

"I'll make sure that happens."

Gina stared at him for a heartbeat before she nodded.

Ryan didn't shake his hand when he drove away. Max scanned the parking lot for Benjamin's Jeep, even though he knew it wasn't there.

"Do you think he went to Aspen's?"

"I don't know. They aren't speaking to me after last night."

Max noted the flash of pain in his friend's eyes. Bennett was another victim of his recklessness.

"I'm sorry." The words were starting to taste bitter in his mouth, but they were all he could think to say.

"Let's go over there and see," Bennett said with a resigned sigh.

ASPEN OPENED the door with their face a mask of fury. Their eyes were red and swollen from crying. They took one look at the two of them on the doorstep and started to slam the door in their faces.

"Aspen, please," Max said. "I know I fucked up. I know my apologies don't mean shit to you, but I am sorry. I'm trying to make things right."

"He's gone," Aspen said, their voice low and flat. "I don't know where he went."

This wasn't good. Benjamin leaving without telling Aspen where he was going showed the depths of how badly Benjamin was hurt.

Aspen's gaze flickered to Bennett, who stiffened at Max's side. They shook their head, another tear starting to form in the corner of Aspen's eye as they shut the door on them.

They went back to the *Faunus* in silence, each navigating their own grieving process. When they arrived back at the ship, Max stopped Bennett as soon as they set foot back on board.

"I'm going to get a hotel room. I can't stay here. I'll understand if you want to go your own way. I'm sorry, Bennett. I never meant to hurt you."

Bennett sighed, rubbing the back of his neck, his frustration simmering beneath the surface. "I'll make us a reservation," he said, his tone heavy with resignation. His gaze flicked to Max, a mixture of hurt and anger clouding his eyes. "You're my best friend, Max. I'm mad as hell at you. At the entire situation." His voice was gruff, betraying the deep disappointment he was trying to contain. "I'm withdrawing my resignation. I spoke out of anger and disappointment." He poked Max in the chest. "I'm trusting you to make it right. Don't let me down."

"I will." Max pulled Bennett into a hug, his chest tightening with a mix of gratitude and fear. He couldn't lose Bennett—not his friendship, not the solid, grounding presence he'd been through everything.

Max started packing the moment he reached his cabin, his hands trembling as he yanked clothes off hangers and shoved them haphazardly into his suitcase. His chest felt tight, each breath shallow and uneven, while a dull ache throbbed behind his eyes. Lack of food and sleep caught up with him. He swore softly under his breath as he fumbled with the zipper. Max exhaled with relief when they left the ship without encountering his parents. He didn't have the strength for another fight that day. Not when he had so many battles ahead of him.

Soon after, they arrived at the hotel, a tall glass-and-steel structure on the waterfront.

"You should try to get some sleep. You look dead on your feet," Bennett said the moment they stepped into their suite. "You're no good to anyone if you can't even keep your eyes open." When Max tried to protest, Bennett silenced him with a pointed look, his expression leaving no room for argument. The suite had two bedrooms, and Max stumbled into the closest one, exhaustion overtaking him the minute his head hit the pillow.

He woke up to the late afternoon sun streaming through the window and a view of the ferry leaving the dock, filled with tourists and commuters heading home after a day at work in the city. Rubbing his eyes, he left the bedroom but drew up short when he saw his dad talking quietly to Bennett at a small table by the wall of windows overlooking the sound.

"Dad? What are you doing here? How did you know we were here?"

Bennett got up and went into the small kitchenette, avoiding making eye contact with Max as he passed.

"Don't be upset with him. I reached out to Bennett."

Max sat in the chair Bennett had vacated. He folded his hands on the table. "What do you want?" he asked, his voice still raspy from exhaustion.

Bennett returned and set a cup of tea in front of Max. He took a sip of the hot sweet liquid with a grateful nod in his friend's direction.

Phillip leaned forward. He'd aged even more since that morning, looking more tired and worn than Max had ever seen him. "I'm leaving your mother."

His stomach sank. "You've been married for almost forty years."

His dad nodded. "We have, and a lot of those years were good ones. But something changed. It was so subtle it took me a long time to notice it. What happened yesterday and today…." He sighed. "I can't ignore that. I can't stop thinking about what you said yesterday about your heart not being an asset. I had no idea your mother bought Hyas House. I never imagined she'd try to manipulate you that way. I used to look at her drive and determination with admiration. But it's turned into something ugly. I asked her to apologize to you, and she refused." He clasped his hands on the table, the skin stretched taut over his knuckles. "I'm sorry."

Max looked at his father in shock. He knew there would be fallout when he left the company, but he never expected his parents' marriage would be part of the collateral damage. He exchanged a worried glance with Bennett.

"I'm not sure what to say."

"I'm not here to ask you to come back to Huntington Outfitters. Of course I'd like it if you came back, but after everything that's happened, I respect your decision. I want to help. What can I do?"

Max tapped the rim of his cup, thinking. "I need to figure out how to get Hyas House back to Benjamin."

His dad sat back with a calculating glint in his eye. "I can help with that."

Phillip booked a room on the same floor, and the three of them ordered room service. Max spent the evening with his dad, tearing apart their lives so they could build new ones. Max fell asleep that night with his heart full of hope that he could find Benjamin and show him that the new life he planned for himself wouldn't be complete without Benjamin in it.

Chapter Twenty-Eight

"I don't think this is a good idea, Max." Bennett hovered behind him on Aspen's doorstep.

"I have to try."

Aspen answered the doorbell with their grandmother standing behind them, both of them red-faced with anger.

"You have a lot of nerve—"

Bennett came forward, moving to stand in front of Max. "Aspen, please give him a chance to tell you why he's here."

With a grunt, they opened the door wide enough for them to come in.

They followed Aspen into the living room. "Go ahead and sit down," Aspen said, sitting on the sofa, their grandmother taking her place at their side.

"I don't suppose you'd tell me where Benjamin is?"

Aspen's face fell, their voice teary. "I wouldn't if I knew, but I don't. That's how much damage you've done, Max."

How much more fallout would there be from his actions? Guilt sat like lead in the pit of his stomach.

"I understand," he said quietly.

"Then you can go," Aspen said flatly. Their grandmother put a protective arm around her grandchild, glaring at Max and Bennett.

"There's something I'd like your help with."

Aspen's eyes flashed with anger, and they jumped up, that anger rolling off them in waves. "Do you think I'd help you with anything?"

Max held up his hands. "I didn't say that right. I've got something to do, and I thought you'd like to be there when I do it."

Aspen pressed their lips together. Lifting their chin, they glared at Max with defiance.

Max pulled an envelope from the inside pocket of his blazer. "This is the deed to Hyas House. As of this morning, my mother has signed it over to me. I'm going there now to evict Rochelle and her children. I thought you might like to be there when I do."

Some of the anger dissipated from Aspen, replaced by a malicious gleam in their eye. "Keep talking."

"When I find Benjamin, I'll sign the house over to him."

MAX ARRIVED at Hyas House with Aspen, Gwen, and Bennett alongside him.

Max hadn't known what to expect when he saw Benjamin's house for the first time, but the moment it came into view, he understood why he cared about it so much. One look and he'd fallen in love.

The house had a simple, understated elegance. Its low profile hugged the landscape, with wide front doors framed by slim slats of dark wood that gave it a mid-century modern charm. From a distance, it exuded timeless sophistication, like something plucked from the pages of an architectural magazine.

But as they drew closer, the cracks in its façade became impossible to ignore. The rich wood of the front door was warped, curling at the edges as if weary from years of weathering. The paint on the exterior walls, once smooth and vibrant, was now peeling and cracked, exposing faded layers beneath. It was more than a house; it was a relic, beautiful even in its neglect, carrying the weight of stories that begged to be revived.

"He tried his best to take care of it while Rochelle nickel-and-dimed him," Aspen said.

Max didn't bother to knock—why should he? It was his home now, and he had no intention of asking permission to step inside.

Even though it was his first time in the house, the moment he crossed the threshold, he knew everything about it was wrong. The dark colors, the gleaming brass accents, the heavy velvet drapes—they all felt suffocating, a far cry from the warmth and character the house deserved. It wasn't a reflection of what Benjamin's mother created or what the space could be. It was someone else's vision, layered over what should have been a safe and loving home for Benjamin. He didn't think he could be more disgusted by Rochelle and her children. He was wrong. What he saw made him shake with restrained fury.

Beneath the horrific decorating, the house was stunning. Benjamin's mother designed the house to take advantage of the view. Since Benjamin told Max about the architect who helped his mom with the design, he'd done more research on Benjamin McAdoo, whose influence on the design could be seen everywhere. From the built-in floating shelves on either side of a fireplace, the combination spanning an entire wall of the living room, to the vaulted ceilings and open floorplan that honored the Cedar Plank houses that inspired it, Hyas House was a masterpiece. Or at least it had been, and it would be again.

Monaco came clattering down the stairs. Her hair hung in loose curls with straight ends that stuck out at different angles like straw. She was wearing a pair of DGD leggings and a jogging bra in a garish combination of lime green and bright orange.

She saw Max and froze, her eyes growing wide as she stared at him for a second before turning on her heel and running back upstairs.

"Mom, he's here," she screeched, with an inflection that made Max flinch.

"Who's here?" Rochelle peered over the railing of a balcony fronting a long hallway with multiple doors Max assumed led to bedrooms. When she saw Max, she started to smile, until she noticed Aspen and their grandmother with him. She marched down the massive staircase that was designed to make the stair treads appear as if they were floating in thin air.

"How dare you enter my home without permission."

Aspen scoffed under their breath, "Bitch, please."

"This isn't your home," Max said.

He noted with satisfaction how the confident mask Rochelle wore so well slipped. "Excuse me. Your mother—"

"My mother," Max cut her off, "has given Hyas House to me."

"We had an agreement. She can't," Rochelle sputtered.

"She can and she has. Did you honestly think any of the agreements you made with my mother are still valid?"

There was a knock on the door, and a man poked his head in, announcing, "Locksmith."

"Go ahead and get started," Max called out over his shoulder.

"I'll sue you." Rochelle seethed.

"For what?"

Monaco and Milan clattered down the stairs to flank their mother. Max sneered at Milan's attempt at an enticing smile.

Max made a show of looking at his watch before addressing Rochelle. "The movers will be here in twenty minutes." The doorbell rang. "Ah." Max smiled. "They're here early."

"Mommy, make him stop," Monaco whined.

Rochelle's mouth dropped open, her eyes darting around the room wildly. Max guessed she was trying to figure out how much she could take within the time he'd given her. He caught the moment when she decided to try bluster and intimidation one more time.

Rochelle lifted her chin, and her eyes flashed with hatred that Max thought must have been the same censure Benjamin endured every day. "How dare you treat a widow and her children this way. I—"

"I'm treating you with the same courtesy you've shown your stepson all these years."

Rochelle glared at him, her nostrils flaring.

"I'll call the sheriff if I have to," Max said, his gaze unflinching.

Max clenched his fists at his side, silently daring Rochelle to challenge him. She'd learn the hard way he wasn't bluffing.

Seconds ticked by before Rochelle turned on her heel and marched upstairs.

"But Mommy—"

"Shut the fuck up and get your suitcases," she barked at Monaco.

It shouldn't be enjoyable to throw someone out of their home. But in this case, it was the best Max had felt since Benjamin left. He listened to Monaco and Milan's frantic screeching, their footsteps as they ran from room to room, doors slamming. After a few moments, he went over to Aspen. "Can you show me where he lived?"

Aspen nodded.

"Gwen, Bennett, do you mind keeping an eye on things for a moment? You can tell the movers everything goes."

"Happy to," Gwen said.

Max followed Aspen to the garage and through the narrow doorway at the back. Max thought he was prepared to see where Benjamin lived. The reality of his situation took his breath away.

"How old was he when he moved in here?"

"Thirteen," Aspen said. "Rochelle told him he was old enough to stay out here on his own since he was a bar mitzvah, and that meant he was a man." Aspen wrapped their arms around themself. "He never got to have a bar mitzvah, though. Rochelle cancelled it after Benjamin's dad died."

Max seethed. He'd never wanted harm to come to anyone before the way he wished it on Rochelle. "I'll destroy her."

"I'd be happy to help with that."

Max didn't realize he'd voiced his anger out loud. "I'd appreciate it."

It took only a few steps to cross the small, cramped room. Max paused by the narrow window, the sole source of natural light, and imagined Benjamin as a little boy, sitting here alone. The thought tightened something in his chest, the weight of it almost unbearable.

When he reached the twin bed tucked into the corner, something inside him shattered. The sight of it, a bed too small, too plain, too lonely, brought a flood of emotions he couldn't contain. He sank onto the mattress, the springs groaning softly beneath his weight, and dropped his head into his hands.

The sobs came hard and fast, wrenching their way out of him. Max cried for the boy who had been treated with so much indifference and contempt, who had been given so little. He cried for the unfairness of it all, for a childhood stolen and replaced with loneliness. And he cried because for the first time, he understood what it meant to lose everything you've ever loved.

So caught up in his anguish, he didn't notice when Aspen quietly slipped out, leaving him alone in Benjamin's room.

His tears slowed, and Max wiped his eyes with the back of his hand, his chest aching from the effort. The room was too quiet, the silence pressing in like the walls themselves. He drew in a shaky breath, but the weight of the emotion that crashed over him lingered, heavy and raw. Before he left Benjamin's room, Max pulled out his phone and sent him a text. He hadn't responded to any of the ones he'd sent so far, but Benjamin hadn't blocked his number, so Max kept sending them.

Rochelle and her children were running back and forth from the house, throwing clothing haphazardly into their cars.

Max checked his watch. "Time's up," he snapped. "Get the fuck out."

"What about the rest of—" Milan pointed to the house.

"Get. Out," Max said between clenched teeth.

He walked back in the door. Milan chased after him, and Max slammed the door in his face.

"Do you want us to keep packing up?" one of the movers asked.

Max pinched the bridge of his nose. "Yes. I don't want any of their things here."

Bennett, always in tune with his moods, said, "I'll take care of it."

"What happens now?" Gwen asked.

Max paced slowly around the room, taking in every detail. The dark colors on the walls and the heavy drapes. "I don't want Benjamin to come back to the house like this," he said, his voice quiet but resolute. He hesitated before glancing at Gwen. "Would it be too much if I brought in painters?"

Gwen's expression softened, her eyes warming with understanding. "No," she said, shaking her head. "I don't think it would be too much at all."

MAX LEANED on Gwen and Aspen for advice, carefully considering which repairs would have the greatest impact while still leaving the house ready for Benjamin to shape with his own vision. Instead of hiring painters, he decided to take on the work himself, buying supplies and dedicating long days to priming and painting.

With every dark, ugly wall he covered with a fresh coat of paint, his sense of purpose grew, the physical labor becoming an unexpected form of therapy. The rhythm of the work steadied him, giving him an outlet for his grief and a way to channel his love for Benjamin into something tangible. Each wall he restored felt like a small act of healing, a quiet promise of a fresh start.

Chapter Twenty-Nine

Waves crashed onto the rocky sand. Benjamin welcomed the chill of the water washing over his feet while he watched surfers bobbing in the water, waiting to find the perfect wave. He'd been in the small Canadian coastal community of Tofino for two weeks. He thought he'd find comfort in the sound of the ocean, spending his days walking the beach. But he stared at the endless stretch of the Pacific Ocean still numb and unsure what to do.

He'd texted Aspen and let them know he was safe but didn't share where he was. Aspen and his lawyer were the only people he'd been in contact with until that morning. Max's messages went unread and unanswered.

Turning away from the ocean, Benjamin got back in his Jeep, checked his watch, and grimaced. He'd have to make good time if he wanted to catch the next ferry back to the mainland. He'd be back in the US.

On the ferry he leaned on the railing, lifting his face to the sun. The warm air ruffled his curls, and he ran his hand through them, a memory of Max doing the same thing bringing a lump to his throat.

"Excuse me?" A young Black girl who looked like she was in middle school approached him. "Are you Benjamin Colton?"

He straightened from the railing. "I am."

She grinned at him with a mouthful of braces. She looked over her shoulder and called out. "Mom, Dad, Jaden, come here." She turned back to Benjamin. "You don't remember me, do you?"

"I'm sorry, I don't."

"That's okay, I was little then."

A slightly older teenager, a man, and a woman joined the young woman. "Well, I'll be," the man said.

Benjamin recognized the older version of a couple he'd met on the trail many years ago. "Mr. and Mrs. Jackson?" He looked at the kids again. "And you're Jaden and Ayesha, all grown up."

Wes Jackson shook his hand with a broad smile. "Oh my goodness, it is so good to see you."

His wife, Donna, pulled Benjamin into a hug. "Oh, honey, you don't know how many times we have thought of you over the years."

The Jacksons ushered him over to one of the benches lining the deck, all talking at once, sharing tidbits of their lives and how that first encounter on the trail when Benjamin stepped in to stop them from being bullied turned into a love of nature that had Jaden studying forest management at the University of Oregon.

"I tried to find you after that day. But you disappeared, and then I started seeing the posts for Big Dipper Adventures, and I knew it was you."

"We've been following what you've been doing, honey, and we are so proud of you," Donna added, looking at Benjamin with motherly approval.

"Thank you," Benjamin said, his voice with thick with emotion.

Wes's expression grew serious. "I read about the Huntingtons buying DGD. How do you feel about having your father's company sold?"

Benjamin started to explain how the company had changed over the years and wasn't anything he had a connection with anymore. Maybe it was their comforting presence, or maybe it was because he was too tired to carry the burden alone anymore, but Benjamin kept talking, telling the Jacksons about his father's patents, his fears and doubts about the future.

Wes looked at him thoughtfully for a few moments, then reached into his back pocket and pulled out his wallet. He retrieved a business card and handed it to Benjamin.

"All those years ago when you came across us on the trail, I was where you are now. Maybe not in such a big way, but as that man stood there yelling at us, telling us we didn't belong, I was paralyzed by fear. If I confronted him, would the situation escalate? Could I defend my family and protect my family at the same time? Then you appeared and got in that man's face, completely fearless. You didn't stop there. You took us under your wing, giving us guidance and more. After meeting you we gained the confidence to keep going, keep climbing. That day has led to so many wonderful days of us being out in nature, finding peace and hopefulness, spending time with family. You gave us a gift that is priceless."

Benjamin swallowed past the lump in his throat. Biting his lip, he fought back tears at Wes's compliment.

"I'd like to repay the favor. I don't know anything about patents, but I do know about money management. I want to help you restart production on the equipment that your dad designed, adaptive equipment for people with disabilities to help them get out in nature. It's something we desperately need right now. There are too many people who are trying to take this country back to a time when minorities and people with disabilities were separated and not given access to the same opportunities." He put his hand on Benjamin's shoulder and looked him in the eye. "This is important, and I want to support you."

Benjamin looked down at the card in his hand.

Westley Jackson

President, North Star Advisory Group

"I-I don't know what to say."

"You don't have to say anything right now. The number on the card is my direct line. Why don't you give me a call next week, and we can talk more."

Their reunion came to an end when the announcement over the loudspeakers informed them that they were approaching the dock and it was time for everyone to return to their cars. Benjamin said goodbye to the Jacksons with hugs and handshakes and a promise that he would come to dinner once things had settled down.

Benjamin drove off the ferry, his mind a jumble of possibilities. He realized his trip to Tofino hadn't given him the peace he was looking for because he had run away from his problems instead of facing them. He drove back to Seattle. When he arrived, he couldn't resist the temptation to make a detour around Lake Union. He pulled up to the empty berth where the *Faunus* had been docked. For a moment he wondered if the whole thing had been a nightmare. But a fresh batch of messages from his lawyer and the business card in his back pocket made it all too real.

His next stop was Aspen and Gwen's place. Aspen came running out of the house to tackle Benjamin on the walkway before he even made it to the front door.

"You're back," they sobbed. "I'm so glad you're back. I know all about nursing broken hearts and all that stuff, but please don't ever run away again."

Benjamin returned Aspen's hug. "I'm sorry. I needed some time. I had to get away from everything and try to sort through the mess I made of my life and figure out what I'm going to do next."

Aspen punched him in the shoulder. "You did not make a mess of your life."

The front door opened. "Children, come inside. You can work all of this out over coffee and chocolate babka."

"Yes, Bubbie," they both said in unison.

Aspen put their arm around Benjamin's waist and held on to him tightly while they walked up to the front door, refusing to let go even as they squeezed through the door frame together.

Some of the grief he'd been feeling lessened as he sat in the warm comfort of Aspen and Gwen's kitchen.

"You're staying here until you figure things out," Gwen declared with a stern look that said she was not going to put up with any arguments. She handed Benjamin a cup of coffee and placed a plate of babka on the table. "It's a good thing I was already making brisket. You look awful. We have brisket sliders for dinner tonight."

"Thank you, Bubbie,"

Benjamin took a sip of coffee. His eyes growing wide, he wheezed and started coughing. Aspen turned to Gwen. "How much whiskey did you put in that, Bubbie?"

"As much as I needed to. Don't ask questions," she said. Then she opened her laptop and started to type furiously.

Benjamin looked at Aspen with a raised eyebrow.

"She's been on an absolute tear since the party," he explained.

"How does this one sound?" Bubbie asked. "DGD Designs bills itself as a high-end activewear company, but under the management of Rochelle Termaine, it's more like an expensive experiment in how not to run a business. Rochelle, who refers to herself as the 'Visionary of Athleisure,' seems to spend more time trying to fit in those ridiculous 'bad boss bitch' lady suits than actually running a company. If you like overpriced chaos wrapped in spandex, DGD Designs is the train wreck you've been waiting for. Good luck receiving any orders you've made. If I were you, I'd hold on to your floating debris better than Jack did in *Titanic*, because ever since the *Faunus* sailed away, this company looks like it's a sinking ship."

This time Benjamin's coffee went straight up his nose. "Oh my God!" His watery eyes went to Aspen, who was watching him with their hand clapped over their mouth, shoulders shaking with laughter.

"I warned you she's been on a tear," Aspen said between giggles.

Gwen leaned over and patted Benjamin's arm. "Don't you worry, honey. BirchBitch206 has got this covered."

"Bubbie," Benjamin wheezed, "I'm saying this because I love you. You are gonna have a shitload of stuff to atone for at Yom Kippur this year."

Gwen continued typing as she spoke. "Honey, I'm already atoning for making out with that hunk on the last Big Dipper Adventures senior hike. This is a drop in the bucket."

"Bubbie!" Aspen and Benjamin exclaimed in unison.

Gwen's head popped up from her laptop, and she shrugged with a twinkle in her eye. "Honey, when you come across a silver fox in the wild, you'd better trap it."

Aspen put their head in their hands with a groan.

With a belly full of chocolate babka and coffee doctored with whiskey, Benjamin's eyes began to grow heavy. Aspen insisted that he take a nap, and they would talk more when he got up. Benjamin gratefully climbed into the bed in the guest room, a room he realized was *his* room—the walls painted a warm white, the bedding in shades of forest green, little knickknacks spread around the room that were all things special to him. He slept better than he had in the last two weeks, knowing he was in a loving home.

Benjamin woke up to the rich aroma of Bubbie's brisket and fresh rolls. His stomach grumbled in anticipation. His clothes were freshly washed and folded on top of the dresser. After a shower and a shave, he felt a little more civilized. He gathered his laptop and a notebook and went back to the kitchen.

Aspen was ensconced in their favorite place, the corner of the banquette seat, leaning against a collection of colorful pillows.

The minute Benjamin sat, Aspen scooted toward him, clearly still needing to reassure themself that Benjamin wasn't going to leave again as they pressed themself against Benjamin's side and leaned their head on his shoulder.

"Feel better?" Aspen asked.

"I do. And Aspen, I'm sorry. I shouldn't have cut you off the way I did. I was so angry and hurt, and I didn't know what to do."

"I understand. You hurt me, though, and I'm angry with you for that."

"That's fair."

"You two have a bond that's unbreakable," Gwen said, leaning against the door frame, watching them with a wistful look in her eyes. "You'll always find a way back to each other."

Benjamin and Aspen shared a smile as Gwen joined them at the table.

"What's next?" she asked.

"I'm going to grow Big Dipper Adventures. Now that I don't have to worry about Rochelle or—" He took a shaky breath. "—Hyas House, I can do whatever I want." He showed them Wes Jackson's business card. "I'm going to take him up on his offer. I want to have a branch of Big Dipper Adventures that sells adaptive outdoor gear. Not only the equipment my dad designed, but clothing, tents, and other gear."

"I've been wanting you to do something like that," Aspen said.

"It's going to take a while, even with the money I've been saving and you've been investing," he said with a nod to Aspen. "I'll have limited funds to work with."

"We'll invest," Gwen said.

Benjamin turned to Aspen. "I was hoping you'd consider coming on board as a partner."

"CFO and head of tech infrastructure?"

Benjamin held his hand out. "Deal."

That night, after they mapped out a business plan and a new social media strategy, Aspen climbed into bed with Benjamin. The same way they'd done since they were kids, they propped themselves against the headboard, holding hands.

Finally Benjamin asked the question that had been haunting him since he returned.

"Have you heard from Max or Bennett?"

Aspen lifted their head from his shoulder. "Do you want me to tell you the truth or lie?"

"Lie."

Aspen let their head fall back. "No."

Chapter Thirty

It wasn't hard to find the person he was looking for when Benjamin walked into the little coffee shop. Phillip Huntington stood up and held his hand out when Benjamin approached, eyeing him warily.

"Thank you for coming." He shook Benjamin's hand.

"I'm still not sure why I did," Benjamin admitted.

Receiving a text from Max's father came as a shock. Benjamin debated Phillip's request for a meeting for a day before he decided to meet with him and hear him out.

"Understandable," Phillip said.

Benjamin declined his offer to buy him a coffee. Folding his hands on the table, he met Max's father's gaze. "The *Faunus* is gone. I didn't expect you to still be in Seattle."

"My plans have changed. I'll be staying here for the foreseeable future."

Benjamin wrinkled his forehead. "Why? Huntington Outfitters is based in New York."

Phillip gave him a mysterious smile. "I can tell you about that later. I asked you to meet me so I could apologize. I'm sorry, Benjamin. I took you for granted. I didn't bother to learn anything about you."

"Okay," Benjamin said slowly, trying to figure out where the conversation was going.

"I've been doing some research. And finally paying attention to the reports Max wrote about Big Dipper Adventures."

Benjamin tensed. "It's not for sale."

"I didn't ask you here to try to buy your company."

"No, you'll take my idea with or without my consent, right?"

Phillip's mouth turned down. "What makes you think we would do that?"

Benjamin repeated what Rochelle told him the night of the party.

"I wasn't aware of that. You don't have to worry. It's not going to happen. After our meeting when you dropped that bombshell—" Phillip sighed. "—DGD is shut down. Your stepmother's and her children's contracts were cancelled. New lawsuits are being filed against them daily. Rochelle has already filed for bankruptcy. An IRS investigation has also been opened against her."

"I can't say I'm sorry to hear it, but that doesn't mean Huntington Outfitters isn't going to start their own version of Big Dipper Adventures."

"I can assure you that's not going to happen either. Huntington Outfitters is being sold."

Benjamin sucked in his breath. "What are you talking about?"

"Kathrine and I are getting a divorce. As a family we've decided the best path forward is to sell the company."

"Huntington Outfitters is your family legacy. What about Max? All he's ever wanted is to run the company."

"It was my grandfather's and my father's, not mine," he said with a sad smile. "I realized Max and I have been doing a lot of talking and spending more time together than we have in a long time. Dreams change, Benjamin. Max has a new challenge now, something that he's passionate about."

Benjamin shook his head, trying to digest what Phillip told him.

"Benjamin, I hope you and I will get to know each other better too. I'd like to learn more about you. I already can see why my son fell head over heels in love with you."

Benjamin's eyes flew to Phillip's face. Phillip nodded at him with a knowing smile.

"I-I'm not ready yet. Max broke my heart, and I don't know how I'm supposed to move forward from that and trust him again."

"Would it help to know that he quit Huntington after you walked out of the boardroom that day?"

"He did?" Benjamin asked in a shaky voice.

"He did. I've never seen my son so determined and focused as he's been since that day. I've always been proud of my son, but I'm...." He shook his head, with a sparkle in his eyes that reminded Benjamin of how his dad looked at him when he could name all the stars that summer. Love and pride. "I've never been so proud of him as I am now."

"What happens now?"

Phillip's smile returned. "Some of that depends on you." He reached into the messenger bag hanging from his chair and took out an envelope. He placed it in the middle of the table, tapping his finger on the top "This is for you. It's not a bribe. What you decide to do when you know what's inside is up to you. Max will respect your decision, and so will I."

Phillip stood up and held his hand out to Benjamin. "Like I said, I'd like for us to get to know each other better. Maybe we can meet for coffee again sometime."

Benjamin took his hand. He sat for a long time after Phillip left, staring at the envelope. Eventually he picked it up and left the coffee shop.

THE TRACK was empty. Did he want Max to be there?

Benjamin parked and got out of his Jeep, his phone gripped tightly in his hand. He started walking. Every once in a while, he'd start to dial, his thumb hovering over Max's name, and then let his hand drop again, his conversation with Phillip replaying in his head along with flashes of memory of his time with Max. He stopped walking and sat down on the bleachers. His knee bounced with a mixture of fear and anticipation. He exhaled, his breath shaky, and opened his phone, pulling up the texts from Max that he had let go unread.

The first few were apologies. He winced scrolling through them. They were too painful to read. But then he saw the next text, and it shattered him.

Has anyone hugged you today?

And the next.

Has anyone hugged you today?

Has anyone hugged you today?

Has anyone hugged you today?

Every night since he'd left, Max had texted the same question.

A sob broke free. Then another, and another.

All of the fear and anger he'd held in came pouring out of him. He cursed his stepmother, Max, even his parents for leaving him so alone and abandoned. He knew it wasn't their fault. They didn't leave by choice, but the hurt was still there.

Finally he dragged his exhausted body and mind back to the Jeep and sat for a long time before he even had the strength to start the engine.

CHAPTER THIRTY-ONE

THE ENVELOPE sat in the middle of the kitchen table. When Benjamin returned, he had put it there without a word. And now Benjamin, Aspen, and Gwen formed a semicircle, staring at it as if it were a coiled snake ready to strike.

Gwen glanced at Benjamin with a raised eyebrow. "Well?"

Benjamin chewed his lip, staring at the envelope. "I'm scared to open it, and I'm scared not to."

"Do you want me to poke it with a stick and make sure it's safe?" Gwen said.

"Not helping, Bubbie," Aspen said with a frown and a slight shake of their head. They turned to Benjamin. "Before you open it, let me ask you something. Are you afraid because opening that envelope might mean opening your heart again?"

Benjamin answered with a jerky nod.

Aspen clasped his hand and gave it a comforting squeeze. "I know it's scary, and I know too many people in your life haven't given you a reason to trust. I don't think you'll be able to move forward if you don't see what's inside."

"You're right. I know you're right." Benjamin reached for the envelope. His heart pounding, his hand shaking, he slid his thumb under the flap, broke the seal, and pulled the folded sheets of paper out. When he did that, a key dropped to the floor. That was enough—he didn't have to unfold the papers to know what he held in his hands. But he did, and there it was, the deed to Hyas House.

"Oh, honey." Gwen put a hand to her cheek, reading the deed with tears in her eyes. "That's what I wanted it to be, but I can't believe it."

Gwen's words gave voice to the unspoken ache Benjamin carried in his chest. When Phillip handed him the envelope, a small, trembling whisper had stirred in his heart, daring him to hope. But hope was fragile, especially when dreams had been shattered so thoroughly that they'd crumbled into dust. Like the birth of a star, it would take time. Time for the scattered fragments of hope to gather and for something new, something luminous, to take its place.

Aspen reached down and picked up the key. "Benjamin," they said softly, holding it out to him, pointing to where a tiny Big Dipper had been engraved at the top of the key, along with the words Follow the Stars Home.

Aspen's and Gwen's arms went around him as he went to his knees, sobbing. Phillip was right. The rest was up to him. Did he dare to hope?

It was early in the evening by the time Benjamin had collected himself and made the drive back home. For so many years, coming home had filled him with sadness and longing. Now he had too many feelings to process. The key slipped into the lock, and he opened the door. The smell of fresh paint greeted him. The walls that Rochelle had painted shades of gray and black were restored to a fresh, crisp white. The furniture—chrome, oversized, upholstered in leather and velvet— was gone. The floors underneath his feet had been refinished to their original, natural golden-brown hue. Benjamin's entire body shook as he wandered through the main rooms. There was still work to do, but enough restoration work had been done that the house felt like the home he loved. Along the way, echoes of laughter and his parents loving voices returned in his memory. When he moved to the expanse of windows overlooking the lake, he saw a lone figure standing on the dock.

Benjamin watched him for a few heartbeats, standing quiet and still, his longing growing stronger until it guided him downstairs. The yard had been pruned, the grass cut. He toed off his shoes so that he could feel the earth under his feet, hoping that would keep him tethered and grounded for what was to come.

Max turned when he approached. His hazel eyes were shadowed, and a few days' worth of stubble covered his face. A pair of worn jeans dotted with paint splatter sat low on his hips, and his T-shirt was rumpled, more paint on one sleeve.

"I wasn't waiting for you, I swear. I like to come here in the evenings. It's a beautiful view," he said, looking into Benjamin's eyes, his voice breaking.

Benjamin didn't stop moving. He walked straight to Max and wrapped his arms around him.

"Benjamin," Max breathed, burying his face in his neck. "I'm so sorry. I promise if you give me another chance, I will always choose you first without hesitation or question. You're my North Star, and I'm lost without you." He drew back so he could look into Benjamin's eyes. "Has anyone hugged you today?" he asked, his voice trembling.

Benjamin took Max's face in his hands, eyes searching his. "I'm scared. Scared of letting you back into my heart and terrified of what will happen if I don't." He held Max's gaze for a heartbeat, and then his lips were on Max's, soft and hesitant. He tasted the saltiness on his lips, unsure if it was from Max's tears or his own.

"I didn't give you the house to try to get you back," Max said when they broke apart. "The house is yours. So much of my life is a mess right now, but the one thing I am certain of is Hyas House belongs to you. I couldn't live with myself if I didn't get it back to you."

"Thank you," Benjamin said, smiling over his shoulder at his home.

"I thought I knew, Benjamin. I was so arrogant thinking I understood what this house meant to you. I didn't know what it meant to lose something that was a part of your soul until you left. I hope you don't mind the work I had done. I didn't want you to come home with any trace of your stepmother in the house. There's a new roof, and the electrical and the plumbing have been done." He shifted his feet. "And the dock is new, but the rest is for you to put back the way it was."

"Some things can't be put back the way they were." He kept his hand on Max's cheek when his face fell. "It's good to keep some of the old, but maybe it's time to also embrace something new."

He smiled when he saw the spark of hope return to Max's eyes. Some of the tension he'd been carrying melted away. Benjamin leaned forward, resting his forehead gently against Max's.

"I love you, Max. It's frightening how much I love you. I thought I could restore Hyas House on my own, and now I can't imagine being here without you. I know you have a life in New York, but—"

Max stopped him with a kiss that laid claim to his mouth and reassured him Max wasn't going anywhere.

"I'm not going back to New York. My dad and I are going to stay in Seattle. He's been working with a real estate agent to find a place here."

"And what about you? Have you been looking for a place to live?" Benjamin asked, stroking the short golden hairs covering Max's cheek.

His eyes flickered toward the house, giving Benjamin the answer he hoped for.

Max licked his lips. "Not yet."

"Wrong answer," Benjamin said with a smile. "Stay with me?"

Max nodded, a tear clinging to the corner of his eye. "I have a present for you."

He held Benjamin's hand, weaving their fingers together as he led him back into the house. Benjamin followed Max upstairs. He drew up short in the doorway of the room that had belonged to his parents. A small lamp on the floor cast a warm glow in the room. A mattress covered in soft sage-green bedding was set against one wall.

"You'd want to pick out your own furniture, but I wanted you to be able to spend the night here." Max went over to the windowsill and returned with a small package wrapped in brown paper and tied with a blue string. "It's a housewarming present." Benjamin took the gift from his outstretched hand. "I bought it on impulse. If you don't like it, it's okay," Max babbled anxiously.

Benjamin opened the box, and his heart filled to the point he thought it was going to burst.

"I made sure the scroll is kosher."

"Max, stop," Benjamin said, lifting the mezuzah out of the box. "It's perfect."

Max exhaled. "Really? Are you sure?"

Benjamin ran his fingers over the tiny silver stars inlaid in a piece of wood stained midnight blue. "It's perfect," he repeated, pulling Max into another hug.

Their lips connected again, their kisses a mixture of comfort, longing, and need.

"Stay with me," Benjamin whispered against Max's lips. Not a question this time.

Max nipped at his bottom lip. "Always."

This time their lips met with urgency. Their hands fumbled as they tugged and pulled at each other's clothes. Benjamin let out a low moan when Max gently pushed him down on the mattress and he could feel the weight of Max's body on his. He wrapped his legs around Max and rutted against him. "I missed you so much," Max whispered as they reunited with soft words and lingering touches.

Lying with his head against Max's chest, Benjamin listened to his heart beating in sync with his. "This is the first time we've made love in a bed," he murmured.

Max ran his fingers through Benjamin's curls and traced the stars behind his ear. "I wouldn't mind making it a habit. But I still want to go camping with you."

Benjamin put his arm around Max's waist, gently nudging him until they were on their sides, face-to-face. "Are you sure you won't want to live in New York?"

"Positive. This is home. There isn't any place else in the world I can call home if you're not there. This is where your heart is, and now mine too."

"I know what I want to do now with Big Dipper Adventures."

"I'm listening."

Benjamin shared with Max the ideas that had been bouncing in his head since reuniting with Wes and his family.

There would still be challenges and hard work ahead. Both on the business and on themselves. Benjamin confessed that he wanted to start seeing a therapist, and Max supported his decision, telling him that he and his father were going to do family counseling as well.

The conversation about their lives and business turned to his vision for the house and then turned back to long kisses and loving touches once more.

Epilogue

Max came up behind Benjamin and wrapped his arms around his waist. He pressed a kiss on the tattoo behind Benjamin's ear. "Everything's almost ready?" he asked.

"It will be if you let go of me long enough for me to get the challah out of the oven before it burns."

Max gave him another quick kiss on the cheek and squeezed his waist before he left the kitchen. It seemed they were always touching, finding each other, gravitating toward each other. Benjamin knew part of it came from Max's lingering insecurities, wanting to prove to Benjamin that he would always be there for him. Benjamin pulled the challah out of the oven and set the perfectly braided golden loaf on its platter. He paused for a moment when he entered the dining room, taking in the friends and family gathered for Shabbat dinner. More than repairs, paint, and new furniture, it was the Friday nights spent with friends and family that made Hyas House home again.

Phillip stood from his chair and cleared a spot for the challah plate next to the candlesticks. "You've outdone yourself, son," he said, giving Benjamin an affectionate pat on the back.

Phillip had decided to make his home in Seattle, buying a small houseboat on Lake Union. He thrived in retirement, had joined a nature conservancy club, and sat on the board of Big Dipper Adventures. He bought a kayak of his own that was often found tied up at Benjamin and Max's home, where he was a welcome visitor. A father figure that Max and Benjamin had both come to treasure.

Summer faded into fall, and it took all winter for them to get their lives sorted. Instead of Huntington Outfitters being sold, the board asked Max to return as president and CEO. He kept his apartment in New York for occasional business trips but worked mostly from an office he'd established in Seattle. Now he focused on making Huntington Outfitters a more inclusive and sustainable company. It had been a bitter fight with his mother, who was determined to stay in control. But with the board's unanimous vote to remove her, Kathrine's fight was over. She refused to engage with Max or Phillip. Kathrine Huntington remained distant and resolute that she'd only had her son's best interests at heart and hadn't done anything wrong. She retreated to their family estate in Connecticut that Phillip happily gave her in their divorce settlement.

Aspen, Noah, and Gideon joined Benjamin as he struck a match and lit the first candle.

"Baruch ata Adonai Eloheinu, Melekh ha'olam, asher kid'shanu b'mitzvotav v'tzivanu l'hadlik ner shel Shabbat."

"Y'all are getting good enough you could start a boy band like the Maccabees." Gwen laughed.

Benjamin picked up the wineglass next, and they sang the next blessing. He put his hands on top of the challah for the final blessing. He pulled off a piece and held it to Max, who wrapped his hand around Benjamin's wrist as he took a bite, looking deep into his eyes. They would have a lifetime of Shabbat in this house, and Benjamin would never get tired of this small moment that meant so much.

They sat down for dinner, and conversation and laughter swirled around them, but when Benjamin caught sight of Aspen, sitting between Charlie and Able, who were trying to coax them into conversation, his heart dropped. There was one person missing from their Friday night dinners. Bennett had returned to England. No one quite knew what had happened between them. Benjamin was tight-lipped, and Bennett was silent. Max shared his concerns with Benjamin. They knew Bennett's return had something to do with trying to save his family's estate, Goulding Hall, which had been terribly mismanaged by his older brother, Mark. Max's emails and messages received only terse responses.

Gwen leaned close and whispered to Benjamin, "How much longer are we gonna let Aspen mope around like this?"

"I'll try to talk to them again."

The front door opened, and Ryan, Dylan, and the kids bustled in. "Sorry we're late," Dylan said, bouncing his daughter in his arms. "I swear we try, but with two it gets out of hand so quickly."

"What're y'all gonna do when there's three?" Noah said with a mischievous smile.

"We're going to call their honorary guncles to babysit," Ryan said.

"Now look what you've done." Gideon glowered at Noah, but his attempt at being stern was ruined by the way he put his arm around Noah's neck and pulled him in for a kiss while he admonished him.

Laughter filled the room from everyone except Max. His attention was on Ryan—who was sitting with his daughter in his lap, bouncing her on his knee—with an unreadable expression.

Ryan and his family took their seats at the table. Benjamin and Max had ordered from a local woodworker a table big enough to hold all of their family and friends. There would always be a seat for everyone.

"Congratulations on the award," Ryan said. "We've got green across the board!"

Phillip spoke up with pride. "Benjamin deserves it. The adaptive equipment he's providing has changed so many lives."

Benjamin ducked his head. It was still hard for him to get used to the accolades and being the public face of Big Dipper Adventures. With guidance from Wes and Phillip, and Max's unwavering support, Big Dipper Adventures had grown over the past year beyond Benjamin's wildest dreams. The company was recently honored with an industry award for the innovative designs his dad created that were now being manufactured and distributed nationwide. The campground accreditation program grew from the three campgrounds in their pilot program to over a hundred certified campgrounds. Max was also getting much-deserved recognition with a recent article about the changes he'd made at Huntington Outfitters. Staff meetings in boardrooms had been replaced with nature hikes and company camping trips. A stipend for camping equipment and national park passes were now perks that every employee enjoyed. The newest Huntington Outfitters catalog sat on the coffee table in the living room. This time the photograph on the cover wasn't staged. It was a picture of Max and Benjamin sitting by a campfire with their arms around each other, loving looks in their eyes and smiles on their faces. The picture had been taken with a phone on a tripod instead of by a professional catalog photographer.

Wes's son, Jaden, would be joining the company—working with the campground accreditation team—when he graduated next spring. In the meantime, he'd spent the summer guiding hikes as an intern.

Max pulled Benjamin's chair closer to his and put his hand on Benjamin's thigh. "Happy?"

Benjamin put his hand on top of Max's, lacing his fingers with his. "Very."

The front door opened again, and Jason and Joy joined them. Benjamin looked around the table, his heart so full he thought it might burst. When dinner was finished and the table cleared, Max took Benjamin by the hand.

"Come down to the dock with me."

Benjamin stopped when they walked out to the backyard and he saw the dock lined with luminaria. Max answered the question in his eyes with a smile, pulling him with him toward the dock. When they reached the end and stood surrounded by candlelight, the dock gently moving with the waves, Max took Benjamin in his arms. "Benjamin, I've wanted to see the night that we were fully reunited, but I knew I needed to wait to give you time, to give us both time. But we've restored the house. I think maybe we have restored our hearts too." Max knelt on one knee. "Benjamin Colton, will you spend the rest of your life with me? Sleeping under the stars, filling this house with a family of our own, letting me love you?" He reached into his pocket and pulled out a small velvet box. He opened the lid to reveal a reciprocal band. Like the cufflinks Charlie had given Benjamin, the band was embedded with diamonds in the shape of the Big Dipper.

Benjamin reached down, grabbed Max's hands, and pulled him up into a crushing embrace.

"I love you so much," he whispered against Max's lips.

"Is that your way of saying yes?"

Benjamin nodded. "Yes."

Max stood back, cupped his mouth, and shouted, "He said yes."

He'd been so focused on Max, Benjamin hadn't noticed their family and friends gathered on the deck watching them. A cheer went up, and the pop of a champagne bottle opening echoed.

Hand in hand they made their way back to the house, stopping every few steps to kiss until the catcalls became calls to hurry up so they could toast the happy couple.

Benjamin looked at the man at his side, unable to imagine what his life would be without him. With Max he'd learned to embrace the future and make peace with the past. Benjamin would still have moments when the years of loneliness and struggle would come back to haunt him, but he didn't have to face them alone. They would navigate the trials of life together.

When they were finally alone, Max pulled Benjamin into his arms. "Has anyone hugged you today?" he murmured, his voice filled with warmth and love.

Every day with Max ended this way, the familiar question a quiet promise. Benjamin smiled softly, leaning into the embrace, his heart full. "Yes," he whispered.

Max's eyes met his for a heartbeat before he tilted his head and pressed a gentle kiss to Benjamin's lips. It was soft, lingering, and Benjamin knew in that moment he'd always have this. Max's arms around him. Max's endless ways of showing he cared. Max's love.

Keep Reading for an Excerpt from
Dreidel Date
by Eliana West!

Chapter One

"I FORGOT TO tell you." Zach's best friend since they were seven, Becca, leaned across the table, her round, dark brown eyes bright with excitement. "A paralegal at my office has been talking about a new rabbi at a temple in the valley, and I think we need to go check him out."

Zach hummed and took another sip of his mimosa. "And why would we do that?"

Becca's husband, Ben, elbowed his wife. "Stop trying to play matchmaker, Bec."

"Zach needs to settle down." Becca swirled the stalk of celery in her bloody mary.

Sunday brunch day was a tradition they'd started as soon as Zach moved to the same city as Becca and Ben. Sunny LA meant even in early November they could sit outside under blue skies while they sipped bloody marys and mimosas as Bec and Zach gossiped, with Ben joining in now and then. God bless Ben, who completely understood that when he and Becs were together, he was solidly relegated to third-wheel status.

"Why? Why do I have to settle down? I'm happy. I'm having fun." Even to his own ears, his declaration rang hollow.

Happy? Maybe, depending on a sliding scale. Having fun? Not so much. Tinder hookups were becoming more trouble than they were worth. Why spend hours prepping for someone you weren't sure you were going to connect with other than you liked the way their abs looked and the size of their dick on your phone screen? The idea of reaching his sixties and still swiping left or right was depressing. As he approached his late twenties, his small circle of friends were engaged, married, or having kids. For some reason, in the last few months, Becca had made it her mission to play shadchan, transforming herself into a Jewish matchmaker.

It wasn't much of a transformation. From the minute they met on the first day at Camp Kokhav HaTzafon, Camp North Star, Becca took on the role of Zach's social secretary. If she hadn't, he would have happily spent his time in the bottom-bunk fort he'd created using his sleeping bag and sheets, with his nose in a book or drawing.

Becca pulled the bright green stalk of celery out of her glass and jabbed it in his direction, flinging splashes of her bloody mary on his T-shirt. The red splatters blended in with the tie-dye lettering that spelled out If God Hates Gays, Why Are We So Cute? "You aren't taking advantage of your carefree twenties, and they're going to be over soon."

"Gee, thanks, Bec. I love being reminded that I'll be thirty in two years."

Thirty and still alone given the current state of his love life.

"Honestly, Bec, you make it sound like I took away your hopes and dreams," Ben said, giving his wife sad puppy-dog eyes behind his tortoiseshell glasses.

Becca leaned over and gave her husband a kiss. They were camp sweethearts, and no one doubted they would wind up together after all the summers they spent making out in the boat shed. Even though they were separated by less than three hundred miles—the distance between Seattle and Ben's hometown of Eugene, Oregon—you'd think they'd had an ocean between them the way they greeted each other the first day of camp every summer.

"I'm lucky. I got to spend my twenties with you and be carefree together," she said, giving Ben another placating kiss.

Zach groaned, rolling his eyes as the two of them started making out. He downed the rest of his mimosa and rapped his knuckles on the table. "Excuse me, third wheel here. Can you please wait until after brunch before you give each other tonsillectomies?"

Becca eyed him. With her lips still against Ben's, she winked before slowly separating from him. Ben gave Zach a sheepish smile, his face slightly flushed. Zach might give his friends a hard time, but the truth was, he was jealous as hell. He'd love to have someone to kiss like that, the kind of kiss that made the rest of the world disappear. The kind of kiss he'd written about but never experienced. He'd had his fair share of kisses, but so far none that rocked his world the way he fantasized about. None that made him feel the way his fictional characters did.

Becca turned to her husband. "Babe, that would be a fantastic idea for a show. A renegade doctor who specializes in tonsillectomies becomes the new chief at a failing hospital."

Ben took his time chewing the bite of omelet he'd put in his mouth. He swallowed and took Becca's hand in his. "Sweetheart, we've talked about this. You are a wonderful, talented, and amazing entertainment lawyer. I love you want to help me, but you come up with the worst show ideas I've ever heard."

Zach nodded in agreement. Becca's talents were many, but her creativity was always a bit off the mark. But her desire to support her husband's burgeoning career as a network executive came from the heart.

"Fine." Becca sat back and folded her arms in front of her, a small scowl on her face. "But one of these days I'm going to come up with something that you can use in a show or Zach can put in one of his books."

Zach and Ben exchanged a look, both schooling their expressions, trying to appear hopeful. Becca's ideas were notoriously bad, but they came from a place of love. Bec was equally as passionate about seeing Zach on the *New York Times* bestseller list as she was about supporting her husband's career.

"You never know," Zach said.

"Speaking of books, congratulations. I saw the new issue of *Book Nymph* in the window of the bookstore by my office the other day." Ben nodded to the cocktail napkin Zach had been doodling on. "Is that an idea for your next book?"

"Maybe." Zach glanced down at the ghostly image he'd drawn. He'd been toying with the idea for a new graphic novel series about a ghost who teams up with a human to start a ghost matchmaking agency. Together they paired ghosts who needed a place to haunt with people willing to invite them in. He liked the idea and was pretty sure he would do something with it, but he wasn't ready to share it with anyone. Not yet. "I haven't decided."

"You'll have a lot of disappointed fans if you don't write another *Book Nymph*. Did I tell you I saw a copy of the first issue sitting on one of the senior partners' desks? In a million years I wouldn't have thought a stodgy old guy would be reading a gay graphic novel," Becca said. "I asked him about it, and he told me he's been reading it along with his grandson as a way to bond. Isn't that sweet?"

Becca's story touched him. Zach was always in awe of the impact his work had.

"Don't worry, I have no plans to stop writing Ren and Alden."

Ren was the fictional hero Zach started doodling in middle school who loved a character from his favorite book of fairy tales so much the character came to life. It eventually became a bestselling graphic novel series. *Book Nymph* followed the nymph Alden's and his human boyfriend Ren's adventures as they helped other book characters escape from the pages to unite with their true loves in the real world. The series started off with a small following, but when a book blogger discovered *Book Nymph* and gave it an enthusiastic review, the series took off. Everyone was curious about Edward Brandon. The two people sitting across from him were the only ones who knew it was Zach hiding behind the pen name.

The tenacity that made Becca a successful lawyer also made her an annoying friend at times. Once she latched on to an idea, she didn't let go. "So, you'll come to temple with us next week, right?"

"Come on, Bec, you know I'm not religious. I stopped going to temple after my Bar Mitzvah. I don't think a rabbi is my type."

Dating exclusively in the Jewish community wasn't an issue for Zach. Religion wasn't a deal breaker for him. He wanted something deeper to connect him with a partner beyond a shared religion.

"We all know you only agreed to a Bar Mitzvah for the presents." Ben gave him a wry smile. "But maybe it's time to give it another try."

"I agreed to have a Bar Mitzvah because my parents promised me a new tablet with a stylus and the latest graphics program."

Becca slapped his arm. "Don't be gross."

"The point is going to temple isn't my thing."

Becca and Ben exchanged a glance that had Zach's spidey sense tingling. They were up to something.

He narrowed his eyes. "What's going on? Why is it so important for me to go to temple?"

"What's so wrong for me to want my best friend to be happy, and if there's a hot single rabbi that I think is perfect for him, I—" Becca's eyes grew wide and she grabbed Ben's arm. "Babe, I—"

Ben shook his head. "Nope, don't even think about it. I am not making a show about rabbis dating."

"But—"

"Bec, we're focusing on Zach's love life right now, remember?"

Becca's gaze turned back toward Zach with laser focus. He could keep arguing, but it was going to make life easier if he gave in. He was willing to sacrifice a Saturday morning of sleeping late and lying in bed drawing the next adventures of Ren and Alden to listen to a sermon from a sexy rabbi if it would placate his friend and get her to stop meddling in his love life for a while.

"Okay, I'll go, but—" He grabbed another cocktail napkin and scribbled on it. "—only if you sign this."

He handed her the napkin and watched. Her eyes scanned what he'd written, and her lips pursed.

She tried to hand it back to him. "Absolutely not. This is not a valid legal document."

"Sweetheart." Ben gently pulled the pen Zach was holding out of his grasp and handed it to his wife. "Just sign it."

"You too." Zach waved his fingers at Ben.

"I don't think…. I'm not as bad as Bec," Ben sputtered.

Zach raised an eyebrow. "Really? What about that lighting tech you insisted was the man of my dreams?"

Two bright spots of pink appeared on Ben's cheeks. He grabbed the pen out of his wife's hand and scrawled his name on the napkin before handing the pen back to Becca, muttering, "I thought when he kept talking about how much he liked big cats, he was talking about lions, not that he was a furry."

"He was cute. I don't have anything against furries. Not my kink, and he wasn't my type."

"No dating advice or setups for six months is excessive," Becca said, using her lawyer voice. "I propose an amendment."

"Sign it or I make it a year."

With an angry scowl, Becca signed the napkin and tossed it toward him. Zach folded it neatly with a smug smile and tucked it into the pocket of his turquoise-blue khakis.

"I'm taking back all of your Hanukkah presents." Becca pouted.

"On the one in a million chance things work out with this rabbi, I promise you'll never have to buy me another Hanukkah present again."

Becca's lips curled into a sly smile as she picked up another napkin and began writing on it, presenting it to him a minute later. "Sign it."

He took one look at the contract she'd hastily written out and started laughing.

I, Zach Kravitz, exempt Becca Greene from buying Hanukkah gifts in perpetuity if I fall in love with the rabbi at Town and Village Temple.

Signed:

"I'll email you my Hanukkah list for next year after we go to temple next week," he said, signing his name with a flourish.

He handed it back, and Becca mimicked him, making a show of folding the napkin and putting it in her purse.

"We'll pick you up at nine. It's thirty minutes to the valley."

Zach groaned. "Seriously, a temple in the valley?"

"Encino isn't the end of the world."

"No, but it's geographically inconvenient. Strike one against your rabbi."

Becca wadded up her napkin and threw it at him. When they parted ways after lunch, Becca waggled her fingers in his face with a stern reminder that they'd be picking him up for services next Saturday.

SCAN THE QR CODE
BELOW TO ORDER!

ELIANA WEST, the recipient of the 2022 Nancy Pearl Award for genre fiction, is committed to embracing diversity in her writing. That means she doesn't limit herself to a single genre. Instead, Eliana welcomes every story that comes her way with open arms. She aims to create characters that reflect the diversity of her community, with a range of social backgrounds, ethnicities, genders, and sexual orientations. Eliana loves to weave in historical elements whenever she can and fearlessly engage in challenging dialogues. Eliana believes everyone deserves a happy ending.

From small towns to close-knit communities, Eliana West loves stories that bring people from different backgrounds together through the common language of unconditional love and acceptance. Eliana is a passionate advocate for diversity within the writing community. She is the founder of Writers for Diversity and teaches classes and workshops, encouraging writers to create diverse characters and worlds with an empathetic approach.

When Eliana isn't plotting her characters' happy endings, she can be found embarking on adventures with her husband, traversing winding country roads in their beloved vintage Volkswagen Westfalia, affectionately named Bianca. Whether it's traveling abroad or exploring locally, Eliana and her husband are always willing to get lost and see where the adventure takes them.

Eliana loves connecting with readers through her website: www.elianawest.com.

AN EMERALD  HEARTS NOVEL
BE THE
Match
ELIANA WEST

An Emerald Hearts Novel

A senseless accident leaves Ryan Blackstone a single father. His son, Leo, survives, only for the hospital to discover he has leukemia. Ryan's only hope to save him is a bone marrow donor.

A donor registry reveals a perfect match for Leo but unearths an unsettling family secret: Ryan's wife's brother isn't dead. Then they meet, and Ryan realizes Dylan could save him as well.

Dylan McKenzie stopped thinking about his family's betrayal when they kicked him out twelve years ago. They would rather say he is dead than gay. So the news of his sister's death comes as a shock. Dylan is afraid being pulled back into the family will hurt him again, but meeting Ryan and Leo upends his plan to keep his heart closed.

Ryan almost lost everything. Now he must decide if he can gamble losing his family to have everything he's ever wanted. Together, he and Dylan could be the perfect match.

SCAN THE QR CODE
BELOW TO ORDER!

A HOMEMADE Hanukkah

An Emerald Hearts Novella

Noah Stern's patients at Seattle Children's Hospital don't mind his OCD quirks. He loves his job as a physical therapist. Working with children is easy. Checking in on Gideon "the Beast" Wilder at his remote mountain cabin as a favor for the owner of the Seattle Emeralds proves to be anything but easy. Gideon seems determined to live up to his nickname. But beneath his surly demeanor, Noah glimpses a man who is longing for love.

Seattle Emeralds star player Gideon Wilder doesn't want company, especially a physical therapist with a charming smile and eyes that sparkle when he laughs. Noah Stern's arrival on his doorstep is an unwelcome interruption, complicated when an avalanche traps them together for Hanukkah. Gideon came to his cabin to nurse both the physical injury that ruined his soccer season and a heart broken by failed relationships. People he dares to love always leave him. Noah will surely do the same.

With each homemade Hanukkah gift, Noah tames the Beast. When the snow clears and Hanukkah comes to an end, Gideon's fear takes hold before he realizes that Noah's presence in his life has been the greatest gift of all. Will Noah accept Gideon's belated Hanukkah gift—Gideon's heart?

SCAN THE QR CODE
BELOW TO ORDER!

STRUCK BY Lightning

SARAH BLACK

Marcus always thought life had a plan: paint by day, avoid commitment by night. But when he's literally struck by lightning in front of his apartment, things take a wild turn—especially when his cute, quirky neighbor, AJ, crashes his UPS truck after witnessing the whole thing.

AJ, a free-spirited dreamer with a big heart, heroically performs CPR to save Marcus's life. As they navigate the aftermath of the bizarre accident, their small neighborhood community rallies together. Tenesha, the outspoken single mom next door, along with her hilarious son Po and their mischievous dog Marco, become unlikely friends to both men.

While Marcus struggles to recover and AJ faces his own insecurities, the group leans on each other for support. As sparks of romance start flying between Marcus and AJ, the pair soon realize that fate might have more in store than either of them imagined.

When chaos threatens their lives again, AJ steps up, proving that lightning can strike twice—but love, once ignited, is there to stay.

Filled with humor, heart, and unexpected twists, *"Struck by Lightning"* is a feel-good rom-com about finding love when you least expect it and the beautiful messiness of community.

SCAN THE QR CODE
BELOW TO ORDER!

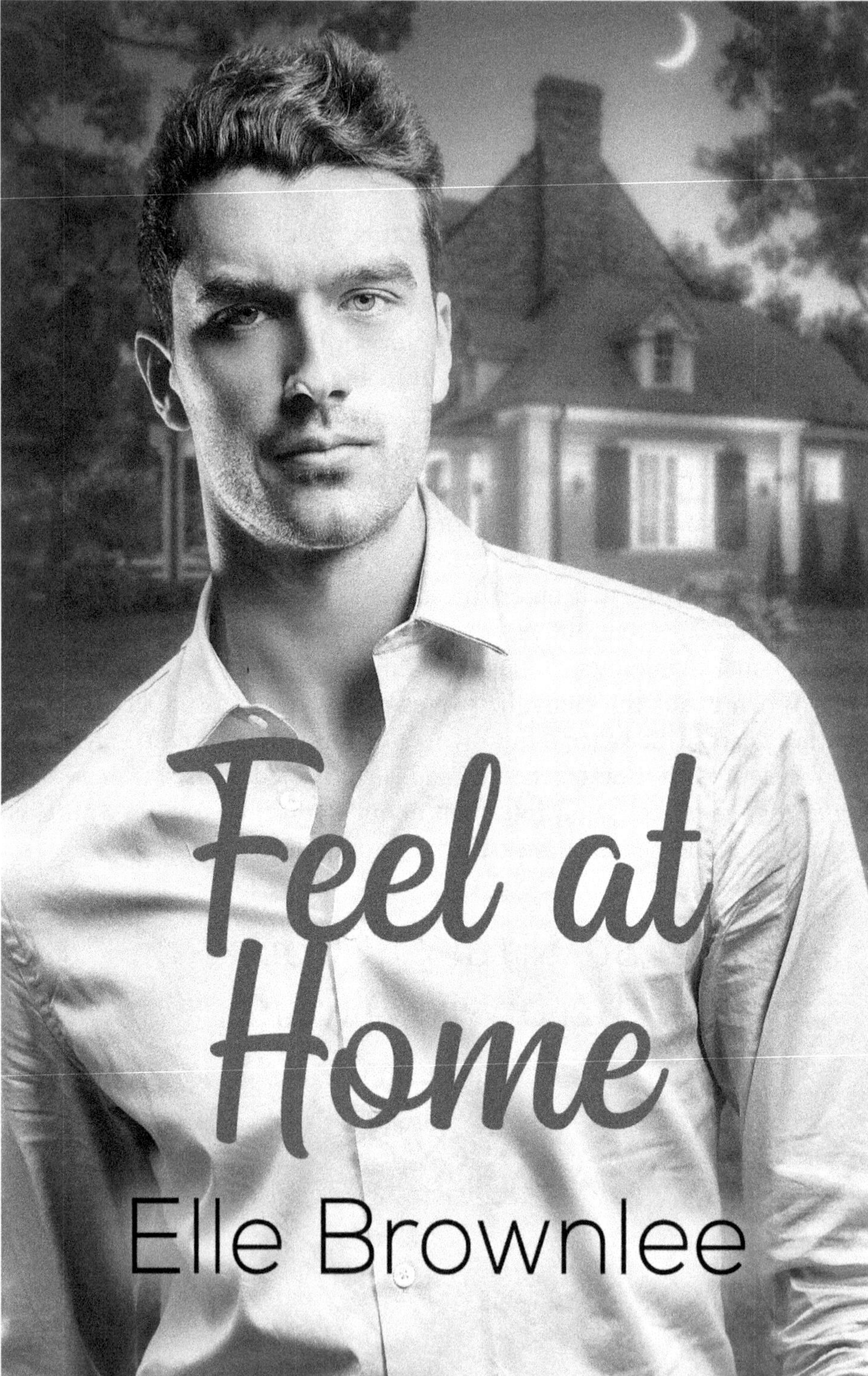

Feel at Home
Elle Brownlee

Solitary photojournalist Philip Conyers is out of money and out of time.

One year after pausing his work chasing stories across the globe to buy and fix up his dream house, a series of events has him flat broke, creatively clogged, and out of options. Philip must sell—and then is stuck as months pass without any offers.

Enter tech millionaire Zak Springer. He needs space and quiet away from New York City to think up the next big idea, and Philip's upstate place is the perfect retreat. He wants to rent it for six months, price is no object, and oh yeah, Philip is welcome to stay. What can Philip do but agree?

Living with easygoing Zak proves interesting for Philip, a dedicated loner. Despite their different circumstances, Zak understands him in a way no one ever has, and the attraction that simmers between them is undeniable. With their days together numbered, Philip decides it's safe to indulge in a fling—until he realizes he never wants this life in his dream house with his dream man to end. Can Philip open his heart as well as his home, or is he doomed to lose them both?

SCAN THE QR CODE
BELOW TO ORDER!

ANDREW GREY
LOVE
AT FIRST SWIPE

Darby Wright has fought for his independence ever since he lost his sight as a child. But even now that he has his own home and a good job, his overprotective mother doesn't believe he can handle himself. Darby's determined to prove her wrong, but there are some things—like finding his guide dog's potty accident—where an extra set of eyes would come in handy.

Enter See For Me, an app that connects blind clients with sighted volunteers. See For Me is designed for just this sort of emergency, and it's through this app that Darby meets Reynaldo. Lust at first voice turns to more when Darby and Reynaldo run into each other at a local sandwich shop, where Renaldo seems as nice in person as he was in app.

With Reynaldo, Darby can feel his world expanding. Reynaldo doesn't just support him but understands him and sees Darby as more than his disability. But will being with Reynaldo mean giving up Darby's hard-fought independence, or will it mean gaining something more than he ever dreamed?

SCAN THE QR CODE
BELOW TO ORDER!

FOR **MORE** OF THE **BEST** **GAY** ROMANCE

www.ingramcontent.com/pod-product-compliance
Lightning Source LLC
Chambersburg PA
CBHW071525120726
47907CB00013B/1078